THE DEVOURING GOD

Also by James Kendley

The Drowning God

THE DEVOURING GOD

JAMES KENDLEY

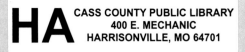

HARPER

VOYAGER
IMPULSE

An Imprint of HarperCollinsPublishers

THE DEVOURING GOD. Copyright © 2016 by James Kendley. All rights reserved under International and Pan-American Copyright Conventions. By payment of the required fees, you have been granted the nonexclusive, nontransferable right to access and read the text of this e-book on screen. No part of this text may be reproduced, transmitted, downloaded, decompiled, reverse-engineered, or stored in or introduced into any information storage and retrieval system, in any form or by any means, whether electronic or mechanical, now known or hereafter invented, without the express written permission of HarperCollins e-books. For information, address HarperCollins Publishers, 195 Broadway, New York, NY 10007.

EPub Edition MAY 2016 ISBN: 9780062360670

Print Edition ISBN: 9780062360687

10 9 8 7 6 5 4 3 2 1

To Elizabeth Lawhon Kendley,
who always put good books before all that other stuff
that didn't matter

CHAPTER 1

Monday Evening

Despite his faith, the old man was terrified. His breath echoed ragged in the enclosed space, and his heart hammered in his chest. He was alone in a basement, he was sure of it; his escorts had led him down stairs and through a narrow tunnel, and now he was waiting to be punished for his mistakes, his treachery, and his cowardice.

A honeyed voice from the darkness said, "Abbot, you may remove your blindfold."

The abbot's liver-spotted hands trembled as he untied the silken kerchief. He blinked in the glare of a naked lightbulb suspended in the gloom. When his eyes adjusted, he found himself alone in a room the size and shape of a tennis court, a basement room as he had guessed. The walls were white with a floor of durable rust red. Folding tables and chairs stood stacked against the far wall. The bare concrete floor sloped slightly away from him to a steel-grated drain running the length of the room. A track in the ceiling ran parallel to the drain. Rusted pulleys in the track suggested a machinist's assembly line or an abattoir. He imagined briefly that he had been led there to be murdered, and that his blood would be washed into that drain, but only vanity would lead him to believe himself worth murdering.

A cracked and yellowed projection screen hung from the pulleys. At one end of the drain, to the abbot's right, a low, ornate iron door was set into the irregular stones of the wall. The other walls were modern cinder block, but that wall, plastered and painted though it had been, betrayed much older construction, and the ornamentation of the door itself suggested prewar fabrication, perhaps late-nineteenth-century Meiji era. It was as if the whole building had arisen around this older structure.

The iron door was midnight black, shining with oil or varnish. It had been cared for.

There was nothing else. He turned. The double doors behind him had closed, and there was only a folding table—no, a human skull on a folding table.

"Is it—" His voice echoed in the darkened space. "Is it the Cinematographer?"

"As promised," the voice answered from the darkness. It seemed to come from all around the abbot, buzzing and whispering from the shadows themselves. "Please, feel free to examine it. Take your time."

The abbot's hands were steady as he reached for the skull, but his pulse fluttered in his belly.

The bone was cocoa-brown and unmarred under thin shellac. The cranium and jawbone were wired together in an everlasting grin. The crooked teeth were inlaid with brass, and the eye sockets were inset with sleepy ovals of ivory and stained wood. A silver band embossed with a death's head motif marked the seam where the skull had been sawed open and the brain removed. The abbot pulled, and the skull cap popped off in his hands—the discarded grail of a bloodthirsty Hindu goddess. The interior of the cranium had been lined with beaten copper to make an airtight cavity, and a cylindrical brass key lay on a bed of green felt within.

"Does this key unlock the shrine?"

The darkness laughed, and a man stepped into the pool of light beneath the naked bulb. His suit was so black that it seemed to stay behind, melding him with shadow. "The shrine needs no lock. The lock that key once fit was reduced to slag decades ago."

The abbot glanced at the double door. It had not opened, so the man in the suit had been there all along, somehow concealed in the empty room. He was clearly the one called the counselor. Such a man's time was very valuable, and even the abbot himself had to avoid wasting it. The abbot quickly reassembled the skull, raised it to his forehead, and chanted a brief verse from the sutras.

"He's quite unable to hear your prayers, you know. He lost his ears in the Himalayas almost seventy years ago."

The abbot looked up to see the counselor's small, derisive smile. Such impiety could be a test of the abbot's responses, or it might be a mockery of the heresies spouted by their common enemies. The abbot could only reply from his faith: "My prayers are not for the ears of the living or the dead, but for those of the Eternal Buddha, who is beyond life or death."

"An interesting proposition, but we are concerned with only two alternatives: life or death."

"The life or death of our cause if news of the . . . ah, the *other* relic becomes public?"

The counselor grinned. His teeth were huge, yellow in the incandescent light. "The life and death of Japanese citizens. Productive members of society. Consumers and taxpayers. We must retrieve the artifact, and we must retrieve it quickly."

"You have the resources of this huge corporation at your command," the abbot said. "Why do you need us?"

The counselor waved at the darkness. "All this is really . . . well, let us just say that recovery of the artifact requires a different sort of power. That is where your organization comes in."

"I don't understand."

"It's not necessary that you understand the levels of power involved, but you must witness the effects of the artifact itself. This footage is the work of the cinematographer whom you so revere. Each frame was painstakingly colored by the same skilled workers who tinted Japan's famous postcards. An important cultural legacy indeed, especially since those skilled workers were liquidated at the project's conclusion." The counselor addressed the darkness: "I will leave the room, and then the projector will start."

He slipped out into a brief glimpse of sickly green corridor.

The abbot heard, for the first time in many years, an old-fashioned motion-picture projector whirring and clattering to life. His own silhouette sprang up fat and black on the projection screen hanging on the rust-frozen pulleys above the steel grate in the floor. He stepped out of the beam and turned to look for the projector. There was a cinder block missing in the wall behind him, a hole pouring forth the chatter of sprockets and the flickering stream of moving images.

The abbot turned back to face the screen. The footage was disturbing from the first but not horrifying, not even when he began to suspect what was about to happen. When the blood began to flow, the abbot couldn't help but pity the artists whose final work in this world had been hand-tinting this monstrous reel, laboring frame by frame toward their own doom. He forgot all about the workers when the artifact's true effects became clear, abundantly and gruesomely clear, and his body attempted to betray him. His hips pivoted as if to turn him from the screen, but he dared not look away. His hands rose to cover his eyes, but he dared not raise them higher than his cheeks. His lungs pushed air through his vocal cords as if to make him scream, but he dared not make more than a small, mewling moan easily drowned out by the ratcheting noise from the hole in the wall behind him.

The screen went dark. The abbot stood in silence, his hands still on his cheeks, stunned and shaken by what he had seen.

The counselor stepped into the light again. "So you understand why we must regain the artifact."

The abbot started. He had not noticed the counselor's return. "So it's t-true," the abbot said in a stuttering, wheezy voice. "The rumors about the starfish killings are true."

The counselor assumed a pained expression. "Starfish killings indeed! I called them the *jellyfish* killings. What else would you call murders with boneless victims?" He sighed. "Even the best marketing sometimes goes to waste."

The abbot didn't know quite what to say.

"Abbot, you have a special relationship with the ones who will retrieve the artifact for us. One of them at least."

The abbot stiffened. "I know the men of whom you speak. They are heretics. Madmen. They cannot be trusted."

The counselor tilted his head. "The same has been said of you and your followers, Abbot."

The abbot crossed his arms. "I will not contact them."

"They are already engaged. They are on our side,

working for the health and welfare of the Japanese people."

"Their betrayal of the *Lotus Sutra* condemns them to the Avichi Hell. I cannot intervene."

The counselor laid his forefinger on the abbot's wrist. "You will save them. You will bring them back into the light of truth."

A relief and a certainty swept over the old man. *I will save them.*

"You will help feed them information they need to recover the artifact for us."

"I will bring them back to the light," the abbot said. Then he growled: "I will bring them back to the light or I will kill them myself."

The counselor laughed with genuine amusement. "Abbot, your enthusiasm is commendable, but killing won't be necessary. If our mutual friends fail to retrieve the artifact, why, within a few weeks there will be no one in Japan left to kill."

CHAPTER 2

Monday Evening

Tohru Takuda found his wife, Yumi, watching the lights dancing on the Naka River.

She leaned with her elbows on the footbridge's concrete balustrade, her hands clasped, her expression serene. The neon signs of the entertainment district on the river's east bank reflected from the rippling river. It was beautiful, he thought, as he crossed the footbridge to meet her. She was beautiful, and he loved to see her in a moment of peace despite all the trouble he had brought to their lives.

The abnormally long rainy season was finally over, and it was a steamy, lazy late summer in Fukuoka. It was a gorgeous southern city stretching in a low, flat crescent around Hakata Bay like a lazy cat sunning itself on a windowsill. Fukuoka lent itself to an easy pace of relaxed industry, and this summer's fashions and pop songs accentuated the atmosphere. Okinawan music played everywhere Takuda went, even now drifting from a convenience store across the river.

If only he were wearing sandals instead of jackboots, it would be perfect, he thought. If only he were wearing shorts and a Hawaiian shirt instead of a security guard's coveralls. If only he were a decorated prefectural police detective on holiday instead of a wandering hunter of demons and monsters.

Yumi looked up at the sound of his footsteps and smiled at him. "I was going to meet you at the pachinko parlor, but I got distracted here."

He joined her at the balustrade and put his hand on her hip. Her eyes were wide, clear, and untroubled. Her hair was slightly wavy in the sultry air, as it had been ever since the rainy season started. "You don't need to be in the pachinko parlor," Takuda said.

"Neither do you," Yumi said. "I'm sure something else will come along."

He looked out across the shimmering water. There were jobs available, of course. Fukuoka was on the cusp of becoming a world-class city, a metropolis of promise and possibility. It was a perfect time to be there. Unless you had pitched over your career to destroy a cursed beast that had murdered your son and your brother. Unless you and your friends had continued to stumble across monsters to slay, communities to liberate from hauntings, demons to send back to the deepest, hottest hells. Unless you had to move every few months when you became unemployable.

He watched Yumi watching the water. *At least she still sees me for what I was*, he thought, *not what I'm becoming.*

She seemed not to be thinking of him at all. She looked out across the ripples with the same wistful expression she wore when viewing fireworks or cherry blossoms. She didn't have to say it. Nobody had to say it.

This will not last.

Today or tomorrow or next week, no one knew when, some new beast would appear to be slain. Then Takuda, the ex-priest Suzuki, and their young cohort, Mori, would be drawn into a new horror, and soon after, they would be forced to wander again. In the three years they had all been together, they had already moved five times.

Takuda sighed. "Let's go home," he said. He hated the thought of going back to the cramped little apartment they shared with Suzuki and Mori, but it was better than standing on the bridge contemplating the inevitable future.

She nodded. They went back across the bridge the way Takuda had come, ready to cut through the bar district to catch their bus, but at the end of the bridge, she pulled at his sleeve to turn south. "Let's take the long way home," she said. "Let's find a place for you to lay down your staff and relax for a while."

That road led past tawdry little clubs, pachinko parlors, and adult shops, but it also led to posh little hotels designed for lovers like Takuda and Yumi, people who seldom found privacy.

"Are you sure?" he asked.

"We have enough," she said. He slung his oaken staff over his shoulder. She took his arm as they threaded through the crowd of office workers and secretaries. "Don't worry."

He smiled, for the first time in days. *Maybe things aren't so bad after all. Maybe we can stay here for a while this time.*

He stole a glance at Yumi as they walked along the river. She still looked happy, but there was a tiny crease between her eyebrows. Not as serene as she seemed. Takuda looked back at the road in front of them. *It's coming,* Takuda thought. *She knows it, whether I want to admit it or not.* He squeezed Yumi's hand. *We have tonight, at least.*

" . . . So I must talk to someone about this strange desire. It is not natural . . ."

The foreigner's Japanese was stilted and bookish, and he refused to be interrupted. Yoshida muted her phone and rested her head on the desktop. As she moved, her clammy cheek made a slight sucking sound on the cool plastic. The pencil lying beside her call log rocked slightly with her breath.

It was only 11 o'clock at night.

"The words I must say are very simple, but the meanings are complicated . . ."

He would have to wind down on his own. These late-night callers usually needed healthy sleep more immediately than medication or therapy. If they weren't violent or suicidal, the goal was to get valid contact information and then try to tuck them in over the telephone. Even a few hours seemed to help.

The foreigner spoke more quickly, as if to tell his secret before his spirit weakened. "There is a boy," he said.

Yoshida bundled her sweater into a pillow.

"I met this boy, a student, at the college where I teach, and I have strange thoughts about him." His whisper had a hollow, metallic echo, perhaps from calling on a cell phone. "Never before have I had such thoughts."

If the caller paused for a breath, she would confirm for him that he was not the only man who liked men. A little late in life to be finding out, but perhaps he had been preoccupied with his studies. She laid her head on the bundled sweater.

"I want to do something I have never done before."

She smiled. The foreigner couldn't know it, but that was the setup of an old, old comedy routine.

"His . . . his bones," the foreigner whispered. "I want to lick his bones. I want to peel off his flesh and lick his bones clean."

Yoshida's eyes snapped open. All of a sudden, sleep was the last thing on her mind.

The foreigner was breathing hard. "Pardon me, but if you wouldn't mind answering a question . . ."

Yoshida grunted in numbed response.

"Well," the foreigner said, "how tall are you? Are you a long-legged woman?"

Haruma stood forlorn in the darkness. The girls from his study group had promised him a party, but instead they were performing a silent and complicated dance in a dim, stinking restaurant, and he was beginning to hate them for it.

He had tried to join in at first, but he bungled the pattern again and again. The girls were weaving in and out, stepping in perfect unison without even looking at each other. They had obviously practiced this dance for hours and hours, practiced so they could do it with only the greenish glow of the exit sign to guide them. Perhaps they wanted to impress him, but it really wasn't working.

Close order drill was sort of a Japanese specialty, as far as Haruma was concerned. No flair or originality on display here, just the same lockstep precision of a Tokyo crosswalk, the great ant heap in motion.

"Girls, this is great," he said, rolling his eyes in the dark as he clapped his hands. "Think of how much better this would be with music and exotic drinks. I know places we can go to show everyone!"

They didn't look at him. They hadn't brought him here to dance with him or entertain him or even let him take part. It was all clearly designed to make him more separate, to make him more the outsider. Haruma was used to being the outsider. Maybe the girls thought he felt at home with them at school, flirting harmlessly and joining in their breathless conversations about boy bands and fashion, but he was always on the outside. Every time one of the girls mocked him to establish her own place within the circle, his place was clear as day. Outside.

Haruma's deepest resentments led him only as far as avoiding those who had hurt him. He had learned not to hate, and he had learned not to feed his anger. The lessons reminded him of the teacher . . .

"This is boring," he said. "Girls, thank you for the display, but I'm going to get some dinner at the Lotus Café, on Meiji Avenue across from the Black Gate. You should join me. My friend Koji will serve us. He'll appreciate a tale about your dance in the darkness." And Koji would be much, much more entertaining. Flamboyant and witty, utterly hostile toward pretension and imposture, Koji was currently the brightest light in Haruma's life. Koji was only a waiter, but he had become what Haruma only hoped to be.

"Well, I'm going, then," he said to the echoing darkness, the shuffling of feet. They didn't even look at him. "Stupid," he muttered as he stepped into the pattern. The pattern tightened on him. Inexplicably, the girls quickened into a faster lockstep. Up close, even in the greenish half-light they looked disheveled, unkempt. They brushed by him on all sides.

He didn't know how many there were—he hadn't stopped to count. There had seemed to be seven when he first walked in, but they had multiplied, or other girls had come out of the woodwork. It made no sense. They were two-deep all around him.

All at once, they grinned. Their mouths popped open in painful-looking grimaces, baring their teeth in spastic smiles that stretched and contorted their lips. They grinned and grinned in a humorless, skull-like rictus identical on every face.

"That's horrible," he said. "This isn't funny."

He began to shove his way out. He was pushed back at every turn with no seeming effort. They simply moved with him, still milling about him two- or three-deep no matter where he turned, still grinning the horrible grins.

He pushed with all his strength, trying to break through. The crowd absorbed his push, and he felt a shocking, burning pain that ran up his arm. He pulled back his hand and stared at it. It was dark brown—blood. It was crimson blood, brown in the greenish half-light. It pumped out of his forearm, through the slit in his sleeve. He had been cut.

He swore at the top of his lungs, then gasped at sudden, blinding pain in his leg. He went down to one knee. The girls stopped their dance and turned inward toward him, grinning their horrible grins. He was at the center of the circle. They bore down on him, and he screamed as they stripped him of his flesh.

CHAPTER 3

Tuesday Morning

"Just smile this time," Ota shouted over his shoulder as he and Takuda weaved among shoppers and stalls in the crowded market street. "You scared the Mitsugi Carbon guys so badly that they don't even return my calls."

Ota was a small, bandy-legged man, and he scooted through the street market like a fox in underbrush. Takuda followed his employer patiently, even when he had to squeeze sideways between fishmongers' carts and vegetable stands. It didn't really matter if Ota got too far ahead. Takuda caught up quickly because the crowd parted before him. There was nothing obviously different about Takuda. Those who noticed him at all saw a larger-than-average Japanese man in a security guard's jumpsuit. Yet shoppers stopped in their tracks to let him pass, sometimes fumbling for change, sometimes fussing over their children, sometimes just staring into space. This was how he knew he was being summoned: Answering the call to action was always the path of least resistance, as if the universe were smoothing the path ahead of him.

It's always very easy, he thought. *Always easy till it gets very, very hard.*

Ota shouted over his shoulder again: "The section chief will be there. They're all in a tizzy, what with all the stupid rumors about this starfish killer, and we're there to make them feel safe. Now remember, it's a tiny office with one old woman manager and a college girl answering the phones, got it? Street level converted apartment, main room plus two eight-mat rooms, bathroom, and galley kitchen—front door, kitchen door, and bathroom window. When the time comes, you walk around, act as if you're checking it out, and then go back to your spot. Got it?"

"Yes, I've got it."

"Good. Just be quiet, okay? Stand there looking relaxed and ready, and let me do the talking. This is our first call from one of these little local governments, and we want to shine here. That's why I'm bringing you." Ota guffawed, looking back at Takuda. "With you, they wouldn't even need a door. You could just stand aside to let people in or out."

They emerged from the market into the main street. A tall, thin priest stood on the corner with his brass begging bowl, so while Takuda and Ota waited for a break in traffic, Ota made the bowl ring with pocket change.

"For luck!" Ota was excited about the meeting.

The priest blessed Ota, but then his eyes met Takuda's. His smile wavered, only for a second. Takuda shook his head. He didn't even look over his shoulder at the priest as he followed Ota to the work site.

It was a simple apartment block, old but clean. The signboard affixed to the door read:

Mental Health Services
Fukuoka Prefecture
Satellite Office 6

The office seemed crowded when Takuda and Ota stepped in. A middle-aged woman at a desk in the front room stood in response to Ota's cheery greeting. This was, Takuda assumed, the "old woman manager" Ota had mentioned. A long-haired man sitting in the guest's chair at the manager's desk didn't acknowledge them at all. Takuda thought he might be a mental patient, but he was very expensively dressed to be seeking assistance at a satellite office in broad daylight. The "college girl" was busy at a desk in the room beyond the kitchen. She did not look up from her paperwork.

Takuda looked for an unobtrusive place to park his oaken staff. It was shoulder-height on him, stouter than most fighting staffs, and he carried it everywhere when he was in uniform. Even Ota, who boasted about

Takuda nonstop, would be amazed at how efficiently deadly Takuda could be with that staff. But it wasn't a great calling card. He leaned it gently against the wall beside a filing cabinet.

The section chief entered from a room labeled *Consultation Room*. He introduced himself as Hasegawa. He was young and athletic-looking for a section chief with the prefecture. He invited them into his makeshift office in the consultation room, he and Ota exchanged business cards, and they sat down to talk while Takuda slid the door closed behind him.

"This is difficult business," Hasegawa said. "This caller, this crazy foreigner, has indirectly threatened one of my staff, and it sounds like it's related to the starfish killings, but the prefecture won't do anything about it. They've sent that long-haired boy out there, that Detective Kimura, to ask some questions, but they won't offer any protection. My hands are tied, so I have to hire private help."

Takuda was surprised that the long-haired young dandy at the manager's desk was a detective. *Maybe he's some sort of super detective who can wear whatever he wants.*

"I understand your situation," Ota said, bowing where he sat. "Ota Southern Protection Services is here to help in any way possible."

The section chief bowed in response. No one spoke for several seconds.

"Perhaps we should talk about how much help we can offer," Ota said. "Security Guard Takuda, please wait outside."

As Takuda turned to go, the "college girl" slid the door open and backed into the office. She turned without looking and almost rammed Takuda's belly with a loaded tea tray. When she looked up at Takuda's face, she squealed and dropped the tray. Takuda caught it, but plastic packets of cookies skittered off the edge and across the floor.

"Nabeshima, you clumsy girl!" Hasegawa was on his feet.

She grimaced and apologized, bowing backward out the door with her eyes on the floor. As she pulled the door shut, she gave Takuda a quick, wide-eyed stare.

The second stare confirmed it. *She sees what I am, or she sees more than most.*

Takuda slid the tea tray onto the desk.

"Security Guard Takuda has reflexes like a cat," Ota said with obvious satisfaction.

Takuda unloaded the tea tray. Ota shooed him out and took the pot to pour for the section chief. Takuda took the tray and bowed backward out the door, just as the girl Nabeshima had done.

Out in the main office, the office manager and Detective Kimura continued their conversation. Nabeshima stepped forward with eyes downcast, but her jaw was set. "Security Guard . . ."

"Takuda."

"Security Guard Takuda, there are no words to excuse my behavior. I am truly and deeply sorry. Please accept my apology."

She performed a pert little bow, the kind of bow

she probably did on a girlfriend's doorstep before they went clubbing, and she introduced herself as Kaori Nabeshima. He returned her bow as appropriate to his age.

As he straightened, she said, "Security Guard Takuda, what happened to your face? Were you injured in the line of duty?"

The silence was so sudden and complete that the slight buzzing of the light fixture seemed immense. The pair at the desk slowly turned to look.

"What is she talking about?" The detective's whisper was loud enough to hear anywhere in the office. "Is there something wrong with his face?"

The girl's eyes were large and so black that it was hard to tell where the iris ended and the pupil began. They were expressionless. Takuda realized that she had heard and seen strange things all her life, and she was very, very brave to ask him about his face—whatever of his face she could actually see.

Maybe she sees all of it. Maybe it's worse than I think.

"My appearance is partly due to injuries in the line of duty," he said. "I'm surprised you noticed in this dimly lit office. Most adults can't see that well even in broad daylight." He looked down at the empty tray in his hands, trying to seem as relaxed and unthreatening as possible. "With such unusually keen vision, I'm sure you often see things no one else can see. Perhaps it's been that way all your life. It must be tiring."

She stepped backward, blinking. He handed her the tea tray. She almost ran for the small kitchen.

Ota backed out into the main room, leading Hasegawa. "Come for a moment and tell me what you think of the guard I brought you."

Hasegawa glanced up at Takuda and frowned back at Ota.

Ota pushed forward, beaming. "Just look at the protection! I can have this man show up in uniform every evening at sundown. Now, you've really honored us by calling for our help. We're very grateful. We're so grateful that we're just going to charge you the rate for one security guard."

He paused long enough to let that sink in, and then he announced to the room in a stage whisper, "When I bring in Security Guard Takuda, I usually charge for three men."

Nabeshima giggled politely from the kitchen door, and even the tired woman at the desk smirked at Ota's presentation, if not the tired joke itself. Detective Kimura crossed his arms and assumed an indulgent smile.

Ota moved to the center of the room, behind Kimura's chair. "Well, then, there's a great lunch spot right around the corner. Security Guard Takuda, if you'll look the place over and take your station, over there, by the filing cabinet, that will be good for the moment."

Takuda felt all eyes on him as he eased past the manager. Nabeshima flattened herself against a filing cabinet to let him pass into the tiny hallway.

The office was a converted "2LDK" apartment: a living room converted to a front office, two bedrooms converted to Nabeshima's office and consultation room, a tiny bathroom, and a galley kitchen separated from the main room by an old-fashioned hanging accordion screen. Takuda examined the kitchen door and opened it to check the narrow alley. He tested the latches on the windows in the kitchen and bathroom. In the bathroom, he glanced at his face.

The left side of his face was crisscrossed with scars as if he had been laid on a griddle and turned once to make sure he was cooked through. The right side of his face bore several shorter scars and two healed burns, patches of shiny, pinkish skin on his cheek and forehead. Rising from beneath these obvious scars and healthy skin alike, faint lines of puckered, silvery flesh stood in ranks of discrete and unreadable characters, primitive cyphers that banded his head in cryptic ranks. His forehead bulged ominously at what he now thought of as "the corners" where the bone had thickened beneath the scalp, nascent horns ready to burst through the skin.

He kept his face largely immobile in the mirror because the effect was seldom what he intended.

Perhaps this is what the Nabeshima girl sees. Perhaps she sees even worse. Thank the Lord Buddha that my Yumi doesn't see me this way.

"Hey, Security Guard Takuda, don't get lost in that little bathroom. What are you doing, powdering your nose?"

No one laughed at that one. When he went back into the front office, he asked the office manager to move away from her desk so he could check the window beside her. They all stood in silence as he inspected the latch and looked for signs of tampering.

Finally, he turned to them.

"The apartment is solid. The front and back doors are steel, with operational standard locks. The bathroom and kitchen windows are too high for entrance without considerable noise. The window here by the desk is operational and safe. Use the speaker phone, not the headset. No one could get in here before you could call and get out via another exit."

Ota clapped his hands. "But that won't be necessary, because Takuda the Giant will be here."

"That's very rude," the office manager said. She sat down without even glancing at Ota.

Ota seemed not to hear her at all. "Well," he said to Hasegawa, rubbing his hands together, "shall we be off?"

When they had gone, the office manager introduced herself as Kaneko Yoshida. She was brisk and polite. "There's a chair in the storeroom, Security Guard," she said. "Please bring it out. I'm sorry I can't offer you anything more comfortable at the moment."

"Now then," Detective Kimura said to her as Takuda sat, "tell me more about this foreigner who wants your bones."

CHAPTER 4

Tuesday Morning

Detective Kimura leaned forward. "You must have been very frightened, Ms. Yoshida."

Yoshida frowned. "I thought it was a mistake. His Japanese was good, but *bones* had to be a mistake. It had to be. Then he laughed, a very nervous laugh, and it sounded very brittle and metallic. It was like he was calling through one of those old analog cell phones."

"Now listen to me," the detective said. He put his hand on the desk, not close enough to touch her, but she withdrew her arm anyway. "While you're telling me what he said, tell me how he said it. You said you couldn't identify his accent, but try to tell me anything you remember."

"That's what I've been doing," she said. "You haven't been taking notes, though."

He tapped his temple to indicate that he didn't need a notebook. "Please continue."

Yoshida didn't bother to look exasperated. "He was still talking in a rush, even though he sounded a little relieved to tell his big secret. He said the desire is not normal, but it is very comforting, like a place he goes when he is troubled or bored. He says that more and more, he goes there when he is doing something else, and even when he is very busy."

"So he is now in some discomfort. He's really obsessed, and it's getting in the way with his daily life. In a week, he'll be integrated, ready to completely decompensate."

Yoshida sat back. "That's fancy diagnostic talk. Are you a trained psychologist?"

"I've dealt with a couple of cases like this."

She blinked before continuing. "You have the mistaken confidence of the self-educated. I doubt any psychiatric professional would be confident enough to predict a complete psychotic break a week ahead. Anyway, he said he finds himself drawing bones in his journal at night and even in the border of his notepad during staff meetings, and he hopes the dean doesn't see him."

"So he's tenured."

"A foreigner with tenure here in Fukuoka? I seriously doubt that. He may be a full-time employee, but not with tenure."

The detective shrugged to indicate that she might be right.

"Anyway, he had slowed down a little by this point. He said these thoughts are pleasant except for two aspects. First, that these thoughts come from somewhere else, as if someone else desires these things through him, using his mind. And second, that there is a *flavor* or a *tone* to these thoughts that he cannot explain."

"Which did he say?"

"Which *what* did he say?"

"Did he say *flavor* or *tone?*"

"He said both. He said that there is a *flavor* or a *tone* to these thoughts that he cannot explain. At this point, I said he didn't mean *bones*, and he just used the wrong word. Or maybe *bones* meant something else, some sort of slang in the caller's mother tongue. Now I see that I made this a statement instead of a question because I wanted to convince him of the answer. But really, I knew the whole time that he meant what he said. I didn't give him time to answer, and I told him there were many men quite happy to have this desire."

"What did he say to that?"

"Not a word. I told him that in Fukuoka, there was a show club called Tomato Tomato, but I didn't even know if it was open anymore. This isn't Tokyo, and I don't think there's a big gay neighborhood like Shinjuku Ni-chome, maybe just a few isolated clubs. I told him he could ask around at the baths in Futsukaichi, or go ask in town. And I told him his Japanese was so good he could probably meet men online . . ."

"But he wasn't interested in men, was he?"

Yoshida sat back in her chair. "Just that student."

"Was he angry that you thought he was a homosexual? I certainly would be."

"I can only imagine, Detective. No, he was very calm, and he talked to me very politely, as if I were a stranger's child. His Japanese really is good, and he understands sarcasm. He told me that his desire is not sexual, that it is actually something quite pure and reverent. Just saying that he wants to lick the student's bones does not explain the devotional aspect."

" 'Devotional aspect,' he said?"

"Those were his words. I just told you. He also said he is very curious about the texture of the bones, how they will feel on his tongue. He imagines that the cranium, the jaw, and the cheekbones will probably be smooth, like polished ivory, but that the long bones, like the humerus and femur, may have some subtle grain like fine wood."

"Unbelievable."

"He said he has licked various surfaces around his house, trying to imagine how different bones would feel. He asked me if it sounded silly, walking around in the dark, licking countertops and cabinets and doorsills. I asked if he had hurt anyone or acted on these desires, and he seemed not to hear me. He said it was ridiculous to think about the texture because all the bones would be smooth when he had licked them clean."

"A man this disturbed can't stay hidden long. This

THE DEVOURING GOD 29

isn't his first threat, and we'll be able to catch him easily."

After a moment of silence, Yoshida spoke quietly and deliberately. "You can't even trace the call. How can you catch him?"

The detective smiled. "You know, when I worked in Tokyo, we had a system where we could track a cell phone to within one hundred to five hundred meters. We could receive the location circled on a map at any fax machine anywhere in the country."

"And why doesn't that work here?"

The detective just smiled.

"This is an old trunk exchange," Takuda said. They both turned to look at him. "Not only is there no stored information available about incoming calls, there's no way to trace incoming calls without advance preparation and active switching. Even though we have the destination, there's no way to trace to the origin until we can isolate the transfers for that particular call. It will take luck, but we will do our best."

The detective said, "Security Guard, when you say 'we,' you mean . . ."

"Ota Southern Protection Services. We offer a wide range of services, as I'm sure President Ota will tell you."

"I'm sure. Tell me," he said as he turned back to Yoshida. "How did the conversation end?"

"He said that because I thought this was some sort of sexual act, his offering should include a woman's bones as well."

" 'Offering'?"

"His words. He said his ex-girlfriend would be perfect, but she is a little short, and her teeth are crooked. These imperfections would ruin his offering, but it would be a beginning. Perhaps he should start there, he said, just because she is so short. He said, 'A journey of a thousand leagues also starts with a single step.' "

"Ugh. What did you say?"

"I said nothing. I sat there thinking how terrible it was that both this man and I lived in the same world."

The detective was silent.

"He said he still had a question for me, and I reached for the phone to disconnect, but he spoke too quickly." She straightened in her chair as if to collect herself. "He asked me again how tall I am."

The detective sat forward. "Do you think he means to harm someone?"

She frowned. "I don't know how he intends to get a woman's bones otherwise."

CHAPTER 5

Tuesday Evening

Thomas Fletcher went off his medication. Almost immediately, his obsession with Haruma's bones dissipated.

Then Japan came alive all around him.

It started with full-body spasms and white light searing his brain, followed by waking nightmares of blue-lightning death on Osaka train cars and the man who turned himself inside out with his fingernails. He knew the visible world would come alive as well, and he didn't have long to wait.

One morning, he saw a torn sweatshirt thrashing vainly in the eddied currents of a flood drain. It gestured to him for help. Later that day, two plastic bags buffeted by wind from passing cars spun in a mad tarantella above the median before shrieking off into the leaden sky. Coffee puddled in a subway corridor raced in runnels of grout to reach the soothing darkness in the drain hidden in the floor grate. The remainder, stranded, squirmed in the discarded can, rocking as if to spill itself. Thomas averted his eyes, but he somehow saw the can's spastic struggles no matter where he looked.

The awakening of Japan progressed, as day follows night, and the demons and angels he had seen all his life emerged from the crowd.

Thomas told no one. Instead, he spoke of the Japanese themselves. He insisted that they were insane. He insisted with conviction.

One evening, at his friend Tracy's apartment, he told the story of tutoring a mother and her as-yet-unborn child at twice the going rate. He spoke lovingly to a teakettle as if it were the mother's belly. As his audience responded, his pantomime lecture to the fetal scholar became passionate.

Gorgeous Tracy—her eyes were wild with laughter, and her new boy-toy, Benjamin, just grinned and shook his head, even though he was too new in the country to understand the context of the story. "Good Lord, what a country," he said. "A hundred bucks an hour to teach a fetus. That's crazy."

"That's not crazy," Thomas said, shaking his finger at Benjamin. "The Pachinko Lady is crazy."

"That's not crazy," Tracy said. "The Fujisaki Screamer is crazy."

"I give up," said Benjamin. Benjamin was a busy

guy, all busy with business, ready to get busy with Tracy, too busy to let a running gag play out properly. *Bastard.* "Who are these people?"

Tracy started: "The Fujisaki Screamer is a student, about fifteen years old . . ."

"Older," Thomas said.

" . . . and he wears a uniform from an industrial arts high school. He hangs out on the Fujisaki station subway platform and screams really loud. Just unbelievable. See, Benji, it's all about the pressure of the college exams. They call it 'exam hell,' and the kids go to special after- school tutoring centers . . ."

Thomas was well past giving a damn about the plight of Japan's youth. Benjamin, on the other hand, was fresh off the turnip truck. He knew nothing about Japan, and that's the way Tracy liked them, these newcomers who weren't yet exhausted by the life of leisure. She would *teach* him, she said. And then, as always, she would tire of him, and Thomas's time would come around again.

This was the life they had chosen, even though the world was theirs. The Berlin Wall was down, Vietnam was back online, and the Great Wall was up for grabs at pennies on the dollar. They could have been anywhere, doing anything, even building peace and prosperity in Port au Prince or Mogadishu or Beirut, if they had really wanted. Instead, they spent their terrible freedom staying up all night, drinking to the point of physical agony, and screwing like monkeys in the subtropical swelter.

Tracy made it look easy. She was built for a life of ease. She leaned over to fill Thomas's beer, her breasts swinging under her tee shirt, just as they swung when Thomas took her from behind, swinging one clockwise and the other counterclockwise, smacking into each other as her round rump rotated up toward him and he pounded her flesh . . .

"Thomas, dude, wake up."

They were waiting on him. Funny, but he dared not laugh. There was no way he could explain that lapse, so he explained the next Invisible Crazy:

"The Pachinko Lady walks in the middle of a four-way intersection in the rat's maze near Hakata Station. There's a big pachinko parlor on each of the four corners, and she just walks around in the intersection drinking coffee from paper cups. She's there from dusk until at least midnight, and sometimes she's there in the middle of the day, weaving in and out of traffic in a funky old fake leopard-skin jacket, winter or summer. She leaves her coffee cups in the middle of the intersection, and I've counted as many as fourteen. A true java junkie."

"She's a bookie," Benjamin said.

"Her husband went into one of the pachinko parlors one night, and she's still waiting for him," Tracy said. "I've always thought so."

"Yeah, right? She never figured out there was a back door," Benjamin said.

"Or she loves pachinko, but she doesn't know which parlor to go into," Tracy said. "The choices are just overwhelming."

"Or she's a road agent for a black-market organ network," Thomas said. "When pachinko players go around the corner to cash in their winnings, the black suits harvest them. The number of coffee cups the Pachinko Lady leaves in the intersection tells Yamaguchi-gumi foot soldiers how many livers are on ice. That's how they've paid for the new construction over by the prefectural offices. They just started liver transplants at Kyushu University Hospital, you know, the first liver transplants in Japan. If they have overstock from the transplants, they'll have banquets down by the castle ruins. Just like the old days."

Tracy stared at him. Clueless Benjamin said, "Yeah, a lot of strange stuff happens over here, and it's hard to tell if it's really that strange or if being here just softens you up for it."

"I don't know if the Japanese even see the Invisible Crazies," Tracy said, tearing her gaze from Thomas's face. "For us, they really stand out, but they may just fade into the background for the Japanese. Or the very reasons that we notice them makes them nonentities in Japanese society. Anyway, they wig us out."

Benjamin said, "Maybe we're just more Invisible Crazies."

Tracy pursed her lips. Thomas couldn't hear other people's thoughts, not yet, but he knew she was making a decision.

"I mean, you know these people aren't really invisible to the Japanese. They just ignore these Invisible Crazies the same way they ignore us. But I wonder what the Japanese say about us and the rest of the In-visible Crazies when they're at home drinking beer."

Tracy's smile broadened, and her eyes narrowed. The decision was made—Benjamin was history, and Thomas was back in the saddle. Not tonight, though, not yet. Tonight she would drain Benjamin, savagely, until he was wrinkled and blue, chafed, exhausted. Then she would kick him out.

"Um, Thomas, you're losing focus a little there, man."

Thomas had drifted again. Benjamin's expression was woefully concerned, the expression they had taught him to use when he wanted to pretend that he cared about anything he couldn't destroy outright.

Tracy's expression was pained. She saw. She knew.

She cornered Thomas in the kitchen later. She apologized about Benjamin, as if Thomas cared. She told Thomas she would help him find a new doctor.

"That doesn't work," Thomas said. "I've already lost two jobs, thanks to the doctors. The whole doctor-patient confidentiality thing doesn't mean anything here. We aren't people here. We have no rights here."

"Maybe confidentiality wasn't the problem," she said. "Maybe the doctors didn't say anything. Maybe your bosses just saw what they saw. Like Benjamin says, we aren't really invisible."

Just past her shoulder, willowy shapes floated slip-streaming in the polished wooden grain of her cabinet door. As Thomas watched, more and more appeared, whorled and faceless angels shining nut-brown on golden triptychs. One of them, the Boy Who Walks

Sideways, told Thomas their story: *We are very shy. We disappear when we turn sideways.*

They weren't invisible, and they weren't chameleons. They just knew how to disappear.

Thomas did, too.

He left Benjamin to his fate. He rode down to the beach for a little breathing room. *Japan, where it's so crowded the bedbugs are hunchbacks and you have to go to the beach just to change your mind.* He lay in the cool sand, thinking about Tracy bucking and writhing on top of him in the moonlight, and he thought of lovely little Kaori Nabeshima. What a fool he had been to kick her out. What the hell had he been thinking?

Then he thought of the bones again, of Haruma's bones especially, but it was just the shadow of the obsession, and he finally, finally felt like himself again. He had a nagging feeling that he had missed something about the obsession with the bones, but he pushed the thought away. He could still push thoughts away, to some degree.

He unbuckled his belt thinking about Kaori. Stroking himself as he remembered her trying to arouse him in his old farmhouse, he finally responded as wave after wave rolled in. The medication was finally wearing off. He was still thinking of Kaori as he spurted across the squirming dunes. His ejaculate shone like diamonds on the beach, but he kicked sand across it just in case it started to move of its own volition. Just in case.

We aren't invisible . . . I wonder what they say about us. What rubbish.

None of that was important. The oblong moon shattered on silent waves that beat sand with silent futility, one by one, before sliding back defeated into the bay. It always started with waking nightmares. That was just the first day or so. After that, things started to fall into place, and it all started to make sense again. Looking out at the waves, seeing them reaching for the moon, reaching for love and failing again and again, Thomas began to see for the first time that there was an invisible current flowing through his waking world. It was clear as day, just for a second: all human lives as silent waves washing up on the same beach again and again and again until the final, defeated slide back into the cold, black waters whence they came . . .

All for love, all for the moonlight, all for romance!

As he stumped through the sand on the way back to his bicycle, he wondered about the thing under his floor. He should probably return it before he got into trouble. He would just ride back to his house and get it, and he could drop it off where it came from. He had always had the feeling that it wanted to go home. It would probably be smart to help it go where it wanted to go. That would be the sensible thing to do.

CHAPTER 6

Tuesday Evening

It was a quiet evening in Fukuoka Prefecture Mental Health Services Satellite Office 6. Detective Kimura had left. Ota and the section chief had come back after lunch to tell them that everything was set up and that Takuda would take care of them. Despite Yoshida's chilly reception of this news, Takuda thought she would tolerate him.

Nabeshima, defiant in the face of her earlier fright, was more than tolerant. She was curious. She had seen Takuda at least in part as he saw himself in the mirror. Perhaps he was the first . . . *oddity* she had been able to speak to, though she didn't ask again why he looked as he did.

And I'm not asking what she sees when she looks at me. I don't want to know.

At her invitation, he sat across the desk from her. She spoke to him coyly, in a slightly flirtatious manner that made clear she considered him harmless. "I've just finished writing up my notes, and I thought I would pass the time catching up on my email. I have to use the second phone line, though."

"It's convenient, I'm sure."

"Yes, it is, but the connection is awfully slow. Anyway, where shall we go? I think we should look up the security guard. What is your given name, Security Guard Takuda?"

From the front room, Yoshida called out: "Kaori, leave the man alone."

"Oh, I have your name right here, on the paperwork your boss left us . . . Tohru. That's an old-fashioned character combination, isn't it?"

"Not when I was born."

"Ha. Neither was the name Kamekichi, was it? Oh, I suppose you're not that old. Now, from your accent, I'll say you're from . . . Honshu, probably north of the mountains, correct?"

Takuda said nothing.

"Yes, from the mountain shadow . . . Oh, here's your profile, I didn't even see that . . . former prefectural police detective . . . let's search!"

Takuda breathed slowly and calmly as the girl waited for her search results. It was too bad that she had a slow connection. It would be better if the results just came immediately, like ripping off a bandage. Then again, maybe it was better that she would be unable to download posted snippets of video about him and his partners. The print versions of his story were grim, but some of the television coverage was downright lurid.

Nabeshima inhaled sharply. She had found him.

"Ms. Yoshida, come here, please."

Yoshida came quickly, without a glance at Takuda. He sat impassively, waiting for them to finish reading. They were framed by the tall filing cabinets behind them, the older woman reading over Nabeshima's shoulder as their expressions passed from shock to revulsion and, finally, naked fear.

Finally, Nabeshima stared without expression at the screen, as if this was what she had expected all along. Yoshida looked as if she would cry or throw up. He thought for an instant that an expression of pity had passed over her face, but he didn't trust pity anymore. Over the previous few years, Takuda had found that fear overcame pity in most people's hearts.

Yoshida straightened and looked him in the eye.

"It's unbelievable you found work as a security guard. It's unbelievable you found work at all. Does your boss know what you do in your off-hours?"

"If he does, he hasn't mentioned it."

She moved slowly back toward her desk. Passing brought her closer to him, and she hugged the wall as she went. Takuda would have scooted forward to let her pass, but leaning forward over the desk would have spooked Nabeshima.

And Nabeshima was ashen, her pale face lit blue by her computer monitor. "Are you dangerous?"

Not to you, he thought, but the explanation was more complicated.

Yoshida slid behind her desk. She seemed relieved to be closer to her telephone, and she raised her head to look him in the eye, to prove that she wasn't afraid. "You should answer the question. It's a reasonable question."

"As a detective, I used force in arrests, but no one ever accused me of abuse."

"That's work. How about your off-duty excursions?"

"I've never harmed a living human being."

Nabeshima groaned as if that were a particularly bad joke.

Yoshida ignored her. "Are your accomplices here? The priest and the boy?"

"Accomplices? Reverend Suzuki lives with me and my wife. The boy, as you call him, lives with us as well."

"You stick together," Yoshida said.

"We try to work different shifts."

"Your poor wife."

Takuda bowed where he sat. "Yes, my poor wife."

"How long have you been working for Ota?"

"Ota Southern Protection Services. About seven months."

Nabeshima was staring at the screen. "So you and your friends came just after desecrating cemeteries in

Tokuyama. That was after burning down an ancient villa on Sado Island."

"She means destroying an irreplaceable national historical treasure," Yoshida said.

Nabeshima stood and edged past him. She stood in the doorway uncertainly, as if she would bolt if Takuda moved. "Did you burn yourself on Sado? When you and your friends burned that villa?"

Takuda knew she was trying to ask about his face without Yoshida understanding. "That's where I got some of the scars you see, from invisible fire. But we didn't burn anything. No charges were ever filed in that case, not even misdemeanor trespassing. The fire started beneath the flooring, in a hidden chamber."

Yoshida crossed her arms. "You and your friends have never been arrested, even though everyone knows you are criminals. You play on the superstition and ignorance of backward country people."

Takuda frowned deeply. He couldn't help it, even though the invisible scars probably made his face crease in unexpected directions. Nabeshima looked away.

"Your friends are as dangerous as you are," Yoshida said. "The local police who protect you tend to lose their jobs, don't they?"

He just looked ahead. He had been in this situation before, and there was no reason to speak. At least he had held this job for seven months. Sometimes he lost the job before the interview.

Yoshida exhaled as if she had been holding her

breath. "Well, this is unacceptable." She reached for the telephone.

That's when it happened: a slight quickening, a tightening of his muscles, a subtle shift in his own body that told him he was in the right place. As she picked up the telephone, his heart began to slam against his ribs.

"Please put that down," he said.

She hurriedly pushed buttons, pretending not to watch him. As he walked toward Yoshida's desk, Nabeshima slid sideways toward the kitchen.

He towered over Yoshida. She put the receiver in the cradle and sat down slowly.

"You must think this through," she said.

"You are in no danger from me," he said. His body was on fire, but his mind was at ease. "Do whatever you like after the call."

"The call?"

"Yes, the call. It's coming." The blood coursed faster in his veins. Without thinking, he clenched his calloused fist, and the knuckles popped deep in the flesh. "That is, I think it will be a call. Something is coming, and the doors and windows are secure."

"You are truly out of your mind," she said. Anger blazed in her eyes. "Nabeshima, use your cell phone."

"I lost it," Nabeshima wailed from the kitchen.

Yoshida put her hand on the telephone. She was half his size, and she was terrified, but she would fight if she had to. "This is a prefectural office, and you will not stop me from calling for help."

He was dizzy, as if the blood had drained from his

head. The power washed in more quickly and completely every time, and now it left him reeling. "You'll never understand it, but right now, I'm the only help you've got."

Her hand tightened on the receiver. "You don't have to live like this. When the manager gets here, we will all sit down and talk. I know people who could help you."

He laughed aloud. It was probably not a pretty sight, but he was beyond caring. Nabeshima peered around the doorjamb to see what was happening.

Both women jumped when the phone rang.

"There it is," Takuda said.

Nabeshima and Yoshida stared at him while he fished out his cell phone with trembling fingers.

"Didn't you want to record it?"

Nabeshima and Yoshida scrambled to turn on the tape recorder. The section chief had provided them with a microphone that attached to the back of the receiver with a rubber suction cup. Takuda doubted such an old-fashioned contraption would work with a modern phone, but they hadn't asked him. He dialed his partner.

Mori answered on the first ring. "I started the trace just before the call. I've already got him."

"Okay, you knew it was coming, too."

"Yes. I lost my balance, and I had to crawl to my desk, but I got it in time."

"Good. They have an old fax machine on the second line here." Takuda reeled off the number. "Just send whatever you get, please."

"Another minute or so. Ah . . . did the surge come to you, about ten minutes ago?"

Takuda rubbed his forehead. It was beginning to ache. "Ten? It just got to me about two minutes ago, and it almost knocked me out."

"Yes, it's strong this time. I saw shapes and colors I don't have names for."

"Well, call Suzuki. Ask him how long ago it hit."

Mori snorted. "Suzuki won't know. He doesn't feel it, and he has no sense of time. I still don't think he's one of us."

"Okay, okay. I've got to go. Fax it when you've got it."

Mori hesitated, and then he said, "Did you expect this? Did you know this was coming?"

"I thought something was coming. The way was cleared for me," Takuda said. "But tonight, I thought we were just going to trace a nuisance call and help make our friend Ota richer."

Mori didn't respond to jokes like that anymore. He hung up.

Yoshida and Nabeshima were cheek-to-cheek trying to share the telephone earpiece. Nabeshima's retro hoop earring had gotten tangled in the makeshift wiretap cord, but she didn't even seem to feel it.

Yoshida pleaded: "Who . . . wait, calm down . . . who stole what? Kurodama? What is it you're missing?" Yoshida looked annoyed, but she was obviously not terrified, and Nabeshima just looked confused. Maybe it was not the foreigner.

Was I wrong? Was the surge wrong?

As Yoshida tried to get answers from the caller, both she and Nabeshima glanced up at him. They were no longer quite so afraid. They were curious. They wondered how he knew.

Then we're in the right place. His heart sank. Every time, he hoped it was a false alarm, but the surge was always right. *We've got work to do.*

"Well, I can't . . . if you don't tell me who . . . no, no, don't hurt anyone. You're not . . ." Yoshida and Nabeshima both went limp. The caller had hung up.

Nabeshima blinked as if waking. "I know that voice," she said.

Yoshida concentrated on the little handheld recorder as she rewound the tape, so Takuda asked Nabeshima: "Was that the foreigner?"

She nodded. "He was very upset. It's hard to tell, but I think I know his voice . . ."

Yoshida's tape recorder gave a loud snap as it finished rewinding, and she pushed the play button. The three of them crowded in to hear. The caller's voice was unintelligible. Even Yoshida's shouting was muted and indistinct.

She grabbed her pencil. "Okay, let's get what he said. I think he said the Kurodama was gone, and he asked if it was here."

Takuda ran his palm over his scalp. *Kurodama*, black jewel, could refer to a brand of large table grapes, a brand of candies, or anthracite.

Nabeshima shook her head. "That doesn't make

sense. He was speaking in English half the time. It was really tough to understand."

Yoshida hissed, "Then tell me what you understood. Help me get this on paper!"

Nabeshima gave Takuda a helpless look, as if he could do something for her. The fax machine buzzed and whirred. Mori had isolated the source. He left them to reconstruct the foreigner's call.

As the paper edged out of the fax machine, Takuda began to understand why he had been brought to the satellite office.

"Ms. Yoshida, I need your help in here," he said.

She peered suspiciously into the back office.

He held up the fax from Mori. "Please come look at this fax from my associate, the one you call 'the boy.' We both work for Ota Southern Protection Services."

She rolled her eyes.

"We were ready for this call," Takuda said. "Tracing calls from an unknown cell phone is well within our reach, with the consent of the landline owner."

Her eyes widened. She approached, but she kept Nabeshima's little desk between them. "So you know who the caller is?"

"Not exactly. The cell phone owner has caller ID switched on. Your telephone is just too old to display it. Otherwise, you would have recognized the name." He handed her the sheet.

She read it, blinked, and then read it again. "Kaori Nabeshima?" she whispered. "Our Nabeshima?"

They both looked at Nabeshima perched on Yoshida's chair, trying to fill in the details of the foreigner's frenetic call.

Yoshida turned back to Takuda. "If this is some kind of game . . ."

"There's no game and there's no mistake. The call came from a cell phone account in her name."

Yoshida stepped away, watching him over her shoulder for the first few steps, and then she turned toward the front office with the fax sheet clutched behind her back. She approached Nabeshima slowly and carefully with her hand outstretched as if she were approaching a small animal.

CHAPTER 7

Wednesday Morning

His shift over, Takuda went home with the dawn. At his apartment block, his neighbor met him with a bow. "Thank you again. Your family is very generous."

Takuda had his helmet and uniform tied in a bundle on the end of his staff, like an old-fashioned delivery-man. He didn't bother to lower it as he spoke to this neighbor. He always forgot the man's name. "Good morning. You're up early."

"Yes, well, it's off to the market, thanks to your brother."

Off to the pachinko parlors and the speedboat races, more likely. "My brother, the tall one, he gave you money again?"

"Yes, he did. He's very kind. Now we can afford the

basics, even if we can't afford any of the little luxuries that make life so nice."

Takuda didn't have any cash at all, even if he were willing to give it up. He sighed and bowed before starting up the stairs.

Suzuki and Yumi hadn't left the apartment.

"Welcome home," Suzuki said. He bent over the breakfast table to shovel more rice into his mouth.

Takuda slipped off his shoes and stepped up into the apartment. The apartment was the 2LDK style, the same size as the mental health satellite office: two bedrooms, a living-and-dining room, a kitchenette, and a tiny bath. It would have been adequate for three adults of normal size, but Takuda's width and Suzuki's height left little space for Yumi and Mori.

"You gave the gambler next door more money for his vices," Takuda said.

"Perhaps he will learn from the virtue of generosity, which will outweigh and overcome his vices."

Takuda sat sideways so he didn't rub knees with Suzuki. "And there you were begging yesterday. You spent the money my employer dropped in your bowl on the neighbor's vices. Unbelievable."

Suzuki grinned. "I brought in enough for a week's groceries. Yumi and I are going shopping before work."

Yumi bumped Takuda's tailbone as she opened the bathroom door. He stood so she could get out.

Her greeting was warm enough, but she didn't quite meet his eyes. Something was wrong. *It could be anything. The apartment? Suzuki? Her two jobs? What isn't wrong?*

She dished up his breakfast as he returned his attention to Suzuki.

"So, out begging again. What happened to the tutoring job?"

"Oh, they didn't like my teaching style." Suzuki looked slightly guilty.

"Your teaching style? It's a cram school. They don't do anything but test preparation. How can your teaching style have anything to do with it?"

"Well, maybe the disagreement was more about educational philosophy than style."

Takuda tried to control his expression. "You didn't stick to their lessons."

"The testing system is stunting the minds of a whole generation." Suzuki awkwardly lit a cigarette. He had accidentally severed the nerve in the forefinger of his left hand with his own sword, and some everyday activities were still difficult.

"If the police catch you begging without papers, we can't pay the fine," Takuda said.

"The last time a patrolman stopped me, he ended up dropping five hundred yen in my bowl."

Yumi bent over the rice maker. "And what happens now that the rainy season is over? What will you do now?"

"True, the rainy season is the best," he called to her over his shoulder. "Everybody's under cover. I catch them at the bus stops, and they can't ignore me." He seemed to mull the question over. "Still, they were generous enough this weekend."

That was enough for Takuda. "This isn't a game anymore. You don't . . ."

"Please stop. You're wasting your breath on him. He's like a child," Yumi said. "You and Suzuki have bigger problems. No one will be working a week from now. Not Suzuki, not you, not me, not even young Mori. And if it's like what happened in Hagi or Sado Island, we'll have to move. Again. In two weeks, we'll all be begging in the streets." She put Takuda's breakfast on the table, and then she went into their bedroom and slid the door closed behind her.

Suzuki studied his cigarette with a half-smile that signified nothing at all.

It's easy to be happy when you are a complete fool.

"You all talk about me as if I'm not here," Suzuki said.

"You *are* barely here, Priest. You swim in a sea of your own silliness and we just see you when you surface for air."

Suzuki's brow furrowed, but he still smiled. "It must be painful to be bound by fate to someone for whom you have so little respect."

"Fate? Fate has nothing to do with it. You could walk away right now. So could I. So could Mori. We could all go our separate ways and go build normal lives. Eventually, everyone would forget about us."

"We tried that once, and the three of us showed up at the villa. All of us showed up at the same place at the same time. And we did battle, and we won."

Takuda sat forward. "We decided to stay together.

That makes life tough. But it doesn't have to be this tough." He pointed at Suzuki. "You make life tougher." He sat back. "Quit begging. Get rid of your ragged robes. Get a steady job and keep at it, and quit giving money to lazy, drunken gamblers like that fellow next door. Help save up for the next move. You know it's coming."

The smile never left. "But no matter what, I'm still a priest. That's my calling and my inheritance."

"Yes, you're a priest, but you're officially discredited, your temple is gone, and you have no followers. You're a one-man sect. Every time you pick up a stray dog who wants to hear your message, the police get involved because you're still posing as a priest."

"I'm not posing," Suzuki said.

Takuda picked up his chopsticks and prepared to tuck in. "Then find us a temple so we can all stay off the streets. I'm just about out of ideas here."

Suzuki looked at his hands. His little smile was so tight it was almost a frown.

Takuda ate. There was rice, fermented soybeans, egg, and strips of dried laver. They had breakfast on the table, and they had a clean, dry place to sleep. Maybe he was being too hard on Suzuki. They were living one paycheck ahead of disaster, but that was no surprise. It wasn't anyone's fault.

Still, the brooding priest filled half his vision, and he wished there were something else to look at while he ate breakfast. There was no TV, and no one had yet picked up an abandoned newspaper. Takuda just put his head down and ate.

Finally, Suzuki carefully unfolded his lanky limbs and pulled himself out from under the table. He moved to the middle of the floor and called to Yumi.

"We'll leave in a moment," she said.

"Please lend me your phone."

The door slid open a crack and then slid shut just as the phone hit the straw matting at Suzuki's knees.

Suzuki put it on speaker. Mori answered on the second ring.

Suzuki bowed with his palms flat on the floor and his face just a hand's width above them. "Lieutenant Mori, I wish to apologize to all three of you right now."

Yumi slid the door open. She was still combing her hair.

"I beg your pardon for my foolishness and my self-ishness. I have held on to an old dream too long, and it has inconvenienced you all. I beg forgiveness for all the trouble I've caused."

He sat up briskly. His smile was gone for the moment, but nothing had come to replace it.

There was silence all around. Takuda felt a small pang of regret, but they had all given up any semblance of a normal life. Suzuki was just catching up to reality.

Finally, Suzuki said, "Do you have any ideas about what we're facing?"

Takuda told them what he knew. Mori gave details of the phone trace and the revelation that the call had come from a phone registered to Nabeshima, the office assistant.

"It seems as if Nabeshima recognized the voice, but

she denied it later. I left your fax with the women, and I doubt they've even told anyone that the call came from Nabeshima's phone."

"They're playing a dangerous game," Yumi said.

"Well, they aren't fools. It's not our place to tell their boss or ours unless we think they're in danger," Takuda said.

Suzuki looked past Takuda's ear at the bathroom door. His head was cocked to one side, and his expression had dropped back into his usual half-smile. *He's gone already. So much for resolutions.*

Mori sighed over the phone. "Do we even know what we're looking for?"

"We don't," Takuda answered. "And last night, did you even find out where we should look?"

"No, it took longer than I expected to figure out the PIN for her phone. This Nabeshima girl is no dummy. I just had time to narrow the call down to a series of relay stations. The rest of it, account information and so forth, was a breeze."

"Well, the account information doesn't help us. We know where to find Nabeshima. What about the caller?"

"I can get you within two kilometers."

"Two kilometers? That's no good."

"That's good enough," Suzuki murmured.

"That's good enough," Yumi repeated. "Walk around asking for the foreigner. Pretend to be a deliveryman."

"Newspaper salesman," Takuda and Mori said almost in unison.

"I need my phone," Yumi said. "I'll have to go to

work in a few minutes. There'll be no time for shopping this morning, Priest."

He nodded, but he clearly wasn't listening.

When Mori hung up and Yumi left for work, Suzuki sat in thought for several minutes.

"You said that this foreigner said something was missing, that someone had stolen something from him."

"What of it?"

"He didn't say what it was? He didn't say anything about a jewel? A big curved jewel?"

Hair stood up on Takuda's neck. "A curved jewel? He was just angry about something stolen. Why would you ask me about a curved jewel?"

"Because there are no coincidences. Not in our line of work." Suzuki went to his room and returned with a sheet of onionskin paper. "If you find the foreigner, or find his house, keep an eye out for this."

Takuda took the page. The onionskin was crisp and new, as if Suzuki had just pulled it from a pad before folding it. It was an ancient curved jewel, like the dark half of a yin-yang symbol. A single notation in the lower right-hand corner: *Black as night. Inner curve is razor-sharp. This is the actual size.* If the curved jewel really were as large as the drawing, it would be too heavy to wear, too heavy for personal ornamentation.

He sighed. "The foreigner was asking about a Kurodama."

The priest shook his head. "Coal is too brittle to be shaped like this."

"But it's black, it says here. Black as midnight. A black jewel, a Kurodama." Takuda compared the drawing to the span of his hand. "Ancient curved jewels weren't like this. This is huge."

"No, actually, some curved jewels were quite large, but this one is different in other ways. It's a tighter curve, like a comma from an English font, a half-circle, and it comes to a definite point. A very sharp point. The inner curve of the tail is also razor sharp, or it was."

"Priest, you've seen this thing."

"I've heard of it, years ago, from my father. This sheet showed up in my begging bowl. I didn't see who put it there. There was another sheet, but I don't know where it is. Look, there will be characters incised right here, along the blade . . . or the tail, I should say." Suzuki pointed out rough and angular pictographs.

Takuda squinted at the characters. They were so rough and random-looking he had thought they were just bad shading on the sketch. He handed the page back to Suzuki. "Is it some sort of ceremonial knife?"

Suzuki folded it into a small, tight packet. "Ceremonial knife is one way to put it," he said. "It's the fang of the Devouring God."

CHAPTER 8

Wednesday Evening

With Ota's consent, Takuda took Mori along on the next shift at the mental health satellite office. The shift started with their witnessing an argument.

"There are just too many foreigners in this area. Just on the main rail line between here and the city, I see a new language school almost every week. All these foreigners have students they may be attracted to." Detective Kimura looked around the room, his long hair swaying slightly. Nabeshima returned his gaze. It was after hours, and she had been prepared to go before the detective showed up. She was in jeans and a tee shirt advertising Gen-Key, an energy drink:

> *I am a leopard.*
> *We must everyday nutritional,*
> *happy with B_1, B_2, B_{12}. . .*

Yoshida stood in the doorway to the kitchen. In the consultation room, Section Chief Hasegawa shouted into the telephone. Takuda stood at ease by the front door. Young Mori, sitting beside Nabeshima, bent over his laptop trying to reconstruct the foreigner's call from the garbled audiotape. The detective glanced at Yoshida and Takuda, who were both staring off into the middle distance. He turned back to Nabeshima, the only one who seemed to be listening to him.

"There's really no starting place, no reports of disturbing behavior by foreigners. There are a few complaints about noise and public drunkenness. There's one young man who urinates from his balcony, but that's part of a dispute with his downstairs neighbors." He put his hands on his hips. "I might have to go undercover to the clubs where the foreigners hang out."

Yoshida stifled a grimace and went toward the back of the office.

Nabeshima said, "Detective, you would be conspicuous, wouldn't you? I mean, if you went to a club, I'm sure everyone would know you're a policeman."

"No, of course they wouldn't. I haven't done a lot of clubbing since I left Tokyo, but I'm sure I'll catch up. We aren't talking about high school girls here."

Nabeshima smiled. "We might as well be. They're a month or two behind the fashions in Shinjuku, but they're still just girls. Down here, the foreigner clubs are full of community college students."

"Oh, do you know these clubs?"

"Of course I do. I've lived here my whole life, and I can tell you that you would be out of place." She glanced over at Mori. "Could some of our private security force be of use here?"

Mori looked back at her, and she tilted her head at him. His eyes dropped back to his laptop screen as red spots appeared on his cheeks.

The detective sat forward. "I don't think there's any place for private contractors in an ongoing investigation. That tape is your property, and it's not evidence of any crime except a prank call, so you can do with it as you choose. As long as he doesn't tear it up, right? Right?"

Mori looked up long enough to give a slow, measured bow of assent, then returned to his work.

"Anyway, we now have a phone trace in place here and at the central exchange. The second we learn where these calls are coming from, we'll have more direction."

Nabeshima glanced at Takuda. Yoshida drifted in from the kitchen. She stared at Takuda, but he continued to look off into the middle distance. The women were waiting to see if he would tell the detective that the calls had come from Nabeshima's missing cell phone.

The section chief burst out of his office, purple-faced with rage. Yoshida stepped aside in surprise.

"I've just talked to your chief of detectives. The man is a fool! He does not think this is a serious matter! A prank call, he said. Prank call! A mentally unstable man has threatened to polish the bones of my staff's cannibalized corpses as a form of worship, and he calls it a prank call!"

Yoshida and Nabeshima stared at him open-mouthed. The section chief stepped toward the detective, pointing a finger at his face.

"You are personally responsible. Do you understand? These women work day and night to get help for the mentally ill. Day and night! There should be a staff of six here. Do you understand that? We may not get computers or a decent phone system this year because we have to pay for security guards. We didn't get the equipment we needed last year because it was a choice between modernization and hiring another staffer." The finger shifted from the detective to Nabeshima. "Do you know how I could budget for someone as smart as she is? She passed the exams to get into Waseda University, but she stayed here and went to a junior college to help her family. Junior college! That's the only way I could afford her. Capitalizing on the misfortune of others, that's the only way I can get my job done here. Now, you so-called elite law-enforcement professionals tell me you can't protect my staff!"

The finger slowly tracked from Nabeshima to the detective. The finger had been trembling with rage; now it was dead steady. The detective sat back as if pushed.

"I hold you personally responsible for persuading your fool of a boss to do his job. Do you understand this? If you cannot convince him, then you had better find a way to protect my staff yourself." The finger dropped, and the manager bowed deeply from the waist. "I place my safety and the safety of my staff entirely in your hands. As one public servant to another, I implore you to help us at this difficult and dangerous time. Please do your best for us."

The detective leapt to his feet and returned the bow. "Yes, yes, of course, I am doing what I can. How can I resist your passionate and well-reasoned plea for . . ."

"Perhaps we should go together to speak to the chief of detectives." The section chief straightened his tie and smoothed his hair. "Do you have a car, or shall I drive?"

"I . . . uh . . . took the train this afternoon. Greenhouse gasses, you know." Kimura bowed in apology.

"Admirable. I will drive." He nodded to Yoshida and Nabeshima. On his way out the door, he stopped to talk to Takuda. The detective, following too closely, almost bumped into him.

"Security Guard, please convey our thanks to Ota Southern Protection Services. I will call later to formalize the end of your contract." He indicated Yoshida and Nabeshima with a nod of his head. "You may miss being the thorn among the roses here, but I'm sure you will find pleasant work."

Takuda bowed as the section chief and the detective left.

Yoshida turned on Takuda as the door closed. "Why didn't you tell him? Are you going to attempt to blackmail this poor girl?"

"Blackmail her? Blackmail her for what?"

"For our silence. We know who you are. We could tell your boss, and then you'd be finished in this town."

Mori looked up and made to take off his headset, but Nabeshima raised one sculpted eyebrow: *It's nothing.* He almost smiled as he went back to work.

Takuda stood very still. "We just happened to show up when your troubles started, but that's always how it happens. There are no coincidences in this world."

"What do you want, then?"

"We want to help," Takuda said. "We want information we can act on."

"Act on? There's nothing to act on. This has nothing to do with you. A disturbed young man who found Kaori's lost phone has made a couple of phone calls to her workplace. She's confirmed that the number is on speed dial. Some girls are missing, and there are rumors—unconfirmed rumors—of dismemberments. Rumors and unrelated occurrences. Don't you understand that? If you get involved as if this were some ghost-hunt, you will get us all fired, and it might endanger our town."

Takuda frowned at Yoshida. Nabeshima looked away. Takuda said, "What would it take to convince you that we are sincere?"

"Your sincerity is the problem. Your sincerity is ten times more dangerous than most people's dishonesty.

A hundred times. A thousand times. There is nothing you could do to convince us that you are anything but dangerous criminals."

"Even if I retrieved Nabeshima's cell phone from the foreigner's house?"

Nabeshima straightened. She and Yoshida glanced at each other before she spoke. "It would convince me," Nabeshima said.

"Wait," Yoshida said. "What do you two want in return?"

"We just want information about the foreigner and about Nabeshima's connection to him. She has been caught up in something we don't understand, but none of it is her fault."

"Ridiculous!" Yoshida said. "How do you know that?"

"We've all been brought together for a reason," Takuda said. "I'm sure that the reason is not the destruction of an innocent girl's reputation."

"Coming from you, the word *innocent* means so little that . . ."

Nabeshima stood. "Please let me speak to them. Please. Let me tell them what I told you." Her eyes were downcast. Her handkerchief lay twisted like a tiny storm on Yoshida's desk. "I rely on you as my senior. Please allow them to help me."

Yoshida stepped toward her. She watched the tears begin to flow again. Then she turned back to Takuda.

"I want assurances," she said. "And I want information about you and your friends. I want the truth."

Takuda bowed. "I will tell you everything," he said. "Anything you want to know, from the very beginning."

Mori took his headset off completely. "Miss Nabeshima, this is going to be a long story. Let's have some tea, okay?"

Nabeshima looked down at him coolly. Mori's intentions were good, but he had misjudged Nabeshima. Women of previous generations had escaped to the kitchen at times like this to wipe away the tears and soothe themselves with little office rituals like making tea. But Nabeshima was not an old-fashioned girl, and even if she had been, Mori was an outsider. Takuda himself wouldn't have asked her to make tea. He certainly wouldn't have asked in such a casual way, and he certainly wouldn't have asked while she was still crying. Young Mori was about to receive a lesson in manners.

Instead, Nabeshima picked up her handkerchief. "If we need tea, very well," she said. "Come help me carry." She turned toward the kitchen.

Mori watched her leave. He was clearly picturing himself in the cramped kitchen with the pretty young Nabeshima. He stood quickly and straightened his uniform, then followed her without a glance at his elders.

That left Takuda the security guard and Yoshida the social worker. Takuda waited for her to move, and then followed her to her desk. She folded her hands and waited. When he sat across from her, their eyes met. He didn't like her, and she didn't trust him, but that sort of thing didn't matter anymore.

"You let Nabeshima tell me what I need to know," he said. "Then I'll tell you what I have seen. When I finish, you may believe that I am a madman or a liar, as you choose." He looked her in the eye. "When I tell you my story, you must finally choose, for now and forever, whether you believe in devils, angels, and monsters."

CHAPTER 9

Wednesday Evening

After Nabeshima told Takuda about her relationship with Thomas Fletcher, Takuda told Yoshida everything.

He started with the Drowning God, the beast that had plagued the valley of his youth, murdered his little brother, murdered his son, and held a group of the valley's farmers in thrall until 1990. He told her of his return to that valley in that year and how young Mori and Reverend Suzuki had joined him to help fight the creature.

He told her he suspected that the Zenkoku Corporation had studied the Drowning God. He told her that a Zenkoku corporate lawyer named Endo had used Takuda and his cohorts to dispose of the water-imp when they tired of their murderous pet . . .

"Wait a minute," Yoshida said. "This Drowning God was a kappa?" She smirked. "A *kappa*?"

Takuda rolled up his sleeves. "It wasn't as cute as cartoon kappa or as logical as social-satire kappa." He showed her the scars where the Drowning God had sliced his flesh to the bone. "It was as bloodthirsty and merciless as social-satire kappa, though."

She blinked at the scars and nodded for him to continue.

He told her about the next three years of wandering with Yumi, young Mori, and Reverend Suzuki: finding pleasant, quiet little towns only to realize that they had arrived on the doorstep of a haunted villa or the edge of a demon-plagued forest. Even when they tried to ignore the supernatural bits poking into their world, they were pulled into the affairs of the locals, compelled to act against evil only they could end.

Mori and Nabeshima moved quietly on the edges of the conversation. They brought tea and snacks in a surprisingly subdued manner. *Letting the adults talk*, Takuda realized. He felt Nabeshima's eyes on him while he told Yoshida of their various fights with ghosts, demons, and monsters, and he wondered which of the three she considered him.

Mori didn't interrupt Takuda with corrections or additions, which was a surprise in itself. Takuda glanced at him during pauses in his story of their traveling horror show. Each time, Mori was watching Nabeshima. *On his best behavior.*

"What about the swords?" she asked. "One conspiracy site called you 'warriors against the forces of darkness, armed with nothing but medieval weaponry.' What's that all about?"

Takuda glanced at Mori, who shrugged as if to say he wasn't a lawyer.

"Reverend Suzuki had three swords handed down from his ancestors," Takuda said. "Gorgeous swords, true works of art. They came originally from Kuroda clan warriors, centuries before the clan came here. The warriors were passing through Naga Valley on a pilgrimage to Sado Island, and they barely escaped the Kappa with their lives. They donated both the swords and the land for a temple to Reverend Suzuki's ancestors."

Yoshida leaned forward. "That's the temple he was evicted from, accused of embezzlement, malfeasance, tax evasion, and . . ." She checked Nabeshima's computer. "And squatting."

Mori said, "He's not much at bookkeeping apparently."

Takuda grimaced. "Those charges were a ruse. The real story is that his parents disappeared, probably murdered, and his brothers abandoned him there. He hung on long enough to gather us and kill the Kappa."

"Ah. Sweet vengeance. And the three of you run around with unlicensed swords."

Takuda pointed to his staff. "I use that now. My sword was destroyed in the process of killing the Drowning God. Young Mori's sword is licensed. As a fourth-degree black-belt in Iaido, he's legally entitled to have a true blade in his possession."

"What about the priest?"

Takuda hesitated. Now it was time for him to trust Yoshida. "He has a long sword designed for the swallow-cutting stroke, a medieval masterpiece sometimes called a 'laundry-pole sword.' We try to make sure he doesn't cut his own foot off with it."

They were all silent for a moment.

Yoshida stood. "Well, I don't really know what to say about your hobbies. I just hope that the information our Kaori gave you won't end up hurting anyone. There is a disturbed young man. An innocent girl has befriended him. There's no reason to assume there's any connection to all this . . . other rubbish."

Takuda sat back, satisfied. Yoshida didn't seem to believe his story, but it sounded as if she wouldn't be trying to turn them in to the police.

Yoshida called Nabeshima, who gathered her things and prepared to follow.

"Our Kaori is going out," Yoshida said. "I will walk her to the station and return."

Mori all but leapt for the door. "I can accompany you to . . ."

Nabeshima bowed. "No, please. Let us go. We need time to talk, and . . ." She flushed crimson. "I'll see you day after tomorrow. I will. I just have to take care of something." She looked directly at Mori. "Until day after tomorrow." She whirled and sped out the door.

A bemused Yoshida strolled after her. "I'll be back soon. Don't bother to answer the hotline," she said to Takuda. "We don't treat demonic possessions."

Takuda made fists for the simple satisfaction of feeling his knuckles crack. Mori stood staring at the door.

"She doesn't believe us," Mori said. "She thinks it's a racket."

"But she doesn't think we're dangerous."

Mori sighed. "That's something at least." He pulled a folded sheet from his breast pocket and placed it on Yoshida's desk, right across from Takuda.

Takuda stared at the folded sheet. He hated it when Mori casually dropped things on him. These little bits of paper Mori pulled from nowhere were always portents of the worst kind of trouble.

"What is this?"

Mori pretended to study Yoshida's antiquated electric typewriter. "I found it on the floor in our room. I believe it's another sheet that showed up in the priest's begging bowl."

It was new onionskin covered with neat, dense handwriting. He spread the sheet flat with both hands and began to read:

The footage was silent, hand-tinted, a flickering image on a cracked projection screen: eight peasant farmers squatting, filthy and nearly naked, on a narrow spit of sand, a beach on a tiny island or perhaps on the tip of a peninsula. They could have been from any corner of Asia, but one wore braided straw sandals unmistakably Japanese. Beyond them lay three beached military boats, perhaps the boats on which the farmers had arrived. On the horizon stretched the mainland, a harbor city.

Before the farmers stood a low, rectangular stone box. A

thin rope tied to the stone lid was pulled taut by someone or something out of frame, and the lid tipped to the ground. The men gathered around the cavity thus revealed.

One drew from the cavity a knife that appeared to be made of black volcanic glass. The scene cut abruptly to a close-up of the object in the peasant's trembling hand. It was simply a palm-sized stone lozenge with a long, curved blade. The inner curve of the blade glittered. The film then jumped to a longer shot of the men passing the knife among themselves. Seven caressed it, but one held it in his palm and slapped it excitedly. As he spoke, gesturing toward the mainland, the others grew still and listless. Their faces took on a drawn, strained expression. They took the knife from the eighth farmer, who continued to gesture back toward the mainland, and they passed it flat from palm to palm among themselves. They were very still, except for the passing of the blade, and their eyes were downcast. The blade passed from one to another with increasing speed, fairly flying from hand to hand. The men seemed to barely use their eyes; each man released the blade in midair, but another hand appeared at the last instant to catch it, and so one more hand appeared to replace that one. The blade itself traced a flat and repetitive rosette above the sand. The eighth reached out for the knife several times, but it slid away on its own arc just as his fingers reached it. The final time, he jerked back and then rocked on the sand, pinching his right thumb and speaking angrily to the other seven. He tried to wipe the thumb with his own filthy tunic, but the blood did not stop, and he began to wrap it tightly with strips he ripped hastily from his own loincloth.

The seven broke into grim, unpleasant smiles, their mouths broadening in unison as if to a signal unheard by the eighth of their party. The eighth shouted at them. All at once, the jaws of the seven popped open, each man's lips peeling back in a painful rictus. They raised their eyes as one, still passing the knife with chilling precision. Moments before, they had been a ragtag band of quarrelsome farmers, and now they moved as a single creature. As the eighth fell silent and rose to back away from his fellows, the seven set upon him. They quickly overpowered him and pinned him to the sand. While he still lived, they began to separate his flesh from his bones with the stone knife.

The cameraman changed vantage points several times to capture the smallest details of this ritual. The grinning farmers bathed unconcernedly in the spewing blood. The blade passed from hand to hand as rapidly as before save for quick, dipping slices into the meat of their victim. Each farmer engaged his gruesome tasks with both hands, each slicing skin, retracting muscle, and restraining the victim for his fellows in turn, and together they were as efficient and impassive as laundry maids folding sheets. When a bone became disarticulated from the quivering carcass, the stone knife passed on as the bearer of the bone quickly picked away any remaining flesh, severing muscles or trailing ligaments with his teeth before licking the bone spotlessly clean.

The cannibalism, even though there was a great deal of flesh consumed in the process, seemed incidental to this ceremonial cleansing. Even painstaking processes like the disarticulation of the small bones in the hands and feet and the disassembly of the cranium were performed so quickly and efficiently that the knife itself was always in motion, always there when the next bone was in need of freedom from the flesh surrounding it. In the end, the brains were dumped unceremoniously on the heap of hide and organs stretched in a rough five-pointed star on the sand—one hideous smear for each appendage and one for the flayed-open head. The bones, cloven from the flesh and cleaned in a specific order perhaps relayed from the knife itself, were interlocked to form a cantilevered platform on which the cleaned blade finally was placed.

The seven, blackened with the drying blood and offal of their flayed comrade, knelt before their hideous new altar. Their gaze fell then upon the camera operator. The seven stood in unison and the nearest retrieved the stone blade from its ghastly cradle. The camera shook but the cameraman held firm as the seven advanced. Suddenly, bright red blossoms sprouted on their heads and torsos, new and urgent growths in the blackened field of dried blood. They fell as one, shot to pieces.

Immediately a spry old man in priestly robes, accompanied by a young man in an Imperial Navy officer's uniform, stepped into the scene. The old man, the hems of his robes instantly stained with blood, grasped the knife with fire tongs and tried to wrest it from the dead farmer's grip. The fingers would not release. The old man pulled, lifting the dead man half off the ground. The farmer's head lolled on the sand, but even in death, his lips were pulled back in that horrid grin.

Finally, the officer drew his sword and struck off the farmer's hand. The old priest unceremoniously dumped the knife into the stone box, hand and all. As he hauled the lid back onto the box, he indicated where the officer should cut the ropes, and the officer complied. As the priest turned away, the officer cut him down with a single stroke. The old man folded to the ground, murdered too quickly to register surprise. The officer deftly flicked the blood from his blade and sheathed his weapon. He gestured wordlessly to the cameraman.

Takuda sat up blinking. "What's a rosette?"

"A sort of floral pattern that loops out and comes back through the middle, like a chrysanthemum," Mori said. "I had to look it up. Strange character combination."

"So it's possession. This black curved jewel wants a cradle of bones, and that's what's behind the rumors about the starfish killer."

Mori frowned. "It seems to want pain." He took off his glasses and pinched the bridge of his nose. "I've been trying not to think about it, concentrating on Kaori Nabeshima's situation."

I'll bet you've been concentrating on her situation, Takuda thought.

"But the more I think about it, the worse it gets. An object that possesses crowds . . . There's a practical limit, of course, on how many victims could be flayed at once, but is there a limit on how many could be possessed?"

"Well, if this thing is real, it would be very easy to find the possessed," Takuda said, folding the onionskin. "Covered with blood, jaws locked in a grin. Should be easy to find."

"You told me Detective Kimura said the same thing about Thomas Fletcher."

"Well, I hope he was right," Takuda said. "I'm going to track Fletcher down tomorrow."

They were silent for a moment. Mori finally said, "Finding the possessed might not be a problem. Not joining their number, well, that's another question altogether." He put his glasses back on. Takuda couldn't see his eyes for the reflected lamplight. "As I said, there's a limit on how many victims could be flayed at once, but is there a limit on how many could be possessed?"

CHAPTER 10

Thursday Afternoon

Thomas Fletcher lived in a farmhouse at the far end of a village south of Fukuoka, surrounded by low, rounded hills the locals referred to as "mountains." The house was a heap of faded stucco and weathered cedar with a roof of reddish-brown clay tiles. Foreigners would call it quaint. Japanese would call it squalid, and only the very poor would live in it. Takuda hated walking into such places. *One day, I'll meet my match in some dark, unclean place like that old house. I'll die on a bed of broken plaster and rotten straw mats, watching some evil stalk me in the gloom.*

He slowed in the street.

I should just turn around. I should get plastic surgery and become a stunt man. I should get a mask and become a professional wrestler. Anything.

The villagers had noticed Takuda wasn't from those parts. One boy stopped in his tracks to stare and almost got himself run down by a cyclist. A wall-eyed, gap-toothed man in pajamas approached him gibbering, bowed profoundly, and then pointed out the way to Thomas's house. The whole village knew where Takuda was going. Even if it would have helped, he had missed the element of surprise.

He turned around and went back to the station for a cheap lunch.

Takuda picked at his fish. He was edgy and exhausted, but there was nothing else to do. Nabeshima and Yoshida had entrusted him with retrieving Nabeshima's cell phone from the mad foreigner despite their fears.

The women had discovered his identity at the worst possible time. If he had been able to befriend them as a security guard, not a monster hunter, life would have been easier, but there was nothing to be done. He had told them everything, and they were still trying to decide if he was a lunatic or a liar.

It had been worth it. They had finally told him how Nabeshima and the foreigner had become involved in the first place, an old story with a new twist. Thomas was a young foreign teacher at the junior college, and Nabeshima was a bored, bright overachiever attending a fifth-rate school. He was the only challenge in her life, so she pursued him.

He apparently began to act erratic fairly quickly after they became involved. He grew distant and uncommunicative. He began to spend more time with his private students than with her, and his lack of sexual interest in her made her suspect that he was involved with others, perhaps with another foreigner with whom he worked. When she asked him why he did not want sex with her, he started spouting gibberish, she said, and threw her belongings into the street.

Nabeshima told Takuda to look at Thomas's artwork.

"Look at his journals, if you can, and look at his sculpture," she had said. "He's really good. His sculpture is in the lobby of some Zenkoku Sales office."

Takuda had tried not to squirm. "I've dealt with Zenkoku before. What will his art and his journals tell me?"

"That the world doesn't look the same to him as it does to most people."

Takuda looked at her closely. She looked away. He said: "He sees things other people don't. Just as you do."

She did not reply, and she still didn't look at him.

Takuda asked, "How does he have your phone?"

"When he threw my things into the street last week, the phone was gone. I thought that perhaps I had lost it earlier. I decided not to lock the account in hopes that someone would call my home number."

"Any luck?"

She shook her head. She was leaving out important information, of course, but not to protect herself. She still liked the young foreigner even though he had gone insane.

Takuda already knew it was not as simple as insanity. He just hoped he could retrieve the Kurodama before anyone got hurt.

Thomas lived next door to his landlord. In the garden between their houses, melons and small, green-skinned pumpkins lay rotting in the dirt, some of them exploded from the overlong rainy season. Bean pods hung limp and black on the vines. Takuda marched up to the door and rapped sharply, and then he slid it open and yelled out his presence. *"Daily Yomiyuri!"* If he was going to play the pushy salesman, he would do it with gusto.

There was a faint, sharp reek like rotted crab. It took Takuda back to an earlier horror, but there was nothing supernatural about this stench. Thomas's entrance pit was almost filled with plastic bags, all from the same convenience store, each the same size and shape, each sealed with a nearly identical cross of masking tape. Twenty-five bags were lined up five by five, probably waiting for disposal. Takuda stepped in.

"Excuse me! *Daily Yomiuri!* Would you like to subscribe? Special subscription rate today . . ."

The long, narrow front room was darkened. The walls and windows were draped with yellowed canvas bunched and puckered where it'd been nailed to the beams. Pinwheeled spatters of paint had faded so they met and melded with creeping brown water stains and black constellations of mold. In the middle of the back wall, one section of canvas bearing the legend *Welcome to Yokatopia Art Space Bravo* hung in ribbons and tatters, and the wall behind was gouged to the lath. Plaster had been trodden to dust where ruined canvas sagged to the floor.

He felt eyes on him and looked up. There stood a skinny foreigner, pale and freckled, a redhead with watery, red-rimmed eyes. His eyes were so blue as to be almost transparent. Takuda found it disconcerting, but he grinned and bowed. Thomas didn't say anything.

"Excuse me! *Daily Yomiuri!* It's lucky that I found you at home!"

Thomas smiled slowly and cocked his head to the left. "Good morning. You're back."

Back? Takuda smiled and bobbed two quick bows as he reached in his pocket for an order form. "Yes, a lucky day for both of us. Happy to find you here. You know, *The Daily Yomiuri* is the least expensive English newspaper in Japan . . ."

"Back for your money," Thomas said. He stood, head still cocked as if he were a broken puppet.

"Quite right," Takuda said after a pause. Then in a rush: "For the subscription rate this low, there's really nothing like it. Plus, there's nothing like it for a teaching aid. It's a daily lesson plan. That's what teachers call it in Tokyo. A daily lesson plan."

Thomas smiled a little more tightly and looked at the floor as if considering his words. "My lessons don't come from newspapers, and they are not suitable for all students." He paused as if he were mulling it over. "Anyway, I'm losing students for some reason. They aren't coming back anymore. Perhaps my lessons were becoming too difficult."

Perhaps your voice is getting such a sharp edge and your house is becoming so strange and dark and smelly that they couldn't bear it. Takuda smiled and indicated the back wall. "Are you an artist as well?"

Thomas relaxed visibly. "It's what makes life worth living. While I get your money, come see my new sculpture for the Zenkoku Sales office in Oita. It's my best work yet."

Takuda slipped off his shoes and followed Thomas toward his studio, an old glass-ceilinged potting shed joined to the house by a low, narrow passage. Thomas stopped Takuda in the passage and went into the greenhouse alone. Takuda stood in the dark listening to dull ringing, like rocks in an oil drum, then Thomas came and led him out of the dark passage.

The greenhouse studio seemed bright, even though the day was overcast. On a plywood box in the center of the room, a three-headed dog slunk low in a hunting posture. It was huge, flanks all corded muscle, left forepaw raised in midstep. From the hip-wide sternum sprang three sleek, muscular necks, each flowing into a triangular head. Long jaws and thick, ridged skulls, blank almond eyes, and sharp, erect ears made Takuda think of wolves' heads stretched and flattened to reptilian proportions. The rightmost head, tongue lolling, stared straight at him. He circled left to examine the long, even fangs, but his eyes caught in the net of sinew where necks met shoulders. From there, the center head strained low with its nose almost to the plywood, nostrils flared and expression as intense as a human frown. The leftmost head, raised high, stared in ear-pricked alarm at something past Takuda's left shoulder. All three heads watched him light a cigarette.

He walked around it twice, tracing the lines with his finger a centimeter away from the plaster: the delicate slash of nostril; the regimented concavities of the outer ear; the folded musculature of jaw.

Takuda stepped back and then walked around the other way to take in the totality of it. "It's amazing, Mr. Thomas," Takuda said. Takuda turned, and Thomas was staring at him bug-eyed with a bandanna clutched to his mouth and nose. Thomas backed out of the studio gagging into the bandanna.

Takuda turned around twice looking for something that would serve as an ashtray. Bits of string, wire and tubing, apparently sorted out by gauge and length rather than composition, hung neatly on pegboard hooks. Cans of paint stood in regiments on handmade racks, their labels removed and colors hand-lettered on the cans themselves. The oils were in a wire rack beside them, all squeezed from the bottom and rolled around plastic laundry pegs. Not a speck of clay or plaster anywhere, not even on the plywood under the three-headed dog. Nothing that looked like an ashtray. He didn't dare stub it out in the wrong place. Foreigners were apparently very particular about things like smoking and sex and eating meat.

At the sink, Takuda lifted a blue plastic tarp to

reveal the handles of knives and clay tools, scrapers, hooks, and even an old upholstery knife, all with their blades neatly encased in cylinders of plaster. He picked up an entombed tool with a long, cylindrical handle. It was obviously a wood chisel, encased so carefully that it barely wobbled when Takuda rolled it on the counter. The rusting blade within had stained the plaster yellow and palest orange. Takuda laid it back in the sink among the rest. His cigarette wasn't half-smoked, so he stubbed it out near the drain and stuck it back into his pack. If Takuda got the place dirty, he might end up in plaster as well.

The corridor to the main part of the house was dark and narrow, and the walls were rough enough that they snagged Takuda's trousers. He stooped to feel the paneling, and found it chewed and battered. He flicked his lighter long enough to see that both walls were covered at knee height with crescent-shaped gouges, bright and fresh in the age-darkened cedar as if someone had crawled along on hands and knees hacking at the walls.

Thomas wasn't in the main room. Takuda was suddenly very wary. He called for Thomas from the center of the room, listening to the sound of his own breath.

Then Thomas appeared in the opposite hallway, silhouetted by bright sunlight behind him. He held a small object in his hand.

The Kurodama, Takuda thought. His fears about entering the dark farmhouse returned. *He's not mad, he's possessed by this stone knife, and I'm going to have to kill him to get out of this place alive.*

CHAPTER 11

Thursday Afternoon

"**Y**ou're a man after my own heart," Thomas said. Takuda stared at the foreigner silhouetted in the light from the kitchen. "I like that spot, too. Sometimes I just stand there."

Thomas's favorite spot was in the middle of his work: shredded canvas and gouged plaster, a covered easel, a shin-high table with pens and notebooks, a hip-high table with a large plywood box. As Takuda twisted to look back at Thomas, Thomas stepped up to him and put the dark object right in his face. It wasn't a knife, but Takuda jerked back just for show.

"Sir, you scare me to death! What are you doing?"

The object in the foreigner's hand swam into focus: a squat brown bottle, some sort of energy drink. The bottle was nice and cold. Takuda grunted his thanks in what he thought of as a friendly foreign fashion and twisted off the cap. The drink was carbonated, with sweet, high notes like Ramuné soda and an undertone like watered-down cough syrup. Takuda swallowed, because it didn't seem dangerous. The aftertaste was of potting soil and Chinese five-spice. No alcohol whatsoever. Takuda squinted at the label: Gen-Key, a miniature of Nabeshima's tee shirt.

> *I am a leopard.*
> *We must everyday nutritional,*
> *happy with B_1, B_2, B_{12} . . .*

"It's very good for you. You look very flushed. Is something wrong with you? Are you ill?"

"I don't know," he lied. "It happens sometimes, when I've been working too hard. I'm eating enough, but I'm not sleeping." Takuda felt strong as an ox. The Gen-Key had made his guts lurch with the first gulp, and it stuck to the back of his tongue like a hangover. "I'll have to lay in a supply of this stuff."

Thomas edged toward the little table, so close that their elbows touched. He was deliberately pushing Takuda away from his writing. If Thomas was uncomfortable, fine. Takuda hoped he was so uncomfortable that he'd leave the room and give Takuda a chance to look for the phone. Takuda reached past Thomas toward notebooks laid open on the low table. "You draw, and you write poetry. Can I have a look?"

Thomas closed his notebooks one by one. Takuda drew his hand back, and Thomas bent motionless with his hand on the last book. "I'm not interested in showing anyone my notes just now. They really have gone well beyond what you see here." He gestured absently toward the plywood box on the hip-high table. "But there is one little bit of work I can show you."

When Thomas gestured toward the box, he accidentally flipped a loose sheet with his sleeve and uncovered the tiny prize: a cell phone no bigger than a candy bar, opalescent pink and gray with a jeweled strap.

Takuda bowed. "Sir, please give me the money. I must be elsewhere soon."

Thomas didn't move a muscle. "What are you doing here?"

"What do you mean?"

He looked Takuda dead in the eye. "Just that. Just. That."

Takuda bowed at thirty degrees and held position. It made him belch a combination of grilled fish and Gen-Key. "Sir, I don't have time for any games like this. I am grateful for the drink and your hospitality, but I really must be going. The money, please." He held the bow, not knowing whether a foreigner would understand the meaning of such a prolonged attitude.

Thomas snorted as if frustrated with himself. "I was afraid you were here about a girl."

Nabeshima? Why would anyone be here about her? "Ah. I see. You like a Japanese girl?"

"Oh, yes. Kaori and I . . ." He was looking at the torn canvas, and his lips were moving, silently toward torn canvas, broken plaster, hacked lath.

"What are you looking at?"

Thomas snapped back into the moment. "It just takes time," he said. "You Japanese say it yourselves. You are like onions; you reveal yourselves layer by layer."

Takuda had never heard such a thing, but he didn't care to argue about it. "Japanese girls are like onions because they make you cry. Please, sir, the money." *So I can grab the phone and get out of here before I throw up.*

He turned as if Takuda had just walked into the room. "It's an analogy. The Japanese use it to explain that you get to know people bit by bit. It's a cultural difference, and I'm surprised you don't know this after shaking down foreigners. Do you even try to peel us, or do you just chop us up all at once?" He laughed. It sounded like a dog yelping. Takuda had to look away.

"I'll show you an onion," he said. His high-pitched laugh still grated on Takuda's inner ear. He lifted the plywood cube to reveal a pop-eyed, grinning bust. It was as if a maniacal, grayish-green child were squirming its way up through the table. It was made of some sort of plasticene, but it was sleek and striated like carefully folded corduroy.

Takuda stepped up to the table: the bust was a skinless head, like the plastic one from his high school human anatomy class. The detail was perfect. The stretch of the muscles on either side of the pharynx alone was too precise to have come from imagination. The left side of the head had patches of plasticene skin applied but as yet unsmoothed. The fat and flesh had been filled in around the lidless eyes, but the mouth was still lipless, revealing a slight underbite and crooked bottom incisors.

Kaori Nabeshima. Chills slid up his spine like ice water, but his face felt light and flushed. His guts gurgled. Gen-Key did not agree with him at all.

Thomas stood too close behind him. "I'm doing this one inside out. Layer by layer. The onion analogy breaks down in the face of true knowledge."

Takuda's hair stood on end, and his left ear was twitching uncontrollably. Takuda hadn't even known he could move it. He reached up to stop it. "This is interesting," he said, but he was shouting inside, and he was somehow afraid Thomas would notice his spastic scalp. He struggled for something else to say, just to keep from turning around and running. "Uh, why is there dust on it?"

"I don't know." Thomas smoothed his own fingerprints from the temple. "Sometimes you just get to a point where you see the finished product in the unfinished piece." He passed his palm over the crown of the skull. "I don't think I want it to be finished."

Takuda stepped back. "I've got to go." He backpedaled for the door. "If I don't have the money this afternoon, delivery will stop automatically. Today." Thomas turned on his heel without change of expression, then veered back toward the bust after the third step. He put the box over the bust carefully, then went into the bright hallway without a glance in Takuda's direction.

Takuda lunged for the cell phone, pocketed it. On impulse, he flipped open one of the notebooks, found an empty page, and drew a large, comma-shaped symbol like the drawing of the curved jewel Suzuki had shown him.

When Thomas came back, he seemed furious that Takuda had opened his journal. He froze when he saw the half yin-yang symbol.

"Do you recognize that?" Takuda said. "Have you seen anything like that, but made of stone?"

Thomas held out a white packet. Takuda assumed Thomas had put the money in a clean white envelope, as polite Japanese often do, but the bills slipped out of a facial tissue and into Takuda's fingers. Too dirty for Thomas to touch directly. "Right," Thomas said. "Here it is, all of it." He smiled, but his eyes were slits, and his lip was quivering.

Takuda pinched the thin wad hard, spreading the bills enough to count them. He put it into his wallet slowly, not letting his hands shake. When it was all put away, Takuda looked Thomas in the eye.

"Have you seen a stone like that?" Takuda asked again. "A curved jewel?"

Thomas's face twisted with rage, and he opened his mouth to speak, but then his focus began to wander all over Takuda's face. "Your face, up close. You're covered with . . . with writing."

Ah, this poor boy is so special. "I don't know what the writing is, but I mean you no harm."

"You're a devil. You're growing horns. Are those horns?"

"They aren't horns. I don't know what they are. Sir, have you seen the stone knife? Where is it now?"

Thomas backed away, toward the brightly lit kitchen.

Takuda went after him, but he was almost felled by another wave of nausea and dizziness.

"Thomas Fletcher, where is the Kurodama?"

"I don't know!" Thomas shouted from the kitchen. "She took it! They took it! Someone took it from under the straw mats!" He slid the kitchen door shut with a bang.

Takuda came up the hallway, belching and retching. By the time he got the kitchen door open, Thomas was long gone, out the back door.

Takuda didn't tarry over Thomas's notebooks or stacks of student papers. He did move the tables enough to look under the straw mats. There, under the central mat, was an old-fashioned hidey-hole cut into the subflooring. He slid the panel aside . . . . empty. Anything once hidden there was gone.

On the way to the station, Takuda stopped to vomit, spewing the pavement in a shocking arc that made one woman not only cross to the other side of the street but wait to pass until Takuda was done, as if she were afraid he might suddenly hit the far sidewalk. With thin lunch stringing from his lips and the horrid aftertaste of Gen-Key to keep him company, Takuda felt his pocket to make sure the cell phone was there. *A fool's errand*, he thought, *but at least we can make sure no more calls don't come from the Nabeshima girl's phone. And then we may perhaps have some allies. We shall see.*

Takuda slept till late in the afternoon, and he went to the mental health satellite office at twilight, well after office hours, just in time for the night shift. He showed up in uniform, with his staff over his shoulder, but the office was dark. He let himself in and found a note on Yoshida's desk:

> *Security Guard Takuda,*
>   *Miss Nabeshima has been hospitalized.*
>   *The foreigner beat her.*
>   *I will return as soon as I can.*
>   *Yoshida*

CHAPTER 12

Thursday Evening

Most of Nabeshima's face was yellow-brown and purple. Her left eye was swollen almost shut, and her right eye twitched as if she were dreaming of another fall. Iodine, stitches, and tape traced the hospital's work on her shaven scalp.

Yoshida sat in the only chair in the room, so Takuda leaned against the wall and watched the saline drip. "How did her face get so beat up? Did he do that?"

"The wormy little redheaded bastard pounded her with a chisel encased in plaster. He froze when the plaster broke and exposed the blade. She ran, and he chased her, and she got up on the neighbor's roof. She was throwing tiles down on him, and she got him good. He fell right on his own chisel. In under the collarbone and out over the shoulder blade. Lucky he didn't bleed out right there. She broke her leg jumping down, and she passed out from the pain as soon as people came out of their houses. That's what she told the police right before dinner."

"Was Kimura here?"

She shook her head. "No, his boss, the chief of detectives. Section Chief Hasegawa is waiting for Kimura in the lobby. It's going to get ugly. If you want to earn your salary, since you didn't protect our girl Nabeshima, you can at least protect the section chief from his own anger . . ."

Her face twisted, and the tears began to flow. "Stupid girl. Stupid, stupid girl." She reached out to smooth Nabeshima's hair or stroke her cheek, but there was no hair to smooth, and the cheek was a mass of bruises, tape, and oxygen tubes. Her hand trembled in midair for a second before she withdrew it. "Oh, stupid girl."

The saline dripped, and Takuda pretended to watch.

"The chief of detectives was named Ishikawa, by the way. He asked about three men answering the description of you and your friends, asked if you'd been around. He'd heard that you and your friends were some sort of special consultants sent down from the heavens. I didn't tell him where I thought you'd come from."

Takuda bowed slightly. He didn't bother to tell her he didn't know Chief of Detectives Ishikawa, and he didn't bother to thank her for simply keeping her mouth shut.

"Anyway, the section chief brought flowers and candy and a stuffed giraffe. He said the giraffe reminded him of Nabeshima because she had such a long neck, like Audrey Hepburn. So she told me to stuff it all in the trash as soon as he left. He's the one who signed off against her dental benefits and overtime pay, but he's so screwed that he's trying to make it all look nice." She shook her head. "The section chief is desperate now with the chief of detectives around, and he's looking for somebody to blame. He was asking why we all didn't come to him, if we knew the situation."

"What situation?"

"Thomas and Kaori. I'm her direct supervisor, so of course I'm in trouble here, but he's in worse trouble."

"Thomas worked for Zenkoku. This will sink without a ripple, and everyone will be paid off handsomely."

She smiled a tight little smile. "Look at that girl. Do you think she's going to go away quietly?"

She stood and motioned for Takuda to follow her out.

Before he left Nabeshima, he reached into his zippered pocket and drew out her tiny pink-and-gray cell phone. He had wiped the grime from Thomas Fletcher's house from the phone housing, but it still seemed unclean. Still, he thought it might give her some comfort to have it back. He looped the strap around her thin wrist, the one without the IV tubes.

In the corridor, Yoshida turned and punched him right in the sternum. Her fist was small and hard, and the punch was like a solid poke with a broomstick.

"This is your fault. You know about these things, and you could have protected her. Go find out what's happening with this insane foreigner and with these girls disappearing."

"I can't protect girls from their own bad decisions. Anyway, you told me you thought these things were unrelated. You were so sure about this. What changed your mind?"

She stared off in the middle distance, and then she spoke very deliberately: "Kaori says she sees things. What she said she sees corroborates your tales of . . . other worlds." Her eyes flicked to Takuda's face.

Takuda nodded. "The name Nabeshima sort of rings a bell. It's an old family from Saga Prefecture, right? Maybe seeing other worlds runs in the family. They've had problems with shape-shifting cats, from what I've heard."

"Why am I not surprised you would know that?" Yoshida closed her eyes for a second. "She says you're crisscrossed with burning blue scars and great horns are ready to burst out of the corners of your forehead. She says the boy Mori has a bright green globe hiding beside his heart, like a seed ready to burst." She hesitated. "She says she saw the priest begging over on the market street. She says the priest is all smiles, but every time he smiles, the hunger leaks from between his teeth like burning lava. She says the hunger inside the priest is the most terrifying thing she's ever seen."

Takuda frowned. "Did she say . . . can she tell if the priest is good or . . . or not good?"

Yoshida looked astonished. "I'm in counseling, not personnel."

Takuda thought he might slap someone before the day was out, but it wouldn't be Yoshida. He needed an ally. "Thomas Fletcher is unstable, but I don't think anyone could know he was so dangerous."

She snorted.

Takuda pressed her. "Miss Nabeshima sees things, but you know things. You knew something had possession of Thomas Fletcher the first time you talked to him, and you knew he was free of it when you spoke to him again. You heard the difference."

"Don't start talking about pathology versus supernatural evil, please."

Takuda stared at her until the smirk faded. "We think it's an object," he said. "An ancient object that drives people to kill."

"Rubbish."

"People are missing in unprecedented numbers, so many that there's a press blackout. There are rumors of a dismemberment killer, a jellyfish killer."

Yoshida shook her head. "Starfish killer. I've heard of that. There's nothing in the news. A blackout on missing persons wouldn't keep murders quiet."

He nodded. "Maybe not. But think about the phone call you received. What would a corpse be like without its bones? Like a jellyfish, yes? Or maybe laid out in a starfish pattern?"

The color drained from her cheeks.

Takuda continued. "We need to find out about this. Thomas Fletcher may know something. If he's medicated now, he may be able to tell us."

Her face contorted. "He'll be so medicated he can't tell you his mother's name. He's in intensive care in a secure facility."

"Ah. Perfect. You can tell me where he is."

She was very still.

Takuda looked at his boots. "He spoke to me a little this morning. He might speak to me again. He might be able to tell me about the artifact."

"He'll be in lockdown until he's tried or deported."

"And he'll be deported quietly, no matter what Miss Nabeshima says," Takuda said. "I sort of fade into the background. If your young coworker hadn't . . . seen things . . . you would have forgotten I was even in your office. I even fit in when I'm wearing the wrong uniform."

She sighed. Her hand shook slightly as she pushed back her hair. "What if you were already wearing the right uniform? Let's say the uniform of the maintenance staff of a mental hospital?"

"Go on."

"He'll be in a public facility in the southern ward, a place I know well. Near the back door is a custodial staff office where keys hang on a board. The psychiatric and medical personnel, of course, wear formal whites, no scrubs. But the custodians wear jumpsuits much like the one you're wearing now."

He nodded. "We'll stay in touch. I'm sure this will be helpful, even if he doesn't know where the artifact is right now."

When they walked out to the reception area a few minutes later, they came face-to-face with Section Chief Hasegawa.

He had a whole bench to himself, even though several people stood nearby. His mass, his rumpled suit, and his radiating anger drove everyone else away. He was an enraged and desperate bureaucrat in his prime.

He saw Takuda and Yoshida approaching, and he leapt to his feet, his face twisting as if the first words of his tirade were fighting each other to escape his mouth.

And at that moment, the glass front doors whooshed open and Detective Kimura sauntered in from the darkened street.

Hasegawa's gaze drifted from Takuda and Yoshida to Kimura. He strode to the detective and poked him in the sternum with his thick forefinger. "You didn't take care of my staff." His eyes were red-rimmed and puffy. "She says you knew. You knew he was unstable."

Kimura said, "Sorry, but I can't comment on this ongoing investigation."

Hasegawa leaned into Kimura, his face even darker.

Yoshida groaned. Takuda handed her his staff.

Hasegawa had Kimura by the collar by the time Takuda reached them. Hasegawa grunted and strained as Takuda gently forced himself between them, inexorably wedging them apart. "Security guard . . . you . . . oof . . . let me . . ."

It was just a matter of keeping himself between them. He bowed as Hasegawa threw punches past his ribs, murmuring apologies in the politest language he knew, ridiculously polite, period-drama polite, so polite he had never used some of the phrases himself.

Hospital security came just as it was winding down. Takuda bowed and explained that they would all leave soon, and that there was a simple disagreement on protocol. Prefecture business and all. Takuda didn't even have to look to know that Kimura flashed the detective's notebook at that point.

This set the stage for the head of hospital security to step forward and lambaste them all, leaving Takuda to use his most polite Japanese twice in the same day. This was the detective's cue to slip out the door, and it should have been the section chief's time to go as well, but he stood and made his bows beside Takuda, handing over his card and explaining that he was protecting a patient from badgering by police.

"That's the doctors' decision," said the head of security. "It's a hospital, not a bar. You don't go having this sort of dust-up in the lobby."

No one pointed out that the shouting by the head of security was louder and longer than the original scuffle.

When it was all over, Hasegawa thanked Takuda. "It's been twenty years since I got that angry. Thanks for taking care of me there. I would have broken his ass off."

Takuda bowed. Hasegawa bowed in return. "I'll put in a good word with Ota for you," Hasegawa said.

Yoshida drifted up to him and handed him the staff. "I hid this under the couch while you were scuffling," she said. "The section chief owes you a favor, but Detective Kimura owes you his life. You kept him from getting his ass broken off today."

Takuda snorted.

"I'm serious," she said. "Now he'll feel obliged to tell you whatever he knows about Thomas."

"I need to talk to Thomas. That's what I really need."

She said, "Before you go, see if Kimura can tell you something that will unlock Thomas's head."

Takuda frowned. He wasn't at all sure he wanted to unlock the foreigner's head. After the encounter in the foreigner's house, he was a little afraid of what he might find.

CHAPTER 13

Friday Morning

The detectives' office was beige and gray with desks pushed flush together so that work groups sat face-to-face. At the center of the room, a short, balding detective wrote hurriedly in a small notebook. Takuda asked for Kimura. Without looking up, the detective pointed with his pen toward at the other corner of the office where Kimura sat alone at a table.

Kimura had the hippest glasses Takuda had seen since the 1970s, and he grinned when Takuda told him so. "Yeah, my boss hates them." He pointed at the man out at the table. "So I bought more." He laughed a high-pitched hiccuppy laugh and smoothed his hair with his free hand.

Kimura put on one of his business faces. "You know,

this incident with Mr. Thomas and Miss Nabeshima is very serious. When we look at his notebooks, there is a lot that we don't know. I thought that you, as a special consultant, might have some input on this matter."

Takuda looked down pointedly at his coveralls. He almost reached for his staff before remembering that he had left it at home on purpose. "I'm not really a specialist."

Kimura tossed his chin at the busy detective out in the main room. "Chief of Detectives Ishikawa said you are. He said he got the call that you and your friends were sent from the heavens."

Takuda controlled his expression. The euphemism "sent from the heavens" to mean "from upper strata of the hierarchy" was already getting on his nerves. "I think Yoshida of the social services offices would be more helpful," he said.

Kimura smiled and handed Takuda a large binder. "She's not a criminologist like you."

Takuda sighed and opened the binder. It was filled with copies white on black, like photostats. They were splotched with gray clouds of fingerprints and crossed by sheets of scudding stains from the ham of Thomas's hand. He had lettered and sketched with a mechanical pencil, that or a nib too fine to blob or fill.

Thomas drew with a vivisectionist's precision: details of charred flesh peeling from the bones of inverted popes, intricate and sparingly cross-hatched views of the damned abroil on pikes with their bellies ballooned and juices bubbling from burst navels, and one freer rendering of the Greek Titan Sisyphus crushed beneath his stone, blood spewing from his twisted mouth and coiled mass issuing from his anus. In the lower right-hand corner of each page lay clustered fingerprints as if Thomas had paused after each drawing to examine and approve before moving on.

Kimura took notes as Takuda spelled out the classical references in what he saw. He was surprised the detective was so ignorant of European mythology and religion. Even a cursory reading of popular manga would have taught him as much as Takuda knew.

Three pages were drawings of the three-headed dog, but they were rough enough to be just starting points for Thomas's sculpture, if that. The last sketch in that group was a jointed framework. Either he had continued in another notebook or he had been good enough to pull off that sculpture with almost no preparation.

The sketches were interleaved with bits of writing, none longer than two pages. Thomas's longhand was a surprisingly childish scrawl, but his printing was sharp and angular with neither loops nor curves. He wrote in diamond O's and isosceles D's with high ascenders and deep descenders alike barbed as fishhooks, all characters discretely vertical and altogether more like primitive runes than any English writing Takuda had ever seen. He had reserved this sharp, unleaning style for poetry and essays, as if it were a script specially designed for recording madness, but what he wrote in that stilted hand was even stranger than the lettering itself.

Takuda lit a cigarette after reading the first paragraph, a bizarre and disjointed admission of lust for another foreigner named Tracy.

Kimura directed him to one short passage about knives and Thomas's fear of them. He had written that he couldn't go to Nepal for fear of the long, curved *kukri* nor to Israel for fear of the "shining fish" commando daggers, that he didn't sculpt wood because he thought eventually his own knives would turn on him. It may have explained why he encased his knives in plaster, but Takuda didn't think it told the whole story.

Another, much longer essay was on someone named Job. It seemed deliberately convoluted, filled with internal references to biblical names "two lines above" and concepts "forty-three words before." Had it been straightforward, Takuda still would not have understood; this went far beyond his casual knowledge of Christianity. As it was, Takuda just scanned it. It ended on the second page with a nicely shaded cross-section of a boil, that or some geological formation for which Takuda had no name.

The longhand scribbling was in random spots, sometimes wedged into trapezoids between finished drawings. When Takuda noticed this, he flipped through the binder. It seemed that Thomas had filled a one-hundred-page composition book from cover to cover, then had started to fill in empty spots. No wonder the police had copied this journal. If they were looking for proof of insanity, it seemed a likely place to find it.

One page featured a full-sized drawing of the stone knife, in loving detail. The legend in English at the bottom of the page read, *Kurodama, unknown stone, unknown origin.*

Takuda flipped past it. The following pages were detailed drawings of individual bones and full skeletons, some highly detailed and some ridiculously stylized, some dancing in apparently joyous abandon with the legend *Poor Skeleton Steps Out.*

Two facing pages stopped Takuda as he flipped through. On first glance he thought there was an old Japanese print stuck in Thomas's notebook, but the meticulous cross-hatching was unmistakably Thomas's work. Then the whole thing came clear and Takuda's stomach started to squirm. Thomas had drawn caricatures of Japanese people in scenes from Buddhist hell. They were tortured by comically grotesque demons who grinned to show their tusks and fangs while they flayed and roasted emaciated bodies. The flapping tongues of businessmen were nailed to the floor. Nabeshima, unmistakably Nabeshima, was skewered on a demon's pike in a parody of physical love. Others Japanese girls were stacked in tiers on beds of smoking coal.

The caricatures themselves were worse than the tortures inflicted. Nabeshima's face was haggard and bleary. Thomas had drawn her in three-quarter profile, her forehead sloping down to heavy brows, then shoved her pug nose farther up between her eyes to make room for her jutting jaw and hugely outsized teeth.

The squirming settled deeper into Takuda's stomach. He laid the binder facedown on the table and lit another cigarette. Kimura picked up the binder and pointed out some interesting sights in Buddhist hell, including the *Hari no yama*, the mountain of needles, and the *Sanzu no kawa*, the flaming river. Takuda didn't care. He was done.

"But wait. See, it changes."

Kimura turned the page. Willowy, indistinct shapes floated out of slipstreams and waves. They were beautiful, like faceless angels shining white on the black pages. There were arrows and labels to indicate different figures: "the woman in the hallway," "the screaming boy," "the man who stands sideways."

In the angular script:

They are very shy. They disappear when they turn sideways. They aren't transparent, and they aren't like chameleons. They just know how to disappear. One is a woman and she always hides in the wood crying. I hear her just as I fall asleep, and it wakes me up. But I turn on the light, and she doesn't want to be seen. She just cries.

Beneath that, in longhand:

Eleven voices, two that are certainly not mine.

Takuda sat back on the sofa and exhaled. Kimura raised an eyebrow.

"It's interesting, isn't it? He was hallucinating vividly."

Takuda just looked at him across the notebook. "You're not a psychiatrist."

"When I spoke to Mr. Thomas in the hospital, I

thought perhaps he had a borderline personality disorder, but everything else points toward paranoid schizophrenia. And when I went to his house, I thought he
also had an obsessive compulsive disorder. Look."

He laid out another binder, this one full of photos
from the house. It was like a haunted house from a
traveling festival sideshow. Cerberus was gone from
the greenhouse studio, and the plasticene bust was
hacked down to gray-green chunks. The paneling in
the narrow hallway between the studio and the main
room hung in splinters from the lath. Kimura directed
Takuda's attention to a two-page series of photos: the
dissection of Thomas's identical daily garbage bags.
Each one contained an empty Gen-Key bottle and the
plastic box from his daily boxed lunch, a deep-fried
mix from a local restaurant. The next photo was the
mixture of cigarette butts and shrimp tails in each
Gen-Key bottle.

"All schizophrenics smoke," Kimura said conspira-
torially.

Ishikawa, still in the other corner of the detectives' bull pen, barked for Kimura in the local dialect.
Kimura winked at Takuda just to show that he didn't
care what anyone thought, then excused himself to
talk to his boss.

Takuda went back to Thomas's notebook for clues
about the Kurodama. Instead, he found a list of nice
things to say to Nabeshima about her hair, her body,
her work, her English.

At the bottom of the page in scribbled longhand almost too small for Takuda to read, he had written:

KAORI is MOMMYROT.

Beneath that, in his hooked script:

Not MOMMYROT, but like MOMMYROT.

Outside the window in East Park, the sun shone as if in a different world. Takuda shoved the copy of Thomas's notebook in his satchel and stood to leave.

A framed canvas leaned against the back of the couch. Takuda pulled it out and set it right side up. It was in oils, painted from the center outward with the foreground fading into an unpainted grid with mountains, a valley, and a small town penciled in. At the center was the shadow of a cross cast by the bars of an open window. It fell on dirt near the knobby feet of men who slept shadowed in a squat earthen house. Jesus sat on the doorsill in the golden morning light. He was small and wiry, a nut-brown man with a slightly hooked nose, flaring eyebrows, and the large, liquid brown eyes of Arab children. In his right hand he held a knife, and from his left hand dangled a strip he had cut from his ragged cloak. A kitten at his feet batted at the strip as its mother cleaned her paw in a patch of sunlight in the foreground. Jesus looked off to the distance with his brow furrowed and his jaw set hard.

Thomas's head was filled with devils, and brutality poked into his life like jagged glass. Thomas was the anti-Takuda, or Takuda was the anti-Thomas, or something. There were too many pieces, and Takuda couldn't put it all together.

Who can stay sane, seeing what we see? Thomas and Nabeshima and I might someday share a smoke in a dayroom with no shoelaces or sharp objects.

Kimura returned. "I'm taking the notebook copies with me," Takuda said. "Maybe Yoshida can help me with it."

"I don't care. I have more copies. Here," he said, handing over a thin folder. "Here are student papers we don't understand. Maybe she can make something of that." Kimura looked disappointed. "You don't have any ideas about him? I was thinking that you might have some insight."

"The only thing I can tell you is that he would've snapped no matter where he was living."

Kimura laughed, though nothing was funny. "Maybe that is true. But I just wonder why he did not go back home to America."

Takuda left him wondering.

The sun was low, but Takuda sat near East Park, by the museum devoted to Kublai Khan's abortive invasion of Japan, in front of the giant bronze statue of St. Nichiren with his big baby head. Takuda pulled out Thomas's notebook, but he couldn't look again so soon.

Yoshida was wrong. Trying to unlock Thomas Fletcher's mind through his journals had not helped at all. Now that he had a glimpse, Takuda didn't want to go talk to the boy at all. Unfortunately, Yoshida had told him the way, and he even knew which bus to take. He slung his satchel over his shoulder.

Takuda just hoped he didn't have to go any deeper into Fletcher's head than he had gone already. It looked like hell in there.

CHAPTER 14

Friday Afternoon

"What are you doing? It's not break time! Get those boxes into the pharmacy!"

The doctor was an angry little hornet of a man. He shouted at Takuda from the back door of the mental hospital where Thomas Fletcher was being held pending deportation.

Takuda was sprawled on the gravel in the scant hospital garden. He had shinnied up a utility pole two meters from the fence and leapt over the barbed wire. The utility pole was in a blind spot, and Takuda had thought he could land and recover without drawing attention to himself. He hadn't taken into account the ground-shaking impact. They had probably felt it inside. Takuda's virtual indestructibility didn't relieve him of mass.

"Idiot!" the doctor hissed at him. "You've left psychoactive medication within reach of the patients! Come in. Now!"

Takuda leapt to his feet, bowing as he brushed himself off and straightened his satchel. He bowed all the way to the back door. The hospital was a nondescript two-story building surrounded by rice paddies on three sides and framed behind by the aquamarine arc of the expressway flyover. There were only five parking spots, two designated for patient transport and the rest for doctors and prefectural police. There were no visiting hours at this sort of facility.

Takuda's bows as he passed the stiff, angry little doctor were sincere; he was grateful to have entered the hospital so easily.

He stepped up from the entrance pit into a bright hallway painted pistachio green. The staffroom was on his right and the stairs were on his left, just as Yoshida had said. The dispensary was ahead on the left. Across the hallway from the dispensary, by the restroom door, a nurse stood stiffly beside a waist-high stack of small boxes. The delivery.

They go through a lot of drugs in this place, Takuda thought.

The doctor pointed at the stack. "Quickly," he said.

Takuda spared a glance into the staffroom. The whiteboard with the patients' names and room assignments was also exactly where Yoshida had said it would be. Thomas's name, written in phonetic script, stood out among the rest. Room 5 on the second floor, then. He knew the spare room keys would be hanging from a pegboard behind the open door, just as soon as he could get back to them. In the meantime, he bowed as if to duck another scolding from the doctor and shuffled forward to take the first few boxes.

In the dispensary, a slender middle-aged woman smiled as she buzzed him in behind her glass wall. He put the boxes carefully on a long table that seemed to divide the counter from the ranks of shelves that lined the walls. He stared for a moment. It was a lot of medication, three whole walls of medication.

"You're new, so you won't get in trouble," the pharmacist said, "but don't ever let Dr. Haraguchi see you sitting down again. Ever."

When he stood from picking up the last of the boxes in the hallway, he was face-to-face with a young man in coveralls. The bathroom door swung closed behind the young man. He stared at Takuda as if he had met his own double.

"Your partner covered for you," said the nurse guarding the last of the boxes. "You're both new, so you won't get in trouble. Just don't let Dr. Haraguchi catch you leaving supplies loose, especially medication."

The young deliveryman bowed and grabbed the last box from Takuda. Takuda followed him into the dispensary.

"You're not my partner," he hissed as they waited to be buzzed in. "What are you doing?"

"I'm here to check the ducting upstairs." Takuda replied loudly enough for the pharmacist to hear. "I slipped on the gravel in the garden looking for outside roof access, and the doctor thought I was with you."

"You should thank him for covering for you," the pharmacist said as she buzzed them in.

She told Takuda that the only roof access was the locked door at the end of the upstairs ward. He bowed to them both and headed off.

The corridor outside the dispensary was empty. The staff room was empty. The pegboard behind the door was labeled by room. He snagged the keys to "Room 5" and "Roof" and slipped them into his pocket. He crossed the hallway and started up the stairs.

Dr. Haraguchi was coming down the stairs as Takuda went up. Takuda stood aside and bowed as if ashamed. The doctor ignored him.

The desk nurse upstairs glanced up as he passed. "Checking the ducting," he said as he headed for the door at the end of the hallway. It rattled open and squealed as he pushed. It was a broom closet with a door at the far end, a disused emergency exit. The cut alarm wires dangled, so he unlocked the door and stepped out onto a tar-and-gravel roof overlooking the tiny parking lot. A rusted fire escape was at his feet. They had shut off this emergency exit to leave one tiny elevator and one narrow stairwell the only way off the second floor. They really, really didn't want anyone to leave.

He spent five minutes banging around on the roof

just above the desk nurse's station. It was unnecessary. When he came back down, her seat was empty and the door to room 2 was ajar. Takuda went quickly to room 5 and slipped the key into the lock. He went in and eased the door shut behind him.

It was much like a regular hospital room except for the bars on the window and the molded foam padding on every angled surface. Thomas lay manacled on his bed, his mouth open, eyes closed. But for the slow and steady movement of his chest, he could have been dead.

Takuda stood beside the bed. "Wake up," he said. "I need to talk to you."

Thomas opened his eyes and turned his head toward Takuda.

"I need to ask you some questions, Mr. Thomas. I know your Japanese is very good."

The unnervingly blue eyes focused on Takuda. "You're trying to collect for your newspapers here?"

Takuda smiled and shook his head. "That was just to meet you. Do you remember that you lost something?"

Thomas shook his head.

"Did you have something in the farmhouse? Something you were looking for?"

"I was very confused," Thomas said. "But the medication is working. You don't look like a devil anymore." He frowned. "Not really."

Takuda pressed him. "What was taken from you? Was it the Kurodama you spoke of?"

"I shouldn't have taken it," Thomas said. "It called to them, during our lessons. There was something exciting about it. I didn't feel anything from it. They did, though. They were very, very excited, so I brought it to my house."

Takuda leaned forward. "You say you didn't feel anything, but that's not quite true, is it? It gave you ideas."

Thomas hesitated. He licked his lips in fear and indecision.

Takuda leaned closer. Foreigners seemed to like to be touched in such situations, but Takuda wasn't sure, so he folded his hands. "You're safe here. You may be able to help some people."

Thomas exhaled, though Takuda hadn't noticed him holding his breath. "It gave me very strange thoughts about a boy named Haruma, a student at Able English Institute, a community college where I teach."

Takuda nodded. "The desire was very comforting, like a place you went when you were troubled or bored. You drew bones in your journal. You were very curious about the texture of the bones, how they would feel on your tongue. You imagined that the cranium, the jaw, and the cheekbones would probably be smooth, like polished ivory, but that the long bones, like the humerus and femur, may have fine grain like hardwood. You licked different surfaces around the house, trying to imagine how different bones would feel."

"I have been sedated," Thomas said, "but I know

what I have said. I never told the doctors or the police about this. I never told them of this desire."

"You called a mental health emergency hotline. You knew of the hotline through Kaori Nabeshima."

Thomas closed his eyes.

"I saw your house. It was strange and messy, but there was nothing evil there."

Thomas's eyes popped open. "How do you know that?"

Takuda said, "I just know. And I know you fought it. You encased your knives and tools in plaster because these desires frightened you."

Thomas squeezed his eyes shut. Tears leaked at the corners.

"You didn't want to hurt anyone. You fought it. You fought it hard. You are a good boy, Mr. Thomas."

Thomas wept openly. Takuda sat beside him. After a moment, he pulled Suzuki's drawing of the curved jewel from his breast pocket.

"Is this what gave you the desires, Mr. Thomas?"

Thomas opened his eyes. He reflexively reached for the paper, but his restraints stopped him. "Yes, that is it. I didn't believe it was real. I knew the girls wanted it, but I didn't know what it was. It called for me, you know. It wants to be free."

Takuda nodded as if he understood. "Do you know what it is?"

"I have no idea."

"It is called a 'curved jewel.' Such things are sometimes sacred in Japan."

Thomas frowned deeply. "Curved jewel? Isn't that part of the Imperial Regalia, along with the Grass Sword and the bronze mirror?"

Takuda bowed. "You study not just our language, but our culture and history, as well." Takuda felt an odd welling of pride that the foreigner was so interested in Japan, but he shoved those thoughts aside. There was no time.

"And it called to you and gave you these ideas."

"Oh, no. No, that didn't happen until I touched it," Thomas said. "It's smooth, and it warms to the touch like soapstone, but it seems too soft, even though it has an edge like volcanic glass."

Takuda tried to keep his expression from changing. "You touched it directly, but you resisted the desires."

"Yes," Thomas said. "I don't suppose anyone would give in, do you?"

He hadn't quite formulated an answer when Thomas's eyes went round. He was staring at something past Takuda's shoulder.

As Takuda turned on the bed to look behind him, he felt a sharp sting in his neck. He reached up to brush it away, and his hand wasn't responding properly.

"What are you doing?" he heard Thomas saying. It was thin and reedy, that voice, and it seemed to come from a long distance. "What are you doing to him?"

Takuda felt himself sliding from the bed. He ended up on his back, looking up at an old nemesis, a kidnapper and murderer named Hiroyasu Ogawa.

CHAPTER 15

Friday Afternoon

Takuda had thought he was going mad when the scars appeared. Yumi still could not see them. Nor could Suzuki or Mori. The silvery blue scars, pulsing just under the skin as if waiting to burst through, had swollen and spread slowly at first. Later, as their encounters with others like themselves increased, the scars branched and multiplied, crossing and curling around each other in an elaborate script unreadable by anything living but designed, in the end, for writing the story of Takuda's life in madness and despair.

No one else saw them until the night he held the fire demon by the throat.

In that moment, with Suzuki nursing his wounded hand and Mori shouting directions from the flaming villa, Takuda walked toward the surf with a writhing creature of living flame held at arm's length. Arm's length was not far enough, and Takuda was sure he would die. He had always assumed that his last thoughts would be of Yumi or his lost family or the infinitude of the Lord Buddha's love and mercy. These crossed his mind as the flames whipped around his head, but his overriding thought was of the constant and repetitive stupidity of evil: Why would a demon composed of flame choose to terrorize a peninsular village, surrounded by water on three sides?

Idiot.

By the time his feet touched the sand, he realized the flames would not kill him. Tendrils sent to reach down his throat blew out like birthday candles. Great streamers of fire from the demon's mouth singed his eyebrows and hair, but they curled around his head so that he barely felt the heat. Burning gouts hurled against his chest eventually charred his shirt to smoking ribbons that fell off as he stepped into the waves, but his skin was untouched. The only thing that really hurt was the steam that rose around him as he plunged the shrieking demon into the surf. The water boiled up to his thighs as he held the demon under, Suzuki chanting and Mori cursing close behind.

His hands came out filled with wet cinder. As he washed the dead soot into the waves, he knew the demon had not chosen its home, or this world. It had been trapped in a cycle of death and rebirth just as everyone else was. As Suzuki said, releasing the fire demon from this world was the only merciful act he might perform.

Standing in the surf in that moment, he felt something like an echo, a ripple between thoughts. The scorched hairs prickled the back of his neck. There was something behind his mind, behind it or underneath it. When he retraced his thinking to that gap between two thoughts, it closed like a trough between waves, but he knew it was there. He had felt it before, and now it knew he had felt it.

He walked steaming out of the waves, his mind reeling from almost touching the fearsome emptiness within. Suzuki pointed at him and said, "Those scars you've been talking about . . ."

Takuda looked down at himself. Now that he had turned away from the ocean and the moonlight, the scars pulsed bright blue, arcs and jags overlaid by straight, slashing strokes, all in all like primitive characters scrawled in ice by savage scribes. Suzuki poked at them with a long, bony finger as they faded back to their silvery seams. Mori swore he saw nothing, and in the morning, Suzuki said he could not see the scars at all.

Takuda could see them, for all the good that did him. He also felt the huge and silent presence behind the noise of his mind. It neither watched nor waited. Untouched and unshaken, with neither judgment nor reflection, neither impressed nor disgusted by the human world, it was simply there. It was the revelation of a secret reality, the split second containing all that ever was, all that ever had been, and all that ever would be, with the dim memory of life as a dream revolving around that instant. Takuda hated it almost as much as he hated his scars.

He remembered all this as he opened his eyes, but he remembered it as if in a dream, and everything seemed reversed, as if he were the dream and not the dreamer. He looked out of eyes that were undoubtedly his own eyes, but he looked out of them as part of something larger, the massive presence that waited silently in the back of his mind.

And when he looked out of those eyes, he faced Hiroyasu Ogawa.

"You're alive after all, heh-heh." Ogawa didn't looked pleased.

Ogawa was sleeker, fatter, and much better groomed than when Takuda had first met him, in the Oku Village jail in the Naga River valley. Ogawa had been merely an unemployed engineer suspected of attempting to kidnap a little girl, but Takuda had known better. Ogawa turned out to be the henchman of the Drowning God, a procurer for a murderous water sprite, a kappa. Perhaps the last kappa.

"Perhaps the only kappa ever," Takuda murmured.

"What? You're still not making sense. You need more medication!" Ogawa rummaged in the cardboard box on his lap.

Takuda was sitting in a chair, he realized, though he could not feel his own body. He looked down through the unfamiliar eyes to see that his arms were restrained. The chair was metal, held together with predictable weld points. A normal man could work it to pieces given time. With Takuda's strength, he could simply stand up and the chair would fall to pieces at his feet, but he was quite tired.

He looked again at Ogawa, who was holding a glass ampule up to the light. "Why are you doing this?" Takuda asked him.

Ogawa smiled. "Because I can, heh-heh. And I was asked to come see young Mr. Thomas Fletcher." He snapped the cap off the ampule with his thumb, and it tinkled on the floor. He bit the tip of his tongue in concentration as he stuck the needle of a large syringe into the ampule. "Your being here is just a bonus."

Takuda looked over his shoulder. Thomas Fletcher was still manacled to his bed. He looked as if he were sleeping peacefully, but he was not breathing, and his lips were blue. Takuda turned back to Ogawa. "You murdered him."

"No, I executed him humanely. You I murdered, and I'm pretty sure your heart stopped, but you kept right on talking. Lies, lies, lies, about watching from the bottom of a collapsing tunnel as reality revealed itself through implosion. What rubbish you say under the influence!"

One part of Takuda's mind, the part that still feared death, flared into anger, but he was mostly moved to pity for Ogawa. "You can stop all this, you know. You can turn away from this path."

Ogawa snorted and flicked the cap off another

ampule. "This is the path I've been on ever since you helped my wife escape. I never found her, even with all the resources at my disposal." He drew the contents into the syringe more easily this time. He was getting the hang of it. "That was a grave mistake on your part."

Takuda focused with effort and examined Ogawa more closely. Not only was he well-groomed, he was impeccable. His gorgeous black suit reminded Takuda of something, something dangerous . . .

"Counselor Endo," Takuda croaked. "He's your new boss at Zenkoku General. You don't hate me just because of your wife. You hate me because I killed your old boss, your filthy Drowning God."

"Heh-heh-heh." Ogawa's laugh was entirely without mirth as he concentrated on the third ampule. The syringe was almost full. "You and your friends did me a favor, killing off old frog-face." He flicked the syringe with his forefinger and squirted pale liquid into the air as if he were actually concerned about causing an embolism while administering this massive overdose of psychotropic compounds.

"I'm much happier with my new employers." He smiled as he leaned forward and pushed up Takuda's sleeve. "You see, I'm very much aligned with the corporate principles."

The door swung open. "What is this? Who are . . . Oh, no. Oh, no."

Takuda looked up to see Yoshida standing at the door. She stared in disbelief at Thomas Fletcher's body.

As Ogawa stood, the syringe disappeared up his

sleeve. "Ah, good. A health-care professional. I barely managed to restrain this man. I believe him to be responsible for the death of this patient . . ."

"Who are you?" she said. She hadn't moved from the doorway.

Ogawa moved toward her. "Let me show you my identification," he said, feinting a dip into his pocket. When the hand came out, the syringe would go straight for her throat, and she would be dead before she hit the floor.

Takuda was across the room, gripping Ogawa's wrist. The deformed remains of the metal chair still hung to his forearm by frayed restraints, and pieces of broken plastic buckles skittered across the floor.

Ogawa sidled up to him and hissed in his ear, "Think this through with whatever brains you have left, heh-heh. You're the one with pilfered pharmaceutical drugs in your bloodstream. You're the one who's had prior contact with this poor, dead foreigner. You're the one with the strange, spotty record." Ogawa pulled as far away as Takuda's grip would let him. He pointed at Takuda's left hand. "And you're the one with the syringe. Heh."

Takuda looked down. The syringe was in his slack fingers. He looked back at Ogawa's smirking face, and he smiled back as he started to apply pressure to Ogawa's wrist. Ogawa howled.

Yoshida closed the door behind her. "What is going on?" she hissed at Takuda. "Did you kill the Fletcher boy?"

"No, Ogawa killed him. Look at him. He's dead," Takuda said.

She stared past Takuda's shoulder at the corpse on the bed as Ogawa leaned toward him, grunting with pain. "And who is . . . who is this Ogawa you speak of?"

"Shut up," Takuda said as he jabbed the syringe into Ogawa's shoulder. "Here's something for the pain."

Yoshida wheeled on him and pulled the syringe out of his hand. "We have to get out of here now," she said.

"Leave that syringe with him," Takuda said as Ogawa crumpled to the floor. "He won't get in trouble. You'll see."

She slid the wrecked restraints and ruined chair from Takuda's forearm as he gently swayed in place. He slid his satchel off and handed it to Yoshida. "This is the foreigner's artwork. It's awful. Take it."

"Can you walk?"

"I can walk or run or vault or whatever you need me to do. I can break things."

Yoshida closed her eyes. "Well, let's walk out slowly. I can tell them you're a consultant sent from heaven."

CHAPTER 16

Saturday Morning

Takuda slept through the afternoon, all night, and well into the next morning. He woke to a note telling him to meet Mori, Suzuki, and Yumi at the Lotus Café, across Meiji Avenue from the moat of the Fukuoka Castle ruins. He dimly recalled Mori and Suzuki trying to wake him and his own drugged rambling about Thomas and the girls who had stolen the Kurodama. Now they wanted to meet at the café, just down the street from Able English Institute, Thomas Fletcher's former employer. Yumi was probably ready to have a long overdue talk about their living situation. None of it sounded like a good time.

Takuda sat on the straw matting smoking a cigarette, waiting until his eyes focused properly. Ogawa had pumped so much dope into him that he could taste it as it left his body, a taste like burned plastic and synthetic banana flavoring. He smoked an extra cigarette to paralyze his tongue.

When he got to the café, Yumi was waiting with Mori and Suzuki. She smiled at him, a tight little smile. He slid into the booth beside her. The others nodded and did not look up. Mori was haggard, too grayskinned and exhausted for a man his age. Suzuki sat quietly, as if resigned to his fate. Takuda hoped Yumi hadn't started the conversation about their living situation without him.

He spoke to Mori first: "So, any word on Nabeshima's condition?"

"No way to know. Her mother has taken over."

No, not the day to talk about Mori and Suzuki moving out on their own. He stifled a sigh as he picked up the menu.

"Good afternoon. I'm Koji!" Takuda was startled by a grown man introducing himself by his given name. As he looked up, the plump little server bowed with a sunny smile and a flip of his head that turned it into a curtsy.

Ah. He's a girl. He returned his attention to the menu. *Used to be only in the bar districts. Times change, even in Japan.*

"Today's specials are . . . oh, Reverend Suzuki! My goodness, you look absolutely starved." Koji pouted as he moved to Suzuki's side. "Haven't they been feeding you at home?"

Suzuki smiled. "I am a little hungry. What would you suggest?"

Koji bent low to address the whole table. "How about savory pancakes for four? I can move you to a griddle table in the blink of an eye. Pork or seafood, all with vegetables, special today because eggs are cheap." He bounced back upright. "How does that sound?"

It sounded delicious, even though it was a hot day, but it was more expensive than noodles or lunch sets. Takuda looked at Yumi.

She shrugged. "Everybody's working today. Why not?"

Takuda nodded to Koji.

"Excellent! I'll have your griddle ready in a flash." He sped away.

Yumi leaned toward Suzuki. "Do you know that server?"

Suzuki looked away. "I've been in here once or twice. I believe we also spoke once or twice while I was begging for alms near Shintencho shopping arcade."

They watched Koji shout the order into the kitchen and uncover the griddle top on a booth table. True to his word, he was going to hustle them to another table. As they gathered their things to move, Mori said, "The priest can have my share."

Takuda said, "Don't pay if you don't eat."

"He's hungry all the time. He needs it for something. Maybe next time he'll feed me."

Takuda wanted to slap Mori, but it wouldn't have

helped. Mori wasn't going to leave Suzuki alone, not today.

As they slid into the booth, Mori indicated the server with a jerk of his chin. "Priest, is that the kind you like?"

Suzuki glanced at Koji. "I don't know what kind I like. I know I don't like your kind, if that's what worries you."

Mori snorted. "I've got bigger things to worry about."

"We all do," Takuda said. Yumi nudged him with her foot under the table: *Don't say anything now.*

He lowered his head in answer. "Thomas Fletcher is dead."

He told them everything, assuming that the night before had been gibberish. Finally, he said, "He touched the Kurodama, and I think his madness protected him. We will never know what he might have told us."

He had their attention. He pulled out a sheet he had found in his satchel. Yoshida had relieved him of all the copies of Thomas Fletcher's notebooks but left behind one of the student papers.

Mori leaned forward to see the characters. After a second, he took the sheet from Takuda to read it. Suzuki looked over his shoulder. "This is a girl's writing, probably a high-school graduate, based on the characters she uses here and here and here. See?"

They frowned in concentration.

Takuda said, "Would you read it aloud, or would you rather I did it?"

Mori blinked as if startled by the question. He cleared his throat and began:

"*We pass underground with the wind at our feet, and it pushes us along, up the stairs. Thomas is there, but he has three heads. We pass him and walk up the street, past the fishmongers, and we come to the cafeteria.*

"*It is old, but we are at home. The men who work here are no longer men at all, and they are pale and hollow as if made of wax. Their eyes are black holes.*

"*The downstairs room is a greasy, old-fashioned cafeteria, the kind of place with crushed sesame and pickled ginger strips in open jars on the counter. It's disgusting, but we know that it's just a front. Up above the steaming cauldrons hang fly-specked wooden placards with the dishes and their prices written in traditional script. In a the top row, above the noodle dishes and spitted meats and other cheap and nasty dishes one finds in such places, special placards hang facing inward. The names of our special fare is written there.*

"*The hollow men greet us with veneration, and they fall at our feet and rub our legs with grease from our dinner. They anoint us with the food, even though we do not clearly remember preparing the meal. The doors close for a special celebration, and the hollow men turn over the wooden placards to reveal strange character combinations, old characters we have never seen before. We cannot read these characters, but we know that they are the names of the meal we are there to partake of, and we begin to cry and beg for our food.*

"*The hollow men lead us farther, and then we understand that the food is unimportant. The food is just to feed* our bodies while our minds fly around the room. The real reason we are there, the reverent and right part of what we are doing, is glowing within the food, as if the food were translucent fat. Our appetites are gone, and now we hunger for the act of devotion.

"We have a single tooth between us, and we each use the tooth in turn. We use it to slice dirty flesh from the bones, and the bones shine through the filth in our hands. As if we had been born for the moment, we begin to lick the bones.

"We are smeared with the food as we clean the offering. Our human appetites are sated, but we hunger so for the offering that we cannot be satisfied. As the bones shine more clean and smooth, we carve the old words into the bones, even though we do not fully understand. It no longer matters. We are not in school anymore. This is what we were truly born for. Some of the girls become so excited that they begin to perform sexual acts with the long bones. This is to be expected, and in the long run we shall all do so. Everyone will, and then we will pierce our flesh and the flesh of those around us with the shining bones. Japan will become a glittering pile of bone connected with twitching, bleeding flesh.

"We have a single tooth of the Devouring God, but this tooth has a great reach. The more who use the tooth, the more power it will have. There were days when it took entire villages, and then it simply waited for someone to pick it up and carry it to a new village.

"Now, the village will come to the tooth, and more and more people will be under the influence of the Devouring God. We will take the tooth to Tokyo."

Koji cleared his throat. His smile was a bit more

brittle than before. Takuda didn't know how long he had been standing there.

"Here we are. Start with the pork and seafood, and pile on the vegetables when it's done. Everybody wants to hurry and pour on the batter right then, but make sure the cabbage is starting to go translucent. Trust me on that one. I'll bring sauces and mayonnaise in a moment."

"Thank you, Koji." Takuda passed bowls to Yumi and Suzuki. "How much of that did you hear?"

"Oh, I tried not to listen," he said. "Honestly, I'm sure it's very interesting, but I don't understand modern poetry anyway. If it has upsetting imagery, it's not for me." He hugged the platter to his apron. "Really, I do admire scholarly types." He spared Suzuki a speculative glance. "However, I'm in the service industry because I am so much better at easing the troubles of the intellectually gifted. Soothing the worried mind, so to speak. Perhaps that's my gift." He bowed in mock embarrassment. "So sorry for prattling on when there's sauce to be fetched. I'll be right back!"

Takuda returned his attention to the table. He expected jokes from Mori, or even Yumi, but they were focused on the essay. Suzuki stared at the griddle.

He's not embarrassed about the waiter. He's transfixed by the essay.

"What's happening, Priest? What do you make of all this?"

Suzuki passed a bony hand over his shaved scalp. "I don't know."

Yumi dumped seafood on the griddle. Takuda did the same with pork.

Mori held the essay up to the light as if looking for a watermark. He seemed dissatisfied with what he saw.

Takuda spoke softly. "What do you know, Mori?"

Mori frowned. "I know there's an awful lot of paper just magically showing up. From the begging bowl, we get a drawing of a curved jewel, then a description of a man being butchered with it, on matching onionskin. From Thomas Fletcher's notes, we get a college girl's first-person essay about how she was possessed by the Kurodama during her summer semester. What's next?"

Yumi said, "These, from my bicycle basket. I was parked at the station." She spread papers on the table: a cartoonishly simplified English tourist map of the city, a photocopy of a medieval Japanese map, a photocopy of a newer map, hand-drawn but fairly modern, and a flyer for a telephone sex chat club, the kind kids hand out at the train station. Most such flyers ended up in wastebaskets or in gutters. The photocopied maps were on onionskin.

"And this," Yumi said, drawing a flat package out of her bag. It was a summer kimono, a lightweight thing, very thin. "Most of these are pretty bright and hideous, for young girls trying to attract boys at the fireworks show this weekend. But this one . . ." She ran a palm over the plastic. The kimono was cerulean blue, the bright, brittle blue of a late-August Fukuoka sky, with concentric white ripples around lotus blossoms. The sky reflected in a lotus pond, like the one in the moat across the street. It was a gorgeous kimono, just right for Yumi.

Lotuses, a Buddhist symbol. Just the kind of irony Counselor Endo of Zenkoku General would love. Takuda didn't have the heart to tell her where it came from.

From the look on her face as she put it back into the bag, he could tell that she knew. No one said anything for a moment.

Mori reached for the sex chat club flyer. "Well, I think we can discount this one."

Takuda poured the batter over the pork and vegetables. "Check the address before you throw it away," he said.

Mori peered at it. "Oyafuko." The Street of Disobedient Children, the young people's party street southeast of the main shopping district. "That's where Kimura wanted to go clubbing."

Takuda nodded. "Counselor Endo is drawing us a map. It looks like he's even given us an address. If he's throwing us a party, it would be rude not to go."

CHAPTER 17

Saturday Afternoon

After lunch, Yumi went back to work. Takuda, Mori, and Suzuki walked east along the old castle moat. The water was completely hidden by the lotuses, a forest of fleshy stalks rising from the broad green leaves. *A river of lotuses*, Takuda thought, *ready to bloom any day now*. The cicadas shrieked in the trees, and the sun beat down upon them. Takuda bowed his head as he walked on uneven paving stones partly to shade his eyes, but partly in obeisance to that great force in the sky. *This is why the ancients worshiped the sun.*

"The summer sun is really something here," he said out loud. "Not like where we grew up, huh?"

"We're not pagans," Suzuki said.

Mori rolled his eyes at Takuda. Takuda wondered

once again if Suzuki was so empty-headed that he accidentally heard other people's thoughts.

Mori said, "So, you know it's Zenkoku. You know Counselor Endo is dropping all these hints into the priest's bowl and your wife's basket. You know that he knows we're here."

Takuda watched his feet on the paving stones. "I couldn't really tell you what I know, much less what Endo knows." He was suddenly light-headed, and the interlocking pavers of the sidewalk were swimming before his eyes like running water.

Takuda looked up, and he saw steaming columns rising up over the shopping district a few blocks away, a dark and dreaming world that mirrored his own, a world where the sites of the fiercest battles and greatest injustices were the sites of the most fruitful worship and the grandest structures were erected on the bedrock of human misery.

"Okay, what do you know?" Mori's voice cut through Takuda's hallucination, for surely that's what it was. "What are you sure of?"

Takuda stopped. They stood on the sidewalk in front of Able English Institute, the junior college where Thomas Fletcher had worked. It was a narrow building with a broken clock on the face, both hands hanging down to an incorrect and dispirited 6:30. The sky above it was alight with the black fire of invisible prayer.

Takuda blinked and tried to focus on the daylit world. "I know that you weren't able to turn the priest into a swordsman. I know that we've been broke since we quit the police force, and a little money has shown up in one account or another since we started this whole thing."

Mori studied his shoes.

"You know what I'm talking about," Takuda said. "Twenty thousand yen, thirty thousand yen, always with a little change to make it confusing, as if they were strange little dividend payments. Sometimes it's the big donations dropped into Suzuki's begging bowl. Just enough to keep us afloat. It always works that way, and I quit questioning it a long time ago."

Mori frowned. Takuda glanced at the building. All seemed normal except for a girl running from the front door with her hand over her mouth.

"I'm willing to agree that it's been Zenkoku all along," Takuda said. "They're just making sure we don't starve, like a really cheap, unofficial retainer. They knew they'd need us to clean up some sort of mess someday."

"Or they start a mess when we're on the scene," Mori said. "First, rumors about the jellyfish murders throw everyone into a panic, even though there are no bodies, just some missing kids. Then Ota's little security firm gets a fat contract without a single bid. An overworked counselor in a county office gets a phone call related to this Kurodama, and we're right on the spot. It doesn't make sense unless Zenkoku put us in place."

Suzuki had drifted up behind them. "This object,

the Kurodama, has an evil influence, and it might have been around here at some time." He pointed east. "In 1945, the Japanese Army's Western Headquarters was right over there, at the end of the moat. That's where it's said the liver of an American airman was grilled and seasoned with soy sauce for a welcoming reception at the Officers' Hospital."

Mori sighed. Sirens shrieked in the distance.

"The Japanese lawyers said the Occupation made up the cannibalism story, but the vivisection of the American airmen is well-documented. The doctors at Kyushu Imperial University Medical Department removed fliers' organs, pumped their veins full of sea-water, even drilled holes in their skulls and stuck in knives, just to see what happened."

Mori poked his finger into Suzuki's chest. "Listen, Suzuki. I know that story, too. The cannibalism charges were dropped. Dropped altogether. As for the vivisection, it was barbaric, if it happened, but let's not get stupid. The Chinese say that Unit 731 of the Imperial Japanese Army killed thousands of Chinese and Russian prisoners in Manchuria. But Manchuria is pretty far away, isn't it? Kyushu University is on the other side of town, isn't it? Do you think this Kuro-dama causes atrocities at a distance?"

Suzuki shook his head. "I don't understand it yet." He seemed too troubled by his own thoughts to take offense at Mori's rudeness. "There's a connection here. I can taste it."

Mori and Takuda glanced at each other. Mori

moved forward as if to start pushing Suzuki around, and Takuda was stepping forward to intervene when a blaring police car pulled up to Able English Institute.

Then another, and yet another. Uniformed officers poured out of the cars. Detective Kimura jumped out of an unmarked cruiser and raced toward the back entrance, hair and tie and coattails flapping.

Traffic had stopped, so Takuda raced across the street with Mori and Suzuki in tow.

Takuda wanted to follow Kimura, but there was trouble at the entrance. A harried patrolman held the double doors closed as panicked students pushed against them. The patrolman was losing. He would be crushed if he didn't move.

Takuda bowed and murmured that he should be allowed to help. The patrolman didn't answer. He pushed against the doors with all his might, but he was buckling. Takuda eased in beside him and slid the breadth of his shoulders against the doors, displacing the patrolman altogether. He put his foot against the wrought-iron banister and locked his legs. The doors snapped shut. A student squealed through the glass; Takuda gave her enough slack to get her backpack out and then eased back into his duties.

Mori bowed to the patrolman and stood beside Takuda. The patrolman stood back and got his first glance at their uniforms.

"Where were you two?" He obviously assumed they were Able English Institute employees.

Mori bowed again. "We were at lunch, Officer."

"I'm a patrolman, you fool. Don't go anywhere. Your incompetence may have allowed a suspect to escape."

There was a sharp rapping on the glass. Takuda glanced over his shoulder. A lieutenant was waving him away from the door. Order had been restored in the lobby.

He and Mori held the doors open as students began to file out clutching their student identification cards.

The patrolman adjusted his uniform. He glared at Suzuki. "You, are you a teacher?"

Suzuki bowed. "Japanese History and Literature, Grammar, Religion, General Humanities and Ethics . . ."

"Okay, okay. You stay here until the students are cleared from the lobby. All the other staff ran out."

"What happened here?" Suzuki's bony hand drifted to his mouth. "What happened?"

The patrolman hissed out the words between students. "Nothing . . . I can tell you. The ? . . students left . . . No witnesses, no suspects, nothing. Just . . . keep them in . . . until the office manager . . . can check them out."

Takuda said, "Actually, we were called from lunch to see a Detective Kimura. Can you tell me where to find him?"

"Wait right here," the patrolman said. "Don't move."

The patrolman shoved past distraught students. Takuda and Mori peered in after him. The patrolman addressed the lieutenant, who shushed him and continued to watch over the shoulder of a small, elderly man with a clipboard who carefully checked the students' identification cards, glanced at their faces, and sent them filing out the door. They seemed to know him, and he had encouraging words for each student.

The patrolman frowned deeply as he waited for the lieutenant's ear. When he noticed Takuda and Mori peering in, he waved them back.

A forlorn young man came through the door. Takuda clapped him on the shoulder. "Big guy, hold the door open for your classmates, will you? We have to go to work."

The boy bowed and fumbled in his pack to put away his identification. Takuda thought he must be the saddest boy he had ever seen.

"Why the long face?"

The boy shrugged. "I don't know. Fire alarms. Rats in the attic. Murder. Something always goes wrong during the Saturday cram sessions." He glanced up at the broken clock. "They don't even care if you're late for class."

Mori was watching. He let two students go by and then called a cute girl over. He bowed and called her "little sister." "Hold the door open, and keep your classmate company. We need you both to count the students as they leave."

"How many so far?" she said.

"Eleven, including you," said the sad-sack boy.

She sighed. "Twelve."

The boy had brightened. He didn't quite smile at

the girl on the other side of the threshold. "Terrible, huh? These jellyfish murders, I mean. Half my composition class is missing."

Takuda and Mori slipped away from the doors. Takuda motioned for Suzuki to follow.

They squeezed into the alley between Able English Institute and the business hotel next door. There was a breezeway between the main building and a two-story building squatting in the rear of the lot.

"Up there," Takuda whispered, pointing toward the second floor of the rear building. "They're all up on the second floor."

Flashes of light, uniforms blocking the windows—the second floor was crawling with police.

Mori hitched up his own jumpsuit uniform and made an attempt to brush the lint off Suzuki's suit. "Here we go, then," he said. Suzuki watched him with clear amusement. "Here. We. Go."

Takuda led the way through the back door and to the stairwell. When they got to the first landing, a patrolman coming downstairs yelled and raised his gloved hands as if to push them back down the stairs.

"It's okay," Takuda said. "We're here to see Detective Kimura."

"Detective Kimura knows you're coming?"

They nodded in unison, and the patrolman had them wait, holding up his gloved hand as he backed up the stairs as if to keep them on the landing by sheer power of will.

"We won't get in," Mori said.

Kimura was down in seconds. His face was pale and grim. He wore gloves, a mask, a hairnet, and white fiber booties to keep from contaminating the scene. He pulled the mask down to his throat. "The one in the suit, is he the priest?"

"Ex-priest. My order no longer exists. Please call me Suzuki." He bowed to the detective.

Kimura took a deep breath. "Speak to no one here. Be invisible. Understand?"

They nodded.

"Hide the insignia."

Takuda crossed his arms, covering patches on his breast and his sleeve. Mori followed suit.

Kimura studied them. "You used to be policemen. You know how to act. When we get in the door, I'll go straight and you go left to the windows. Don't cross the tape. And watch your step. I think it's all behind the tape, but there are slippery spots. You've never seen so much blood in your life."

Takuda led the way—
to the stairwell. When they got to the first landing, a patrolman coming down daita pulled and raised his gloved hands as if to push them back down the stairs.

"It's okay," Takuda said. "We're here to see Detective Kimura."

"Detective Kimura knows you're coming."

They nodded in unison, and the patrolman had them wait, holding up his gloved hand as he backed up the stairs as if to keep them on the landing by sheer power of will.

"We must go in," Mori said.

CHAPTER 18

Saturday Afternoon

Detective Kimura entered the lecture hall first. Takuda, Mori, and Suzuki followed.

The stink of blood and emptied bowels hit them at the door. Old wooden chairs were tossed in heaps radiating outward from the bloodied center. Blood splattered the foam baffles hanging from the center of the ceiling, the whiteboard, and even the windows. It was as if a student had exploded in the center of the room, leaving behind radiating crimson spatter and a starburst of shredded meat.

Takuda had seen horrible things, and he had confronted evil and chaos incarnate. He had never seen an innocent girl boned like a fish. He assumed from the blood-soaked hair that it was a girl. He was light-headed. Despite his experience, he was dizzy and nauseated between one step and the next. He felt the blood draining out of his face. He looked at the others in the room to draw strength from the living.

Takuda wasn't alone. Patrolmen in paper booties either stared at the purplish mass in the center of the room or stared out the windows.

At the outer edge of the flayed, mounded flesh, a white-clad photographer carefully laid a plastic ruler beside a footprint in blood. The sole was made up of a flattish horizontal zigzag with a large empty circle in the instep. The tread reminded Takuda of tennis shoes he wanted as a child. It was the tread of a fashionable retro canvas tennis shoe popular among girls.

A girl's footprint.

Kimura pulled up his mask as Takuda, Mori, and Suzuki followed the tape to the left, just as he had instructed them.

"Here's a start on the weapon," an officer crouching next to the photographer called out to Kimura. "There are triangular cuts in the vinyl flooring. The tip slipped and stuck into the flooring multiple times as they boned the victim."

"They?" Kimura stared at the flayed mass as if willing himself to do so. "You're sure there are multiple perpetrators?"

"I'm sure of it." The portable lights reflected off his glasses. "We have at least three sets of footprints already."

Kimura surveyed the chairs. "Chief of Detectives Ishikawa, shall I have prints taken on all these chairs?"

Ishikawa grunted from the lectern. "I've already had to restrain your men from doing so. More equipment is coming, along with the experts to use it."

Kimura turned to Takuda. "It looks like the perpetrators left here barefoot and naked. They had to. The footprints stop right at the edge of the chairs, right in front of you. The bathroom was cleaned at around 4 p.m. yesterday. We haven't gotten in touch with the custodian yet. I've got two men going through the trash." He turned back to Ishikawa without missing a beat. "And what can we learn from the blood spatters? Anything interesting in the pattern?"

Ishikawa glared. Kimura's breezy approach was a pose calculated to anger him, and it worked. "You'll be sorry if this information gets to the wrong people. Do you want that?" He indicated Takuda, Mori, and Suzuki with a jutting chin. "Your friends who aren't worthy of introduction—or is it I who am unworthy? Everyone is affected by such rudeness. Do you trust your friends?"

Kimura grinned. "Implicitly," he said. "With my mother's life."

Ishikawa snorted and looked down at his work. "The victim was alive when this started."

Kimura tapped his cell phone case in the silence.

Takuda glanced at Mori. Mori was steady and impassive. Beyond Mori, Suzuki muttered the sutras as he stared at the ruined flesh on the floor. He stared as if—

Merciful Buddha, he looks hungry.

Takuda shook the thought away. He was letting Mori's disapproval of Suzuki cloud his thinking.

Ishikawa held his gloved hand a few inches over the corpse. "The blood on the sound baffles above me and over there on the window are outliers, too high or too far for arterial spray if the victim was on the floor. Otherwise, the only spatter like that is very regular, as if the instruments spun horizontally at about this level." Ishikawa waved his hand palm-downward over the corpse and stopped cold, a look of intense concentration on his face. "Of course. What an idiot I've been."

Kimura peered over the tape and the jumbled chairs. "Something new, Chief of Detectives?"

Ishikawa glanced at Takuda, Mori, and Suzuki. "Nothing to report yet, Detective. Not here, not now."

Kimura smiled a thin, tight smile. "You are thorough and discreet, Chief of Detectives. Experience shows."

Suzuki cleared his throat. "Might it have been a curved blade?"

Takuda, Mori, and Kimura went still. The chief of detectives looked up slowly.

"Detective Kimura, perhaps now it is time to have the patrolmen assist the lieutenant in the main building."

Kimura nodded to the patrolmen. Ishikawa dismissed the crouching officer and the photographer with a gesture. The officer fairly sprinted from the room. The photographer bowed formally and packed his kit so quickly that he fell into line behind the last patrolman going out the door.

As the door swung shut, Ishikawa returned his attention to the corpse. "One of your mysterious friends addressed a very interesting question to me, Detective Kimura. It is a question regarding a very sensitive aspect of this investigation. Yet I still don't know this man's name."

"Detective Kimura has no administrative role in my presence here, Chief of Detectives Ishikawa. Officially, I am not here." Suzuki bowed deeply. "My colleagues are employed by a private security firm. They are also officially elsewhere."

After a few seconds of silence, Takuda and Mori bowed with their arms still crossed. Kimura exhaled loudly.

"They say you come from heaven, but I think you come from hell." Ishikawa stripped off his gloves. "More thugs. More damned Zenkoku enforcers."

Suzuki walked around the perimeter of caution tape toward Kimura. "Chief of Detectives, we are not from Zenkoku. We're not from the governor's office. We're not from the National Police Agency." He lifted his lapels with his thumbs. "Look at this suit. Would they even let me into the commissioner general's office with this suit?"

Ishikawa picked his way through the blood spatters to meet him. "I've gotten over my surprise about who gets into the commissioner general's office." Kimura held the caution tape down as Ishikawa stepped over. Ishikawa unzipped his paper coveralls with Suzuki towering over him. "You don't know anything about the commissioner general's office, though, because you aren't police." He indicated Takuda and Mori with a tilt of his head. "Those two might be. But not you."

Suzuki bowed. "I serve a higher function. I regret that I cannot reveal more."

Ishikawa's face darkened.

Suzuki straightened. "A curved blade, sharpened on the inner edge. You think it might be a linoleum knife, a hawksbill fruit knife, or a fishing knife. At the most extreme, you think it might be a modified scythe."

"Who are you?"

"You also know there were seven assailants. You just realized that a moment ago from the gaps in the spatter."

Ishikawa growled as he stepped backward, stretching the caution tape with his calves. He reached for the cell phone at his belt.

Suzuki said, "Chief of Detectives, we need your co-operation here. If I tell you something you don't know, will you cooperate?"

Ishikawa's growl became a sputtering laugh. "If you don't tell me everything, and right this second, you're going to jail."

Suzuki lowered his head. "As you wish." He pointed to the flayed mass behind the caution tape. "You're not looking for multiple weapons. That was done with a single blade."

Ishikawa released his cell phone. He turned and looked at the corpse as if he hadn't noticed it before. Then he turned his stupefied gaze to Takuda, Mori, and Suzuki in turn.

Suzuki continued: "They whipped a single instrument so violently that they spattered blood in a very regular horizontal pattern. They passed the instrument among themselves so quickly that partially co-agulated blood was flung from the blade. It was a stone knife."

Ishikawa stared. "The tip would have broken off in the flooring."

"It's an antique curved jewel of an unknown stone. The thick part is a flattened orb, an oblate spheroid that acts as a handle. The tail is sharpened along the inner edge, and it comes to a very sharp point."

"Whatever it is, it's obviously sharp. Who wields it?"

Suzuki bowed as if in regret: *That's for you to find out.*

Ishikawa said, "What are they doing with the bones?"

Suzuki bowed more deeply and backed toward the door. "Good day. We must be going now."

Takuda tried to follow, but Ishikawa blocked his path. "You, nameless policeman. You know I can't act on any of this."

Takuda said, "Chief of Detectives, you said 'more toughs.' Have Zenkoku employees been talking about this?"

"Have they!" Ishikawa fished in his breast pocket. "I've got at least three of these." He handed a card to Takuda.

A plain corporate card on inferior card stock: Endo, the Zenkoku corporate lawyer, real-estate speculator, and possibly inhuman monster.

As they left the room, Takuda looked over his shoulder once more. From the door, the flayed remains looked nothing like a starfish, nothing like a jellyfish. He felt as if he should pray, but there was nothing he could say.

He took deep, sweet breaths as Detective Kimura escorted them out the front door of the college. "Your friend Suzuki is gutsy."

Takuda made vague noises of agreement. He wondered if Suzuki's gutsiness would land them in jail this week. It would happen eventually. Mori was right about Suzuki. He was becoming a liability.

As they stepped out of the college's main building, Takuda pulled Kimura aside. "Chief of Detectives Ishikawa said Zenkoku employees had visited him. Why is Zenkoku interested in the jellyfish killings? What do they want?"

"I don't think it's related. They probably just want to make sure they're not caught up in the incident. Thomas Fletcher beat the girl from the counseling satellite office."

Takuda frowned. "Why would they be caught up in it? Because he made sculptures for them?"

"Because he taught for them. Every Thursday evening from 4:30 to 6:30."

Of course he did. "So Thomas Fletcher taught English to their employees. Spring intensives for incoming freshman employees? That kind of thing?"

"No, not just that. It's a perk left over from the real-estate boom of the 1980s. They still offer free English classes to all employees. Sort of a hobbyish, team-building thing. They used to contract with the college, but they contracted with Fletcher's new employees, ActiveUs, after he quit teaching here."

Takuda blinked.

Kimura brushed back his hair. "Fletcher is no longer a suspect in any of this, by the way. He was restrained for two days before he died. It's under investigation. He may have hallucinated something about the jelly-fish killings, but nothing he said was useful."

Ishikawa came around the corner. He stopped when he saw them.

"You know I'm going to report your presence here, don't you?"

Takuda bowed out of habit. "I'm sure you think it's part of your job."

Ishikawa squinted at him. "You say you aren't with Zenkoku, but everyone is with Zenkoku, whether they know it or not."

Some of us more than others. Takuda bowed in assent. "A man would have to be a fool to doubt it."

Ishikawa looked toward the castle ruins across the street. "I don't know what you are, but I doubt you could make this situation worse. You've got training, and your man seems to have training. Just don't let that tall one make me sorry I didn't report you." He glanced at Takuda's uniform. "I know Ota. He's a shill, but who isn't a shill these days? So if you're using him for cover, don't let him get hurt. Call me if you find something real. Don't bother telling Kimura. He's an idiot."

He walked off.

"I'm standing right here," Kimura said as Ishikawa walked away. "I heard the whole thing."

Ishikawa didn't respond.

Takuda took his leave of Kimura and looked around for Mori and Suzuki. They were a block away. Suzuki was standing at a vending machine, and Mori stood next to him as if whispering into his ear. Takuda sped up.

When he got there, Suzuki was red-faced and clearly angry. Mori drew several sheets of paper from his inside jacket pocket and threw them at Suzuki. While Mori pursued Suzuki to continue berating him, Takuda gathered the papers. A drawing of a stone knife, the Kurodama. Maps. Random bits of writing.

"I didn't ask for any of it, any more than Yumi did. I found those sheets in my begging bowl," Suzuki said. "It's why I want to hang up my robes."

Mori said, "It shouldn't be a surprise. Zenkoku has used your begging bowl to keep us alive until they needed us. Now they're using it to drop off clues."

Suzuki smiled as if in pain. "It's not Zenkoku this time. That's my father's handwriting. It appears that he isn't dead after all."

CHAPTER 19

Saturday Afternoon

"You'd better tell us everything," Takuda told Suzuki. "Start at the beginning."

They sat at the window table of the business hotel next to Able English Institute. Takuda and Suzuki faced each other across the table. Mori turned sideways in his chair with his back to Suzuki. He watched uniformed officers come and go next door. He worked a toothpick in his mouth like an angry street hood.

"Then I should start with my father's disappearance in the Naga River valley," Suzuki said. "That was eleven years ago. He had stepped down as head priest two years before that."

"The body never showed up," Takuda said.

"His robes, yes, but no body." Suzuki smiled as if he

were talking about a favorite old television show. "He was carrying his modern translation of medieval documents about the Kappa. You know."

"You thought the Kappa murdered him?" Takuda asked.

"I assumed so. Why else would his robe show up in the valley when he was taking the high road to the capital? Now, though, it makes no sense at all."

"Priest, none of this makes sense. You say this is your father's handwriting. Someone is feeding you documents stolen from your dead father?"

"I'll bet it's Endo," Mori said. "He's obviously taunting Suzuki. He's trying to break our weakest link."

Takuda closed his eyes in the silence following Mori's insult.

Suzuki broke the silence. "Taunting is one explanation. That would appeal to Counselor Endo, of course, but he is focused and disciplined. If he is responsible—and I'm sure your assessment is correct," he said with a bow to Mori, who ignored him, "then we can be sure he is feeding us information to achieve some greater purpose of his own."

Takuda shifted in his seat. "We can't ignore the surge, even though we're serving the interests of Endo and Zenkoku. Even though he's using us, we're doing the right thing."

Mori and Suzuki glanced at each other.

"We have to stop these killings if we can. Maybe we can learn Endo's game in the bargain."

Mori sucked his toothpick loudly. Takuda had to

quell the urge to reach across the table and squeeze the laughter out of him.

Suzuki said, "It's true that I'm an easy target." He ran a fingernail along a crease in the paper. "I have always been an easy target. That's part of my nature, I suppose. That may be why my father kept me in the valley after he moved the rest of my brothers to safety."

Takuda sat forward. "You said they went away to school. You never said your father deliberately moved them away from the valley."

Suzuki smiled sadly. "Oh, yes. I have always been considered the weakest link. If the weakest link is isolated, the chain won't be endangered." He nodded as if to himself, a half-smile spreading and slowly disappearing.

Takuda said, "You aren't the weak link. I know this. The second sight is getting stronger in me. I see you as a great and terrible force, and Endo will regret the day he taunted you."

Mori stared off into the middle distance.

"Anyway, your confidence in me is reassuring," Suzuki said. "Not much confidence has been shown in me. Ever. My father once tasked me with translating a manuscript written by a foreign visitor to the temple. It was not so old, perhaps from the 1920s, but it was written in old-fashioned and difficult English. It was a hard job, and I . . . my father seemed to assume I was failing. He gave the work to my next-oldest brother. Perhaps I was doing a poor job. I don't know. I remember being upset over the whole thing. But I remember the first line best of all.

"After the impossible front matter laid out a ridiculous purpose and an improbable time frame—not only for the author's life, but for the events in the manuscript itself—the manuscript proper started like this: '*I would wish it upon no man that his father dislike him.*'" Suzuki did not bother to say it in Japanese. "Through no fault of my own, that was my fate as well."

Takuda searched his memory for any signs of affection from the old head priest toward any of his sons. The elder Suzuki, shorter and rounder than his son, had never been demonstrative toward anyone, at least so far as Takuda could recall.

"When he sent us away for schooling, I began to think he had some confidence in me. But my brothers never came back. My father and my mother fought about whether I should go as well, and he said he needed me to stay behind and help take care of the temple. She was passionate at first, but she became colder and colder, toward me and toward everyone. When she disappeared, everyone assumed she just left."

"Everyone but you," Takuda said.

"No, I thought so, too. I thought she had *abandoned* us. *Abandon* was the first word in my abridged English dictionary. Now, I don't know. Maybe they fed her to the Kappa. But I always thought she got away. I had to believe that."

"And your brothers?"

"They're alive somewhere. I'm sure of that. They

left for school or work or apprenticeships right on schedule. When my father disappeared, the last link was severed. I never heard from them again."

"These documents showing up in your begging bowl . . . Do you think your father entrusted these documents to your brothers?"

"That's one explanation." Suzuki spoke carefully, as if avoiding some misinterpretation of Buddhist doctrine rather than weighing the possibility that his hidden family had found him.

"Do you think they may have joined your mother somewhere?"

Suzuki shrugged that off, physically discarding the idea. "Wishful thinking. Adding to the idea that she is alive the idea that she might have gathered together my brothers and my father, all of whom I assumed to be scattered to the winds . . ." He shook his head violently. "It's not a possibility."

"Do you think Endo might have . . . captured them?"

"The existence of documents in my father's handwriting doesn't indicate that my brothers ever possessed them, nor does it provide any information on whether my brothers are alive or dead."

Mori wheeled around to the table. "What have they sent you? Everything. Show us everything."

Suzuki brought out a single sheet of onionskin. "This is it. This and the description of the film. I believe that was among the papers you were throwing on the street a few minutes ago. The rest came from

Yumi's basket or the foreigner's notebook." Suzuki stretched out a drawing on onionskin. It was a curved jewel, a knife shaped like the dark half of a yin-yang symbol. The flattened disk was its grip, and its long, wickedly curved tail was a blade.

"Stop lying and keeping secrets," Mori hissed. "Stop acting holy and spill your guts. Now."

Suzuki turned crimson.

Mori made a disgusted sound. "Look at you two. What a pair."

"Enough," Takuda growled.

They both glanced up at him and then returned to their respective miseries.

Takuda pointed to the sketch of the stone knife. "Priest, what do the symbols running along the blade mean?"

"I don't know." Suzuki traced them with his finger. "These are completely new to me. They look like the markings on oracle bones, but they're more basic. More primitive."

Mori said, "What markings could be more primitive than those on oracle bones?"

Suzuki looked surprised. "Oracle bone script is hardly primitive. The Chinese were cutting characters into tortoise belly shells and shoulder bones of oxen almost four millennia ago, and there were more than six thousand distinct characters in use for divination, at least a third of which can be identified as precursors to modern characters," Suzuki said, shifting his attention from Mori to Takuda, as Mori had begun staring out the window again. "The bones had been hollowed out in spots to make them thin enough to crack when heated. A bronze rod from the fire was placed on the bones, one on each hollowed-out spot, one for each question. The bones would crack in a very specific way—a long, vertical line with a shorter horizontal line shooting out from its side, a shape which itself forms our character for 'divination,' you see?"

Mori lit a cigarette. Takuda was too tired to pretend interest. Suzuki sighed and continued: "The really interesting thing is that these bones actually confirmed the existence of the mythical Shang Dynasty, and some of the astronomical events depicted on the bones constitute proof of the chronology."

Suzuki seemed to hesitate. He wasn't running out of steam. On subjects like this, he never ran out of steam.

"What is it, Priest? What's eating you?" Takuda leaned forward.

Suzuki swallowed audibly. "The characters on this drawing are unknown. They won't be found in any collection of ancient or modern Chinese or Japanese characters." He looked up and Takuda caught a flash of some hidden fire in the back of the hungry priest's eyes. Gooseflesh played up the back of Takuda's neck.

Suzuki said, "These characters look exactly like the silvery scars all over your body. The ones that glowed when you drowned the fire demon."

Mori raised his eyebrows. "Maybe you've become the Drowning God now."

The skin on Takuda's forearm tingled as if in response to the thought. *Yes, that's me, all right.* Takuda crossed his arms to quell the tingling.

Suzuki took a deep breath. "So just as in Bronze Age China, characters are cut into bone. That's where we will see them. When we find the bones of the victims, we will find these characters carved with stone. There will be no metallic residue."

"Priest, what is the Buddhist teaching on this one? What do the scriptures say?"

"There is no scriptural view on this one." He scratched at his ear like a dog plagued by fleas. "It all just makes me hungry."

CHAPTER 20

Sunday Evening

Club Sexychat was dead. Of course no one was here on the night of the big fireworks show. A lonesome boy sang "Bridge Over Troubled Waters" on the karaoke stage just under the mezzanine where Takuda stood. If the boy would just step to the right, Takuda could spit beer on him.

"Anubis, what would Paul Simon say about what this boy is doing to his song? Hmm?"

The fiberglass Anubis on his right said nothing. The mirror ball lights played over its sleek onyx snout. Takuda turned to the other jackal-headed statue on his left. "You, too? Cat got your tongue? Perhaps a sexy French cat, *le chat sexy*? Or is that *la chat sexy*?"

Takuda hadn't even finished his first beer, but it had

gone straight to his head. Perhaps the drugs Ogawa had pumped into his system were still affecting him, even though he thought he had slept it off. He wadded up the flyer that had been dropped in Yumi's bicycle basket. No one he had spoken to at Club Sexychat seemed to know anything about Thomas Fletcher, about the missing girls, about the jellyfish killings, about the murder at Able English Institute, and certainly nothing about the curved jewel. Takuda, Mori, and Suzuki had cooled their heels for an entire day, watching the newspapers for details of the killing. So far, it was listed as an accidental death, and the name of the victim had not been released.

That news, along with the rumors of the jellyfish killings, would drive most cities to the edge of panic, but this was Fukuoka, and this was the night of the annual Ohori Park fireworks display. As Takuda had expected, a little flaying and mayhem wouldn't keep Fukuoka folks at home.

But it wouldn't bring them here. The streets were bustling with boys showing off for the girls in their summer kimonos, and Club Sexychat was grimly deserted. Takuda stood sullen and forlorn, flanked by decorative fiberglass gods of death.

Club Sexychat was just off Oyafuko-dori, the Street of Disobedient Children. It had apparently been Excite Disco Pharakos, a clone of a moderately successful club in Kurume, but the model hadn't worked in Fukuoka. Now the dance floor was mostly taken up with twin banks of translucent sarcophagi, actually phone booths in a closed system. There were tokens and numbers and a system Takuda couldn't be bothered to understand that would allow boys to chat with girls anonymously from booth to booth. It was sexy. It was chat. It was sexychat. It was all a bit pathetic.

Two drunken foreign girls screeched off-key and started pulling the microphone away from each other before Takuda could recognize the song. They collapsed into laughter and slipped from the stage onto the dance floor. The Japanese patrons moved back, and an older man watched the foreigners sadly. It was time to go back to his office and do nothing. At his signal, black-clad boys wearing huge silver ankhs moved in and solemnly wheeled away the karaoke machine, an antiquated and monstrous rig more the size of a vending machine than a musical component. They had to stop when one boy's ankh got tangled in the wiring.

Takuda wandered the upstairs, just in case he had missed something. The boilerplate mezzanine led past the old Sphinx Ballroom, an empty space with a free wall dominated by a bandage-wrapped rhino head crashing through a blow-up of Boris Karloff in full mummy regalia. The room was roped off and piled high with funerary jars, hinged sarcophagi, and a stack of bug-eyed papier-mâché cat mummies. The Anubis twins themselves would have been stored there as well, had they not been built into the railing.

The least-used washroom was right beside the Sphinx Ballroom. It was mirrored floor to ceiling, and all the mirrors were etched with Old Dynasty hiero-glyphics and scenes from the story of Isis and Osiris. Isis and Osiris were twins who fell in love in the womb, who loved as brother and sister, as king and queen, as god and goddess, with a deep, unconscious love that overcame death, interment, dismemberment, and reconstitution, transcending mortality and cult to become a binding force of the Egyptian cosmos, binding night to day, life to death, man to woman. The best love story of the past five millennia was right in front of him as he weaved gently at the urinal in the best for-eigner pickup bar in town. The irony was killing him, and he said so to the mirrors.

On the glass wall beside the urinal, Osiris lay supine with the infant Horus standing on his belly and Isis at his feet with her arms raised in blessing. Takuda aimed high to spatter them, growling deep in his throat. He saw his face change in the mirror. It was not dramatic, just a subtle shift, a deadening of the eyes, a sagging of the cheeks. He gave himself a heavy, loose-lipped grin from the mirror, as if some dangerous thing inside him knew it was free to do some property damage.

Takuda zipped his fly and turned the sink on full. He doused his head with cold water. He had seen the glowing scars, and he had seen the fire behind Suzuki's eyes, but he had never seen himself become a beast. When he looked up into the mirror, the beast was gone. It was just Takuda, red-faced and frightened. He grinned in the mirror, just to see what would happen. It was the solid grin of his police academy days, but with an overlay of scarring and a hint of fear at the corners of his eyes.

Maybe the fight to remain human isn't about horns and scars after all.

At the bottom of the stairs, a girl in a summer kimono was climbing onto the lap of a seated statue of Seth. "Hello," she said, wiggling her hips at her friends. "Are you happy to see me?" She turned around and straddled Seth's knees, slipping, looking at her friends with lowered eyelids. They shrieked with laughter and fought over the camera to take her picture.

He turned right toward the bar. Ramses II stood before him, black as the Anubis twins upstairs, probably from the same fiberglass workshop. The pharaoh's belly was broken out in sharp chunks to reveal glowing innards made up of translucent circuit boards and pulsing fiber-optic strands. Above the mugs and glasses, a zoetropic scarab pushed a glass globe of flaring plasma with its rear legs. The stools were thin, inverted pyramids, chic and thematic and extremely uncomfortable. Trying to ignore the girls frolicking on Seth's lap, he turned toward the dance floor, looking for a habitué, someone who might know something about Thomas Fletcher or his friends.

And as he faced the dance floor, one of the sarcophagi lit up. Club Sexychat was open for business.

A plywood sign stood beside the sarcophagus: *English Corner*, with a picture of a cat, a sexy cat, *la chat sexy*, with a phone to her ear and an ankh dangling on her suggestively full bosom.

There was someone in the sarcophagus. Takuda sighed and knocked on Tutankhamen's translucent face. The lid swung open immediately to reveal a girl, a foreign girl, frowning at him from her plush stool. "Buy a token," she said, pointing toward the bar. Takuda nodded and turned away immediately.

He bought three tokens at the bar, enough for about ten minutes of chat. Each was emblazoned with the same four-digit code. He met the gaze of the smirking bartender with equanimity, but he avoided looking at the broken statue of Ramses II. At that moment, he was slightly embarrassed on behalf of Japan as a whole.

And he was very nervous about engaging in sexy chat with a pretty young foreigner, even for all the right reasons. At least she had brown eyes. Green eyes were a little unnerving, and blue eyes were worse. He had drowned a demon, cut a monster's head to pieces, and he was on the hunt for a weapon that forced schoolgirls to kill, but foreigners still made him skittish. He had just decided to live with it.

He dropped onto the stool in the sarcophagus beside the foreign girl's and faced the obviously re-cycled office phone. There was no place to put the tokens. He picked it up: a dull dial tone. He punched in the numbers from the token.

She picked up the phone immediately. "You give the tokens to me," she said.

He left the phone off the hook. Her lid was open a crack, so he handed in the tokens and went back to his sarcophagus.

"I don't want sexy chat," he said. "Do you speak Japanese?"

"A little," she said. "I'm really supposed to speak English, though."

Her accent was understandable. Takuda heaved a sigh of relief. "My name is Takuda," he said. "Ta-ku-da. The characters are 'high' and 'field.' I want to ask you about Thomas Fletcher. Do you know him?"

Static crackled to the slow disco beat outside their sarcophagi.

"I am not Fukuoka police," he said. "Do you understand? Not police. I am higher than police. Bigger than police. Ah . . . higher cause . . . you don't understand me?"

"I understand," she said. "What's the question?"

"First, what is your name?"

"You don't know? How did you find me without my name?"

Takuda couldn't say he had been guided by a flier in his wife's bicycle basket. "Let's start with your name, please."

"Tracy," she said. "Tracy Jenkins."

"Miss Tracy," he said, "how do you know Thomas Fletcher?"

"We work together at ActiveUs. We teach English in the offices of big companies. They send us there like sushi delivery."

Takuda tried not to laugh. She spoke more than a little Japanese. "You knew he was mentally unwell, didn't you?"

"I knew," she whispered.

"You liked him, and you tried to help him."

"I tried," she said. Her voice was breaking. "He wouldn't take his medicine. It hurt him sexually. And in other ways, not just sexually. He said he became . . . ah, sleepy all over."

"Excuse the . . . I'm going to ask a personal question. Do you understand?"

"We are not lovers," she said. "He thinks we are, I think. He doesn't understand reality sometimes." She was truly distraught.

Takuda said, "He's a good boy. I told him so last time I saw him."

She inhaled sharply. "You met him? Is he okay? Is he going home?"

"I believe he is probably home already," Takuda said. The plastic handset cracked slightly in his grip. He eased up so he wouldn't crush it. "He was resting comfortably last time I saw him. There is no pain."

He swallowed his shame about lies and half-truths to a grief-stricken foreign girl and ticked off his questions about the missing girls, about the jellyfish killings, about the murder at Able English Institute, and about the curved jewel.

She sounded stunned. "He is a crazy boy. He chased his old girlfriend. You think he killed lots of girls? Maybe you are the crazy boy."

"Did he know lots of girls?"

She snorted, like a pig. "He was a foreign boy

in Japan. 'Did he know lots of girls?' That's a stupid question."

Takuda persisted: "Where did he meet girls? ActiveUs? Able English Institute?"

"Oh, Able, for sure. He met private students there, girls who wanted to be stewardesses or tour guides, wanted to use their English, and one gay boy who wanted to be a hotel clerk or something."

"Where did he teach them?"

"An old, stinky restaurant that used to be a cafeteria for a big company. The company gave him the space for free."

Takuda closed his eyes. "Zenkoku General?"

"Zenkoku General? I don't know. Just Zenkoku," she answered. "I won't work there. Not again. I'll never go down into that horrible basement."

CHAPTER 21

Sunday Evening

There was a knock on the lid of his sarcophagus. Through the translucent plastic, Takuda could just make out the black sleeve attached to the rapping hand. Counselor Endo of Zenkoku General was moving him along to the next clue.

"I think I have to go, Tracy Jenkins," he said into the handset. "I hope you enjoy your stay in Japan."

The line was dead. He dropped the handset and stepped out of his sarcophagus.

The club had been cleared, and the music had stopped. Endo wasn't there in person. In his stead, a slim phalanx of black-uniformed security guards squared off against Takuda on the dance floor. Tracy's sarcophagus was already empty.

"What did you do with the girl?" Takuda asked the security guards.

The guard nearest the door bowed and indicated the exit with an extended palm, a gesture of almost courtly elegance. Bright spots of light from the mirror ball swam over his Zenkoku Security badge. "The club has been cleared for safety reasons, by order of the regional fire department," he said. "Everyone else has left. Please move toward the exit."

Takuda felt something tight loosen in his chest. Ten of them to one of him. Hardly a challenge, but finally, an enemy he could lay his hands on.

He tossed them like laundry. They maced him and Tasered him before he even reached their ranks, but they couldn't break his momentum, and four of the ten were down for the evening before the others could regroup and circle him. Three of the six still had functional Tasers. It was an effort of will, forcing individual limbs to resist the paralyzing current, but even a tenth of his true strength was enough for these rented toughs. He laughed out loud as he yanked the leads from his own flesh and shocked them with their own weapons. Three tried to pin him with their staffs. He took their staffs away and tossed them up to the mezzanine. One guard, enraged by failure, threw himself on Takuda and tried to wrestle him to the dance floor. He howled as Takuda took him up on it, and he shrieked for his friends to rescue him as Takuda idly applied joint locks. He was testing the suppleness of the fellow's elbow when he heard a familiar metallic clicking.

He looked up into the barrel of an old revolver. Even in the dim lights of the disco Takuda could tell it was a museum piece. He released the swelling elbow and stood to face the lead guard, the one who had stayed out of the fray until he could get a clear shot.

"Please," the guard said. "It's time to move toward the exit."

The pistol was a Russian M1895 with a rounded front sight, at least six decades old. "Be careful with granddaddy's gun," Takuda said. "You'll blow your hand off."

The guard stepped back as he fired past Takuda's ear. The noise was deafening, and Takuda blinked involuntarily. His ears rang, and the pistol was now aimed between his eyes. The guard's hands were rock-steady, and he aimed to drop Takuda where he stood. "Please move toward the exit," he repeated.

Takuda looked back at the jagged, gaping hole in King Tutankhamen's face; the round had destroyed the sarcophagus behind him, so the old Russian pistol wasn't loaded with starter rounds. The other guards had withdrawn, tending their wounded near the karaoke stage. The guard with the gun was keeping out of reach.

It was time to go.

Takuda felt the gun pointed at the back of his head all the way to the door, but every time he turned, the guard stopped two body lengths behind, pistol trained on Takuda's skull. Maybe Takuda was faster than the guard, but he wasn't faster than the bullets.

At the door, he told the guard, "Tell Counselor Endo I want to speak to him."

The guard let the door swing shut. Without taking the aim off Takuda's face through the glass, he jammed the door with his own boot as he reached down to flip the lock. He spun on his heel and returned to his men.

Takuda faced toward the street to see the old manager waiting for him. The manager snapped a Polaroid of Takuda and told him he was banned from the bar forever. Then the old man slouched off toward the Street of Disobedient Children.

Takuda looked around. The alleyway was deserted, with only a garlic-themed restaurant to keep the disco company. Club Sexychat itself was a mess. The old pink faux-marble stairs were faded and milky: they hadn't been made for outdoor use. The sphinxes pieced together from auto chrome were slowly rusting to bits on either side of the golden door, and the rust stains extended down the marble and halfway across the concrete sidewalk. The old *Excite Disco Pharakos* sign was still visible under the sagging and faded banner that proclaimed it *Club Sexychat*. Takuda felt a pang of sadness for Tracy Jenkins, the brown-eyed girl who felt she had to work in such a place.

Takuda followed the old manager to Oyafuko-dori, the Street of Disobedient Children. Oyafuko was lined with restaurants, pubs, karaoke parlors, and game centers. Dusk had filled the street with shifting swarms of orange-haired youths with raucous laughter and too many teeth, small knots of young business people, and the occasional long-legged beauty who slid like silk under the neon. On this evening before the fireworks show in Ohori Park, the street swam with girls in bright summer kimonos. There were sidelong glances for Takuda, bloodied and disheveled and massive. On the Street of Disobedient Children, the kids weren't afraid to let him know he didn't belong.

The phone booths were plastered inside and out with sex service ads. Takuda read them idly as he rang Mori's cell phone. Mori and Suzuki were waiting for the call.

"I just slapped the snot out of ten Zenkoku Security guards. Nine, I mean. The one got the drop on me. But the others, I stuck my hands in their ears and rattled their molars. Most fun I've had since Sado Island."

Suzuki laughed in the background as Mori quizzed him on what he had found.

"There was a girl Thomas Fletcher knew. I couldn't tell her he's dead. Couldn't do it. But I found out that he taught students from Able English Institute in private lessons. Get this: He taught them in a space provided by Zenkoku."

Mori didn't even comment on that. *Silently cataloging everything*, Takuda thought. *That's another thing I hate about him.*

Mori said, "We're on our way. There's a lot of police activity in the area. A lot, but they don't say what they're looking for, and they've gone to cell phones, blackout on radio communication. Stay around there. We'll be there in five minutes."

"Meet me at the pub here on Oyafuko, a place called Fair or Cloudy. It's not cheap, but the people are wonderful. Even for this wonderful town, they're wonderful people. My treat."

"You're drunk," Mori said.

"You're perceptive," Takuda said. He hung up and called Yumi. He left a message that she should meet them at Fair or Cloudy, and that she should wear her summer kimono.

After the answering machine clicked off he hung up and wandered, enjoying stares and the whispers. Adrenaline from the fight had sobered him up, but he was still too drunk and too mussed to be out on the streets. He could have been in the pub bending his elbow in minutes, but he enjoyed shocking the children a little. After half a block, he noticed that they were really disturbed, really frightened. They all averted their eyes when they realized he was staring back. One girl cut away from the crowd. "Please, uncle," she said, a note of terror in her voice. "The police box is empty, and there's a hungry ghost in the park."

It was like being struck sober. He ran to the little park where the kids made out, dodging and weaving through the knots of frightened people fleeing some unknown horror.

The police box on the corner was empty, lights on but no one home. He walked past the darkened kiosk into the park, right to the hungry ghost floating above the grass.

It was a girl in a stained white dress, and she wasn't

really floating. Her feet were so dirty and covered with caked blood that they blended with the shadows. She shuffled in the grass, her arms held out from her body as if to keep the dress clean, but it was too late. The dress was covered with drying blood turned blackish brown in the vapor lights in the park.

"Little sister," Takuda coaxed, unsure what would happen if he got too close. "Little sister, come with me. Let's get you cleaned up."

She looked up at the sound of his voice, but her gaze was blank and uncomprehending. *Just like the police box*, Takuda thought. *The lights are on, but no one is home.* He cursed Ogawa for pumping him full of drugs, and he cursed himself for drinking on the job, even a single beer. He wasn't in control, not in control at all, and he couldn't help this girl, couldn't help this poor little wounded thing who had come to the make-out park, a place that may have been a place of ease and comfort before whatever had happened to her had happened.

Takuda was face-to-face with one of the jellyfish killers.

"*Kurodama,*" she whispered. Her eyes widened and she looked down at her hands. Clotted blood had gathered at her cuticles and the webbing between her fingers. Clots like strips of bark fell to the grass as she picked feebly at her bloody dress. "*Kurodama.*" The bloodstained fingers shook as she started to scrub at the dress. She whimpered deep in her throat as her scrubbing became more frantic, and then she opened her mouth and began to shriek.

He was glad he was drunk when the screaming started. If Ogawa had been there with his evil syringe, Takuda would have rolled up his own sleeve. He gathered the girl in his arms and wrapped her tightly. He couldn't stop her screams, but he could stop her from hurting herself. She could barely breathe for the screaming, and Takuda had to turn his face away from her gaping, gasping, howling maw. It wasn't just the volume. It was what she was doing to herself. He knew it was only his drunken imagination, but he thought he could hear her vocal cords shredding as she screamed.

As her shrieking subsided into gasping moans, black shapes milled in the park shadows. Takuda looked to the lampposts for the first time—most of the lamps were dark. This was all carefully staged, with just enough light for him to find the girl.

Takuda turned and turned with the girl in his arms. The shadows were all around. He could take care of himself, but he didn't know if he could protect her.

Two figures appeared from the Oyafuko side of the park, just by the police box he had passed moments before, and he knew them at a glance. "Mori! Suzuki! Help me here!"

As they began to run toward him, shadows detached themselves from the darkness, shadows in Zenkoku Security uniforms, masked and armed. Also limping and maimed. Takuda had met them before.

They surrounded him, and their leader pulled up his mask. "You can't take care of her. You don't know what's wrong with her."

He looked down at the girl. Her eyes had rolled back in her head. She jerked spasmodically as a thin trickle of bloody drool ran from the corner of her mouth.

"Give her to us quickly," the security team leader said. He motioned, and two smaller figures appeared from the shadows. They removed their masks: grim, hard-eyed women who stared at the girl with an urgency beyond mere concern.

"We have to get her stable," one of the women said.

"Shut up," the team leader hissed. He turned to Takuda. "Quickly. We give the girl the help she needs, and you get what you asked for. Counselor Endo wants to speak to you."

CHAPTER 22

Sunday Evening

The blindfolds came off. Takuda, Mori, and Suzuki were in a posh lobby. Takuda looked behind them to see huge doors of frosted, curved glass sliding silently together.

The floor was formed of concentric, alternating rings of polished marble and rough granite radiating outward from the circular reception desk to walls of matte burnt-umber tile with dark oak trim. Burgundy leather couches, fat ferns, the works. An oversized version of *The Thinker* dominated the lobby from a pedestal in the center of the reception desk. It was Thomas Fletcher's work. He had used beveled edges and precise curves to replace the smooth, natural lines of the original.

Suzuki elbowed Takuda. "The original is from a piece called *The Gates of Hell*. Do you think they get the irony?"

Takuda shook his head as Zenkoku Security forces nudged them toward the elevators.

Counselor Endo waited for them in a dimly lit third-floor conference room. The walls were covered with pages from flip charts, and one whole wall was taken up by a vinyl whiteboard, the warning not to erase it more prominent than anything else written thereon.

Hiroyasu Ogawa lay on a thin mat on the conference table. He was unconscious, pale, dressed in a hospital gown, attached to an intravenous saline drip bag hanging from the fluorescent light fixture.

Counselor Endo was solid and brown and smiling wide with his large, yellow teeth. As the security guards fanned out around the room, the counselor performed the polite and distinguished bow of a successful businessman to his colleagues.

"Good evening," he said. "I trust you had a pleasant time on Oyafuko-dori. Fukuoka is a wonderful town for entertainment, I find."

Suzuki looked around. "That was a very short drive," he said. "We must be in Daimyo."

Mori said, "They turned right and then left. Based on the direction the van was headed, that would put us west, not east. From the traffic sounds as they unloaded us, we're probably in the little strip between Showa Avenue and Meiji Avenue. I think we're in Otemon."

Endo's smile broadened. Takuda hadn't thought

that possible. "Ears like a fox," the counselor said. "Almost as keen as your wits."

"Where are you taking the girl?" Takuda asked.

"I'm not taking her anywhere. After her condition is more or less stable, she will be remanded to a sanitarium, a plush, privatized counterpart to the one in which you foolishly and illegally visited the foreigner."

"The one in which your Ogawa tried to murder me."

The smile didn't dim at all. "Yet he is the one still supine on the altar of modern medicine," Endo said, indicating Ogawa's pathetic condition with a sweep of his manicured hand. "I think you'll agree that it is with him that our sympathies must lie."

"He murdered Thomas Fletcher and he tried to murder me."

Endo raised one eyebrow. "If that is true, then it seems that pharmacology is not his strong suit. In an unexpected lucid window, he reported administering to you a dosage that would have felled an ox, literally. Yet you were up breaking furniture in no time." Endo inclined his head as if examining a curious work of art. "He also said your heart stopped altogether. Did you know that? If our Ogawa did succeed in murdering you, as you so colorfully put it, something brought you back to life right before his eyes."

There was nothing to say. Takuda thought back to the massive presence that had woken him in the mental hospital.

Endo idly poked Ogawa in the side with a meter stick. "You're getting stronger and stronger, unlike your friends. Doesn't that bother you? Young Mori is just getting impatient, and the priest is getting hungrier. He's eating you out of house and home, no matter what ends up in his begging bowl."

He continued into the silence: "So, the girl is safe, the parents—whatever sorry excuse for parents allowed their misbegotten waif to get into this situation—have been notified and compensated for whatever anxiety they were obliged to feel. The foreigner is gone, cleared by his own death and by the testimony of expert consultants of any connection to the recent killings, disappearances, and whatnot. Apparently, a doctor at the mental hospital, a most disagreeable little fellow named Haraguchi, will commit suicide any minute now over the foreigner's accidental overdose. All the blood is washed away." He made a dusting-off motion with his hands. "All fresh and shiny like newborn babes, ready to start again."

"Ready to start what again?" Mori asked.

"The hunt for the artifact, of course, the artifact whose activity wakened your latent talents and disturbed your tranquil working life. Get this taken care of quickly so you can get back to making ends meet."

"It's important to you," Takuda said.

Endo almost frowned. "In itself, no. You see, once ensconced in its usual home, it has a muted and salutary effect on the workplace. Without it, things don't run smoothly. It shares a home with some sharp, aggressive men and women who are expected to go out and make a real difference on an international level. It also shares a home with a group of editors, copywriters, and such who should be beaten to death at their desks. Seriously. They are lackadaisical, pedantic fools who should have been whipped into shape from birth, and even then, they may still have turned out to be the sort of useless buffoons they are today. Some people blame postwar liberalism, but I think they just might be congenital idiots."

Endo poked Ogawa a little harder. "The sharp ones, the international players, are off their game. Numbers are down, and they seem to have lost their hunger, their lust, for acquisition. But even at their worst, each of them is worth a dozen of the copy editors. I don't think you can imagine how those pitiful wretches behave without the influence of the artifact. Just today, two of them came to blows about a reference in a valve manual, and the one nicknamed Ishii the Mutant somehow managed to staple his own tongue."

Ogawa groaned and tried to turn over before falling back into uneasy slumber. "If I had my way," Endo said, "I would turn the girls and the artifact loose on the editors, solving the whole problem at once, but there are rules to be followed and deadlines to be met. My conduct in relation to such antiquities as the artifact are extremely circumscribed. Once again, I need your help."

Takuda said, "It drives children to murder, but you broke one loose from the pack and directed her into our path so she could tell us about the Kurodama, but not where it is."

Endo assumed a pained expression. "*Kurodama* is a word for grapes or candies. Or coal. No jokes, please. It's nameless. It's older than Japan itself, and I mean the islands, not our beloved national identity."

Mori snorted. "No one cares what you call it. It drives mere children to murder. I'd like to shove it down your throat. Just as you used us to kill your pet kappa in Naga Valley, you want to use us to find your Kurodama."

Endo spread his hands in a gesture of helplessness. "Rules are rules, and I must obey the rules. Even worse, I can't tell you where to look. Ironic, isn't it? It's the bedrock of our organization, the foundation of everything we do." A yellow grin split his face. "But I can't tell you anything about it."

Endo's broad, nut-brown face was impassive. Takuda leaned over the table toward him, far enough to catch a whiff of antiseptic and stale urine wafting upward from the unconscious Ogawa. "You're dropping hints about girls and bedrock, laying a trail of rubbish that will lead us wherever you want us to go. Tell us where your wayward stone knife lies, and we'll destroy it. For the victims, not for you."

The counselor rubbed his forehead. "Your strength has completely scrambled what brains you ever had. As you obviously can't follow in the moment, at least try to reconstruct later, between the three of you, the various threads of our conversation tonight."

Takuda leaned in closer, despite the unpleasant odor from Ogawa. "Where is it?"

Endo put his hands in his pockets. "You look at our poor Ogawa with something like disgust, but you are so inferior to him in so many ways. So pathetically ineffective. You want me to draw you a map. You want me to do your job for you."

They heard a sound like thunder. The fireworks had begun.

Endo said, "I could draw you a map, but there would be little use. Things keep on shifting here in Japan." He sighed as if in pain. "This is tedious beyond belief. Please listen so that I don't have to repeat it." He held his hands out as if trying to physically grasp their attention. "I was sightseeing in Fukuoka City's East Ward, just beyond the end of the subway line. You know the old mystery novel *Points and Lines*? It's set there."

Suzuki smiled. "Why am I not surprised you're a mystery fan?"

Endo ignored him. "On the way, I noticed a marker commemorating a poem in the *Collection of Ten Thousand Leaves*. Something about frolicking in the surf and gathering seaweed. That marker is roughly where the beach lay in the ninth century, but it's quite far inland from where the beach lay in the 1950s, when *Points and Lines* was written. And that shoreline in the 1950s is a brisk walk from the shoreline today. You see? Land reclamation continues apace, and the shoreline continues to move. Zenkoku Heavy Materials, I am proud to say, is deeply involved in plans to build an island in the marshlands beyond the present shoreline, once some concerns about migratory birds are cleared away. And they will be. Time marches on, and so does the shore-line."

Mori frowned deeply. "So you can't draw us a map."

Counselor Endo pointed at Mori with genuine en-thusiasm. "You have everything you need. All you need is transparency and a proper sense of proportion."

Takuda turned on Mori. "You've got it? You under-stand what he's going on about?"

Endo laughed out loud. "Young Mori could find the artifact's home on his own, I suppose. He could stop more killings, as you three did with the poor little water-imp." He turned his attention fully on Mori. "It's really too bad that you didn't stop the water-imp before it gutted your sister, but you were just a child then, weren't you? Not all grown up, as you were when you failed to protect the Nabeshima girl from the mad foreigner. She really shouldn't have been there to start with, but there's no stopping a girl once she acquires a taste for the exotic."

Mori's jaw clenched. He took off his glasses.

"Oho, you'll need those," Counselor Endo said, ap-parently oblivious to the security guards unsnapping mace and Tasers. "Keep your eyes peeled. Engage that intellect and find the artifact."

"You don't have to wind him up," Takuda said to Endo. "He's already so disgusted with the rest of us that he can barely stand it."

"Just tell us who's drawing up the clues," Mori said. "Is it the elder Reverend Suzuki? Is he alive? Is he work-ing for you, or is he some sort of captive?"

Endo's smile was beatific. "Yes, you all have your daddy issues, don't you? Your father, Detective Takuda, showed you how a man may be destroyed by monsters. He really let the water-imp drag him down, so to speak." He looked at the ceiling as if considering whether to stretch the pun even further. "Reverend Suzuki, on the other hand, was abandoned for fear of monsters. The youngest son, destined to be the lost one . . . but he stayed home to prove his loyalty, so the whole family had to leave him instead! That was a surprise, wasn't it? And his father didn't stay around long enough to teach him about monsters."

"So is the elder Reverend Suzuki alive," Takuda asked, partly to fill the void left by Suzuki's silence, "or was he drowned by your little pet in the valley?"

"The water-imp was not my pet," Endo said. "It was a nonfunctional aberration, a relic of a failed union of vastly dissimilar entities, a freakish miscegenation that could only cause confusion in this otherwise orderly modern world. I'm grateful to you all for cleaning that up. Anyway, back to your daddies. Detective Takuda's father taught the dangers of monsters by example. Reverend Suzuki's apparently didn't teach quite enough about monsters before his abrupt departure. Young Mori's father, however, taught best, in a much more direct method." Endo absently examined his own shoes. "What better way to teach the danger of monsters than to become one yourself?"

Mori went for Endo over the table, but Takuda pulled him back before the security guards could Taser him.

"Very well, then," Endo said, clasping his hands together as if something had actually been accomplished. "Thanks for playing, and we have lovely parting gifts for you all. First, for young Mori." Two security guards limped forward with a large box. They tilted it forward so everyone could see. It was a ceramic figurine, a samurai in a fighting stance holding a large sake bowl. "A Hakata doll, one of Fukuoka's most renowned local products, a fearsome Kuroda clan warrior. His spear and the glass case are in the box as well." The security guards busied themselves repacking the box as another came forward with a flat, twine-tied packet. "For Reverend Suzuki, another local treat, spicy pickled cod roe. Delicious on rice for any meal." Mori hissed as Suzuki reached for the package, and Takuda held Mori a little more tightly so the hiss became a rushing of air.

"For you, the strongman of the group, something special." Endo himself reached under the table and pulled out a suit bag. "My tailor made this for you." He unzipped it to reveal a suit, shining black, iridescent. "The shirts and shoes are not tailored, I'm afraid, but the measurements should be correct." He zipped up the suit bag and laid it on the table beside Ogawa. "There is also a bottle of solvent for the mace. The smell of it is rather strong, still. I believe that might have been why that poor child you accosted in the park was crying so. And you don't want to make your Yumi cry. She's waiting for you."

Takuda stiffened, and Mori stopped squirming. Suzuki looked up from the package.

"She's waiting for you at Fair or Cloudy. She might be next door at the sister establishment by now, singing *chanson* with the owner's wife. Hurry up and get into your suit," Endo said, smiling like a benevolent uncle. "You don't want to leave her alone with this jellyfish killer on the loose."

CHAPTER 23

Sunday Evening

The blindfolds came off, and the security guards melted into the shadows of the little park.

Takuda brushed off his fine new suit, and Suzuki clutched his packet of spicy pickled cod roe. Mori aimed a kick at the Hakata doll, large and square in its silk bundling cloth, but Suzuki edged in to block the kick. "No, no, no," he moaned. "That's a nice doll. It's a week's groceries if we can get cash back for it."

Takuda scooped the doll up under his arm. "I'm done for the day," he said. "I have to go find Yumi."

"We were set up," Mori growled. "This little jaunt to Club Sexychat, the satellite mental health center, the job with Ota Southern Protection Services, everything."

Takuda nodded. "They even want us to know where their offices are. They took the same route, coming and going." He watched Mori cataloging the information. *He knows something, but he isn't ready to tell us.* "We'll catch up tomorrow. Meet me at the Lotus Café for breakfast. You've got the overnight shift at the satellite office, though it will be pretty grim for you without Miss Nabeshima there. I'm sorry about that." He bowed politely to let them know he was really going. "Good evening." And he turned on his heel and left.

He hoped Suzuki could take care of himself with Mori, but it was out of his control. Takuda had to catch up with Yumi. Counselor Endo's threat about the jellyfish killer was not a direct threat, and Endo knew that hurting Yumi would bring war. Endo didn't want that. Endo had Zenkoku at his beck and call, but Takuda had more power at his command, somehow, though he wasn't sure exactly what it was. Or how he could use it to feed himself.

Takuda sped down Oyafuko, though his new shoes pinched in the heels. He was slowed by the crowd coming back from the fireworks display near the castle ruins.

Fair or Cloudy was homey and cluttered, even at the entrance, a hodgepodge of primitive art mostly by the owner's wife. At the door, he had to wait for one patron, a genially drunken businessman who balked at exiting and clutched at the sliding door as if the club and the sidewalk were moving at different speeds. When he had passed unsteadily onward, Takuda ducked into Fair or Cloudy to a chorus of welcome from the staff.

The owner bowed, beaming. He wore a bandanna on his head, with a brocade vest and jeans, like a cross between an American biker and a Southeast Asian hippie. Takuda thought he would be comfortable wherever he landed.

"Our massive security guard is here," the owner said. "We're safer already! And look at this splendid suit!" He laughed aloud as he bowed again, gesturing for Takuda to follow him. "Please come this way. Your lovely wife is in the stern."

Half the pub, the raised platform tables, had been built with cedar timbers to resemble the prow, midship, and stern of a ship. The owner stopped in consternation when he saw the stern table occupied by a quartet of young women in summer kimonos, all fanning themselves and getting settled in after the long walk from the fireworks display.

The manager, a brown, sharp-eyed little man, came to the rescue. "She's next door, singing with Madame," he said. "Right this way, please."

"Oho," said the owner, bowing with delight. "We have two songbirds tonight. I'll come over in a few minutes to make sure everything is all right."

Takuda followed the manager into the kitchen and up a narrow stairwell. "I hope you don't mind going up the back way, but really, you're part of the family," the manager said.

"That's okay," Takuda said, looking over his shoulder to watch a bearded cook peel a radish he held in midair, reeling a paper-thin, translucent sheet of radish onto a waiting platter of grilled mackerel. "I always find the kitchen interesting."

"I also wanted a quiet place to tell you," the manager said, turning to face him on the stairs.

Takuda shifted the Hakata doll to free his right hand. He liked these people, but he hated being trapped on the stairs.

"Your evening here is on the house," the manager said. "Really, truly. Anything and everything you want, don't hesitate. And I'm preparing a basket to carry home." He looked Takuda in the eye. "Seriously. Don't be shy. It's taken care of tonight."

Takuda bowed and tried to smile. *Counselor Endo is trying to be very generous.*

Yumi was still singing with the owner's wife. Her voice was husky with the echo of a suicide attempt that had damaged her vocal cords, but it was somehow perfect for the evening. Outside it was a summer celebration, but inside this restaurant it was all in French, very breathy and airy and full of Edith Piaf, and Takuda didn't understand a third of it. It reminded him of Club Sexychat, but he wasn't going to let that bother him. He sat in a booth beneath a ratty old ball gown turned into a canopy, and he raised his glass to Yumi when she seemed to be looking in his direction.

Ota, his boss, appeared with a jug of cold sake and

an oversized earthen cup for sharing. "Security Guard Takuda! I waved like a madman from across the room, and you didn't see me!"

Takuda wasn't even surprised. Everyone was out tonight. "I was watching my wife singing."

Ota's gaze jerked to the little platform. "Which one, the redhead?"

Takuda smiled. "The brunette."

"Oho," Ota said, passing Takuda the sake cup. "Nothing against the older one, but you did well for yourself."

"I'm a lucky man," he said as Ota plopped down on the matting and poured for him.

Ota sighed. "Takuda, you're lucky, but you're killing me. Really killing me. Why didn't you tell me about this monster-hunting thing you've been doing on the side?"

Takuda drained the cup before he answered. "You've been very generous to us. Now, please feel free to tell clients that I misled you, or that I gave you false information."

"What? You come into town to ruin my business, and you tell me to lie my way out of it?" Ota shook his head. "Why don't you lie a little bit? It would probably be less trouble for everyone if you started."

Takuda didn't bow. "I'll have the uniforms back to you tomorrow," he said.

"Wait just a minute," Ota said. "I haven't cut you yet."

Takuda poured for Ota, bowing with gratitude even though he had no idea what Ota was going to say.

"You know how I found out about all this?" Ota said after he drained the cup. "Zenkoku called me. Our biggest account, of course. What the hell did you do to them?"

Takuda sighed. One of the security guards had maced him right in the ear, and it was starting to itch. "Publicly, they say my associates and I forced them to retool an antiquated fiber plant in the valley where I was born." He worked at his ear with his little finger. "Privately, they told me they used me to clean up a problem in that valley."

Ota raised an eyebrow. "Monster problem?"

Takuda nodded.

Ota snorted. "Bastards. Shit-eaters."

"That's what I think of them," Takuda said.

"Well, did you know they introduced us to the health office here? They heard the Yoshida woman had a problem, and they recommended us. Isn't that strange?"

"Who did the introductions?"

"Kim, Korean name. Not that there's anything wrong with that. Just shows what a progressive and open-minded company Zenkoku can be."

"For one of the original giants of Japanese industry."

"Exactly. Bastards. Shit-eaters. So they recommend me, and now they start telling me to fire people."

"They told you to fire me?"

"You and the genius. They told me to lose you or I would lose the Zenkoku account."

The sake hadn't hit Takuda yet, and he felt stone-cold sober, unfortunately. "They want me unemployed so I can spend all my time trying to find something for them."

"Well, they don't get it. I told them I would answer them next week. That was so I could scare up a little business to cover the loss of Zenkoku."

"You were willing to lose that account?"

Ota lit a pungent little Japanese cigarette. "They have their own security force. The whole Zenkoku account was a huge retainer, but just a few hours a week for the genius. That's all. Just reviewing tapes and logging them in, then walking the underground parking lots once between the shifts of their regular security force. Light, useless duty."

But it kept Mori in the core of their downtown office, where they could study him. "Did they ask for Mori when they started the account?"

"No. No, they didn't. But you know what? They asked for someone just like him. I mean, just like him. Experience, skills, everything. And the request for a proposal came in from them just a week after you guys showed up."

Takuda nodded. "You told us that at the time. You were pretty happy about the coincidence."

"Well, I'm not happy now. It's very suspicious. Very suspicious indeed. And then they call me and tell me to fire people. Ha! They can all go to hell."

Takuda smiled. "You're not going to fire us."

Ota made a rude noise. "They don't tell me what to do. And I have an iron-clad contract with them. If they want to break it, I'll squeeze them for five years' worth of that monthly retainer. You and Mori, and that priest, you never broke any laws, right?"

Takuda sighed. "We never hurt any living person, and we've never been charged with a crime."

"Ha! Never hurt a living person! I get it! Now look, no reason to be so glum. They can't touch us. I'm such a small fish that I slip through their net, see? They try to ruin my reputation, I just do more divorces and illicit background checks."

"You'll never make a living doing background checks."

"You don't know the referrals I get, Takuda. I know my business, and I know character. I saw that you and the genius were solid the second I laid eyes on you. I wasn't so sure about your friend the priest. But I saw you were someone who could stick around. I saw you could last through a little rough weather and still come out okay. I also guessed you knew how to be a team player. A little teamwork goes a long way."

Here it comes. Takuda bowed. "Thank you for letting us keep our jobs. We've had to move around a lot over the past few years, and it takes a toll on my wife. She'll be grateful."

"It would be nice to give her some long-term stability, wouldn't it? Women get tired of financial stress. Who doesn't?"

Takuda looked up to see if Ota was working him. Ota met his gaze. His eyes were clear and bright, and his expression was neutral, except for a slight wrinkle between his eyebrows.

"You've been there," Takuda said.

Ota didn't smile. "I've been there." He looked at Yumi. "I had a beautiful wife. And then I didn't." He poured for himself, out of turn, and downed it. "Now I've got a wife who doesn't stand for any nonsense. I'm better off, but I did things the hard way." He belched discreetly. "Long-term financial stability is better than any romantic rubbish, and smart women know it."

Takuda exhaled slowly. "And how do you think we could find such a situation?"

Ota clapped the cup on the table like an auctioneer's gavel. "Well, now, are you happy chasing ghosts and monsters all over the country?"

Takuda frowned. "I'm not even sure how to answer that question."

"How would it be to have a home base? A little management? A way to capitalize on your skills?"

Takuda felt his jaw drop. "You don't want this. You think you do, but you don't."

Ota leaned forward. "Listen, when I read through this report from Zenkoku, my mind was racing. Were you three crazy? And your wife, too? No. Was it all just a big scam? No. You're not a scam artist. You're one of the worst liars I've ever met. Really, that's a handicap we'll work on." He reached for the sake. "Anyway, I thought to myself, if he's not crazy, and it's not a scam, it's real." He handed Takuda the cup. "It's real, and it's unique. A unique service to fill a gap that no one, and I mean no one, is filling in the security market."

Takuda managed not to spill as Ota poured.

"We build a framework for this, see, a separate company with you three as owners, all a subsidiary of a little company of my own. You get the support you need, and my subsidiary does the billing. Steady paycheck for big billing."

Takuda didn't drink. "Do you have any jobs in mind, like solving the jellyfish killings or finding a missing artifact or finding the missing girls from Able English Institute?"

Ota looked at him as if he had sprouted wings. "Your record's clean, but you can't be a consultant, not after you've walked away from it. They'll never listen to you. No, no, no. I'm talking about haunted villages and mountain goblins and goose-necked ghosts and shape-shifting foxes." He put his fingers under Takuda's drinking hand, raising it gently. "I'm talking about getting rich hunting monsters. Rich!"

Takuda drank. When he finished, Ota's eyes shone in the pub's dim lights. Takuda said, "But really, you don't believe in all this, do you?"

Ota made a circle with his thumb and forefinger, the shape of a coin. "I believe in this. You have a service, and if there's a service, there's value, and if there's value, we can set prices. You handle the service, and clients will decide the value. Leave the pricing to me."

He was serious. "Not everyone can pay," Takuda said.

Ota leaned forward. "That's the beauty of it. That's the beauty! Pro bono work is everything. You can't advertise the service, not directly. But satisfied customers—the poorer, the better—will start the ball rolling."

Takuda said, "I'll think about it." He glanced at the singing platform where Yumi and the mama-san were wrapping up. "We'll think about it."

Ota clapped him on the knee, complimented him on his suit ("Stick with me, and you'll dress like that every day!"), and prepared to go back to his table. Takuda stopped him. "Why did you come here tonight? Why Fair or Cloudy, of all places?"

Ota said, "Too tired to fight the crowds at the fireworks display, after dealing with these Zenkoku shiteaters, and I like the staff here."

"Me, too," Takuda said. "Exactly."

Servers swooped down on Takuda when Ota left, and the table was covered with hearty dishes and delicate appetizers by the time Yumi arrived.

After he complimented her on her singing, she said, "The evening is on the house."

He told her he had heard. "You're not wearing the summer kimono," he said.

"I leave that to the Fukuoka flowers who're trying to find their men," she said. "I've already found mine."

She asked about the suit, and about the Hakata doll, and he told her the whole story, all except the Russian pistol. She was silent for a moment, and then she sighed and stretched her legs under the table. "The priest is right," she said, examining the Hakata doll's label under the silk wrapping. "A week's groceries at least."

He watched her in the dim light as she examined the box. He hoped they had enough money to go to a hotel that night, even though it would be hard to find a room on the night of the fireworks display. He smiled as he imagined them walking up to a hotel with their silk-wrapped Hakata doll and the basket from Fair or Cloudy.

"It's a pity I can't return the suit," he said. "It would at least pay for a night on the town."

"Oh, you need a new suit," she said, caressing the silk bundling cloth on the Hakata doll box. "Your old detective suits are shiny in the seat and baggy in the knees. And there's no telling when you'll need a nice suit for a funeral."

CHAPTER 24

Monday Morning

When Takuda took a seat in the Lotus Café the next morning, Koji the waiter was almost unrecognizable. He stood at attention in the restaurant foyer as a middle-aged woman leaned forward toward him, whispering with an expression of urgent concern.

Takuda took the booth nearest, just to eavesdrop. Koji didn't take his eyes off the woman's face, but Takuda knew he had been spotted.

" . . . and he mentioned you several times as some sort of mentor. I hoped you might know where he is. I think he and his girlfriends went somewhere; none of them have been in classes lately. It's strange that so many people are missing and there's nothing in the news."

"I have noticed that as well," Koji intoned in a pleasant baritone. Takuda picked up the breakfast menu to hide his amusement.

"The police say there's nothing to worry about, and they say most runaways come home within forty-eight hours, but it's already been more than that."

"Your son is a capable and resourceful young man," Koji said. "I'm sure he hasn't done anything foolish."

The woman smiled a brittle smile and bowed in agreement and gratitude, but her brows were still lined in concern. "I appreciate your concern and your care," she said. "Tell me, in just what way were you mentoring my Haruma?"

"Ah. As I'm sure you know, he is thinking of entering the service industry. Despite my modest role in this fine establishment, I have solid contacts in the catering and convention planning community here in the city. If he . . ."

"This is something his father and I have spoken to him about," she said. "We don't think his aspirations are high enough for his upbringing and his aptitudes. His test scores alone . . ."

"He could be rich and influential in a booming international city like Fukuoka," Koji said, ignoring the woman's exasperated protests. "He's doing the right things by studying English and finance. He's got a good plan, and he's making the contacts to execute his plan. You're very lucky to have such a son."

She bowed without indicating agreement. "I see your point. It's just that his father and I hoped he would be a professional."

Koji smiled. "The real money is in service, if you have the drive and the charm. Haruma has both."

"Yes," she said with an appraising look at Koji. "I'm just so worried that he and his girlfriends ran off without telling anyone. Haruma's harem, my husband calls them. And just to think, the fancy-pants detective that called at our house implied that Haruma might be a homosexual. A detective with hair as long as Yuko Asano's."

Koji chuckled. "Isn't that always the way? Point your finger at someone, and three fingers are pointing back at you!"

She laughed and touched his forearm; his expression softened into the proper paternalistic warmth but without a hint of girlish intimacy. Koji stayed in character as he bowed her out of the restaurant. But as he turned from the door, Koji sagged into a dismayed mass. "There's no telling where that boy is," he muttered as he sauntered past Takuda's table, "but I hope he's run off to Hong Kong. It'll be twenty years before this is a fit town for a flamboyant fellow like him."

"Koji," Takuda said, "I was interested in your conversation with that boy's mother."

Koji turned with an expression of mild surprise. "Interested? You? You hid it so well."

Takuda ignored the sarcasm. "I'm nosy. My friends are nosy. The priest is nosy."

Koji pouted. "And when will I see him again?"

"He's coming this morning. But I have some questions about the missing boy, Haruma."

Koji surveyed the bustling breakfast crowd. "Stand in line. You're the second one this morning."

"I'll make it quick," Takuda said. "Did Haruma have private English lessons with a foreigner named Thomas Fletcher?"

Koji's brow furrowed. "No, group lessons, with a fake and fickle group of little floozies from the ratty little college up the street. Why?"

Someone was bellowing for Koji from the kitchen, but Takuda didn't care if Koji didn't. "Where did Haruma have his lessons?"

Koji wrinkled his nose. "An old farmhouse. Sounded awful. He quit to save the money for clothes."

Takuda nodded. That made sense, but it didn't help.

Koji leaned forward. "Speaking of clothes, I love that suit. I'll sponge off the jacket for you when I have a clean cloth. Somebody had a good time last night . . ." He turned on his heel and bustled back to the kitchen. "Yes, yes, yes, I hear you," he sang. "Koji's coming."

Takuda sighed. He hadn't even ordered tea.

Yoshida arrived a few minutes later. She spilled Thomas Fletcher's journals and his students' papers all over the table.

"I have a lot to show you. I think I know what these girls are talking about." She stopped dead, a thin sheaf of papers in each hand. "Why are you dressed that way? Where are you going in a suit like that?"

He shook his head. "It's not important."

"You look like a different man without your coveralls and your staff," she said, laying handwritten reports out on the table. "These students' papers are . . . Well, first, they're horrifying. These girls are writing dark, twisted horror. It's as if Thomas Fletcher gave them a scenario of dreamlike imagery as metaphors for butchery and cannibalism, and they all did different takes on it. Literally, they each approach the scene from a different direction."

"What does that mean?"

"It means exactly what I said. Violet—he gave them all English names for class. That always gave me the creeps."

Takuda nodded. "I was Theodore."

"I was Alice. Anyway, Violet writes the wind rushes under her feet and carries her to the river of lotuses. You see? It's a dreamlike description of taking the subway to Ohori Park and then walking this way, toward the moat."

"You think they're writing about a place around here?"

"I'm almost certain. Abby mentions the hanging needles pointing to the tadpole. I think that's a reference to the broken hands on the clock at Able English Institute. The six looks like a tadpole."

Takuda didn't quite snort. "That's a bit of a reach."

She frowned at him. "Maybe, but I'm doing everything I can because this is pretty disturbing stuff. Their essays for Thomas Fletcher say they're worshiping. It sounds like they're describing some horrible ritual sacrifice, all about cleaning the bones of the victims. All these horrible little essays are like coded mes-

sages about something called the Devouring God."
She spread them out further. "And there is a pattern
in it. Violet's is a description of the path to a cafeteria coming from the west, along Meiji Avenue. Jane's
comes from the northeast, down and across Showa
Avenue past Enou Temple. I can almost pinpoint the
location, somewhere in Otemon, but not quite."

"You're triangulating. Let me know when you find
the spot."

"That's just it. There's no spot to hit. There's no
restaurant at all in the part of Otemon these routes
lead to."

"Maybe you're not reading it right. Maybe you have
to widen your search a little."

She shook her head. "I just have to put it all together."

Takuda looked around for Mori and Suzuki. They
should have been there by now. Yumi had promised to
keep Suzuki out of the basket from Fair or Cloudy, but
she had a hard time saying no to him. Takuda was getting worried about his basket.

"Anyway," he said, distracting himself from the
image of Suzuki gorging himself on grilled mackerel
and braised tuna from the basket, "what did you think
of Thomas's art and his writing? Could you make anything of it?"

Yoshida puffed out her cheeks. "I couldn't do much
with that. He's an artist, you know? Really, really
good drawings. Can you make a diagnosis from an
artist's work? Some people say they can. One English

psychologist became famous by rearranging the chronology of a patient's paintings of cats to show some sort of progression of schizophrenia, as if it worked that way. The problem was that the patient was painting cute, cuddly kitties at the very same time he was painting demonic neon dragon kitties. Who's to say what's madness on canvas? Art is not structured, like a thematic apperception test." She dropped a sheaf of papers and heaved a deep sigh. "You know, I'm trying to forget that poor dead boy and that poor battered girl and just get on with this." She looked up at him. She was tired. "You told me a lot more as I drove you home day before yesterday. The drugs that murderer pumped into you really made you open up. You're fighting some pretty horrifying people. I've met people in my job who've done awful things, but this, what you're fighting . . . What that man did to Thomas Fletcher and what he was about to do to me . . ." She spread her fingers on the scattered sheets on the tables. Her hands were shaking.

Takuda said, "Don't think about it. Don't do it. Just focus on the job." He felt the dark presence from the back of his mind stirring, and then it pushed him aside. His vision of the bright café around them darkened as the massive mind behind his spoke through his mouth to Yoshida: "Forget. Forget fear. Forget me."

She smoothed the papers with steady hands, as if she had intended to do so all along.

That was quick, Takuda thought. Just a few words, and she. . .

The room brightened, and a jolt of pain shot from his forehead all the way to his canine tooth, a lightning bolt passing through his eye. He swore aloud. "That's the last time I let you speak," he said, rubbing his temple.

"Excuse me?" Yoshida said, incredulous.

"Where are my friends?" Takuda said. He was gasping with the pain. "They were supposed to be here."

"Oh, I told your partner Mori that they shouldn't come. You and I needed to work on this, but it looks like you aren't in any shape. They went home to meet your wife for breakfast."

Takuda swore again as he stood up, holding his aching head. His basket would be empty for sure.

"It's my shift tonight," he said. He held his head with both hands, and he felt the left side of his face swelling beneath his fingers. "I'll be there just after dinnertime. We'll work on it then. If you figure anything out, wait for me to get there, okay? I don't want you charging off alone."

"There's nothing to be afraid of," she said. She was beaming, happier and more carefree than he had imagined she could be. "After all, it's just a few schoolgirls playing some sort of game. Don't worry. I'll be fine."

CHAPTER 25

Monday Afternoon

When Takuda got back to the apartment, the basket was empty and no one was home. Yumi had left a note about smoked salmon, but there was none in the re-frigerator.

When this thing is over, the priest is moving out, Takuda thought as he settled down to sleep. *We just can't go on like this.*

He rolled on the mat for a few minutes till he real-ized he would never sleep with the dull throbbing in his face. When he clicked on the bathroom light, the beast in the mirror horrified him.

A vertical ridge of bone had formed under the skin, running from the bump atop his temple down into his cheekbone and continuing under his lip. The bone ridge would have shut off his peripheral vision, but the left eye had bulged outward to compensate. He bared his teeth at his reflection; the canine tooth was no longer a tooth at all. It was an opalescent fang beginning to crowd out his incisors.

If the other side of his face distorted to match, he would be a bug-eyed demon with contiguous horns and tusks bracketing his face.

He lay on the bathroom floor with the cool tiling against his aching face. *Is this real? Am I mad? Have I gone insane like Thomas Fletcher?* Gently, he felt around in his mind for the dark presence that contained him, using consciousness like a tongue probing a tooth. The great presence remained silent.

He didn't know which was more terrifying, that the dark presence was in his head at all, or that it was so powerful that it could make another person forget just by speaking through his body. Or that its words left bones warped in their wake.

Powerful or not, it would not help him sleep. When he finally slept, he dreamt of dark water for the first time in ages, but he wasn't in the water to save his brother or his son, and he wasn't there to drown a fire demon. He was surrounded by girls, swimming, just out of reach. Lovely girls, naked, with dark hair streaming in the water. They wove around him in an intricate water dance, like the synchronized swimming in old Hollywood musicals, but it was tighter, more controlled, almost mechanical.

Then the dream changed, and he realized that he

was in the center of the rosette, the Kurodama's killing pattern, and he struggled to get out. Then the lovely girls turned on him, and they all grinned. Each had long, black fangs, each mouth full of razor-sharp curved jewels. The girls turned on him and began to bite and slash with those fangs, and his skeleton helped them by turning this way and that to expose itself, to help free itself of flesh.

He woke stripping the sheets off himself, as if he were pulling away his own skin.

He sat up on his sleeping mat catching his breath, wondering how he had come to such a place in his life. Impoverished, disheartened, never sure from one day to the next what would happen. The lustrous black suit hanging from the closet door mocked him as clearly as if Counselor Endo had been standing in it. He almost threw it away right then, but as Yumi had said, he might need it for a funeral anytime now.

He bathed hurriedly and left long before dark. If he had waited just a few moments, he would have seen Yumi and Suzuki at least, and maybe even Mori, but he didn't want to see them. He didn't want to see anyone.

He tried to sit through the last matinee, *Jurassic Park*. It was too loud, and the dinosaurs' teeth reminded him of his dream, and of his own new fang. The young girl's terror reminded him of the hungry ghost in the park. He walked out when he could tell the bloodshed was about to start.

He took a shortcut through the bar district. A Japanese bar district is pitiful in the light of day when neon glitz gives way to peeling paint and filthy pavement. Takuda cut through a narrow alleyway headed for his bus stop.

Coming toward him in the alleyway, a bar matron herded three young, giggling hostesses toward a tiny club. The hostesses were dressed in a weird combination of Tokyo teenybopper fashion and bar-girl trash. They were chatty and silly, country girls just getting the taste of the high life in a provincial capital. One girl, red-haired and coarse, a head taller than the others, stared at Takuda in astonishment. The recognition in her face stopped him cold. The other girls giggled, and the matron bowed and called out her club's hours, but the redhead showed him the corners of her eyes and opened her mouth wide as if to catch his scent. He was not invisible to her, nor she to him, and she wasn't just a girl. She was something more than human, or less, an animal spirit in a woman's body.

He did not bow as he passed, for such a wild thing would only be confused by his lowering his head as if to attack. They watched each other warily, and Takuda turned when he was sure she would not charge at him. The matron shooed them into a tiny bar, and the spirit-girl glanced back for just a second to show him her teeth: *Don't follow.*

Takuda paced back and forth a few times, then went on his way. The redhead was someone else's problem. For all he knew, he and she were on the same team.

Fukuoka Prefecture Mental Health Services Satellite Office 6 was dark when he got there. He let himself in and turned on the lights. Yoshida's desk was covered with papers, student essays with bits underlined and annotated.

In the center of the desk was a city atlas open to the Otemon neighborhood, the triangular bit in the branching of Showa Avenue and Meiji Avenue, across from Ohori Park and the castle ruins. Yoshida had drawn approaches and routes inward from the main roads, all of them converging on a single block.

Among the papers, almost lost, was a note from Yoshida:

> Security Guard Takuda:
> I figured it out. I'll be back by 6 p.m.

It was almost dark. She wasn't back, and if he didn't go get her, she was never coming back.

He snatched the map off the desk. Takuda took a taxi until it got stuck in traffic on Showa Avenue. Then he ran, weaving his mass and his staff through the pedestrians along the way.

The map took him to a building just around the corner from Able English Institute. It looked abandoned, with rust on the shuttered front and blistered paint on the window casements. The awning hung in rags.

He went down the steps to the kitchen entrance, prepared to rip the door from its hinges, but it swung inward at his touch.

He stepped into the darkened kitchen, and the door clicked shut behind him.

The reek of blood and rotting flesh was almost overpowering. Takuda reeled against a shelf, and nested steel bowls gonged gently as he tried to quiet his retching and gagging. This was the strongest stench of decay he had ever encountered, and it was a small, enclosed space.

The kitchen was empty, lit only by the greenish exit light above. He flipped the wall switch—nothing.

He felt his way through the kitchen, staff at the ready. When he swung the door into what he felt sure must be the dining area, the smell of blood was even stronger, though the underlying rot was unchanged.

The cavernous dining area was a scene from hell, worse than anything in the mad foreigner's journal. In the greenish half-light, small, ragged figures shuffled slowly past each other amid heaps of rotting flesh. They were girls, or they had been. They looked neither at each other nor at Takuda as they crossed each other's paths, each trading places in a sinuous and repetitive path through the room. The chairs and tables were stacked against the walls, jammed together in an interlocking pattern up to the ceiling so neatly that he had at first mistaken it for wallpaper.

He watched the girls shuffle past the eyes of the rosette, dark, five-pointed stars of gore, black with blood and drying flesh, and there, the center of the rosette, a man-tall altar of shining bone with a detached jawbone on top, a resting place for the Kurodama. The jawbone was empty. Takuda squinted in a vain search for the black comma, but it was not there. The stone knife was already in motion. One of the girls had the Kurodama, or maybe it was circulating among them, navigating their rosette on its own deadly course.

Yoshida walked past him, her eyes wide with fear.

He felt his mouth go dry. She had survived this long by somehow becoming invisible, as he was sometimes invisible, but he knew that two of them would not escape this place without a fight.

She mouthed something at Takuda. He assumed it was "Help me," but he couldn't quite make it out. He beckoned her forward, and she shook her head subtly. She indicated her blouse front—it looked like a brown silk scarf, which made no sense in this weather. *No, blood.* Bright, slick blood on her blouse, the crimson darkened and muted to brown in the green light of the exit signs.

He knew he would have to go in after her. He prepared to step into the pattern, but she shook her head to stop him. When she came around again, she made a weaving motion with both hands. Takuda cocked his head. Even in this dim light, he could see that she was exasperated. She made the weaving motion again, but this time in a very deliberate manner, as if explaining something to a particularly dim child. She also pointed downward as she wove her hands together, waggling her forefingers and middle fingers in a pantomime of walking, weaving in, joining the rosette.

He exhaled loudly. One of the girls looked up at him briefly, her dull eyes barely visible through her blood-matted hair.

Why didn't they all just attack at once? How did Yoshida get cut, but just get a single cut, not a flaying?

Takuda did not want to join the rosette, but that was the only answer. She must have been cut, then stepped in, masquerading as one of them until she could step out again.

With a feeling of deep revulsion, Takuda stepped into line behind a short girl in a blood-spattered DKNY tee shirt. She stepped behind the next girl they met; Takuda stepped in front of the one after that. They were hideous in their brokenness, their apathy, their bloody dishevelment. This was what happened when people became animals, slaves to forces beyond their control.

Still, it seemed too easy. He was half-again as tall as most of these girls, and twice as wide as any of them, but he shuffled along among them without seeming to draw any attention to himself. The bone altar now blocked his view of Yoshida, but he would come along to a line-of-sight view of her any moment, he was sure.

The girl in front of him suddenly cut right. He realized he had to cut left, and he found himself following a bloody waif who was completely naked except for one yellow rubber sandal. A young man in a bloodied gray summer suit passed him in the rosette without a glance. Takuda somehow thought this was the strangest part of the whole experience so far: the other man had passed him without the flicker of recognition they usually would have shared as outliers in this gang of girls.

It was as if they were asleep, as if they were all asleep, as the Kurodama itself was asleep, like sleeping sharks in shallow waters. The rosette just kept going all the time, the machine in motion, the jaws always chewing, waiting for something to bite.

Takuda was at the outside edge again, at the far side from the kitchen doors, but the next pass would take him straight to Yoshida. He wondered idly if the sleep-walkers stepped out of line when they had to pee, or if they simple soiled themselves as they walked. With the stink of death in that place, there was really no way to tell.

There was a green blur at the edge of his vision, and something thumped on the sodden carpet at his feet. The rosette stopped so suddenly he trod on the naked girl's single sandal. He looked down. The Kurodama lay at his feet, and then it was gone before he had even begun to reach for it. In his mind's eye, a memory of a swift green blur, a tiny hand from the side reaching out to snatch it.

Now the rosette started up again. He looked around. The Kurodama was moving. It had come to him, and it had dropped because he didn't take it. He just needed to rescue Yoshida and get her out of the caf-eteria, and then he could deal with whatever he had to do to retrieve the Kurodama itself. Twenty-something girls and a businessman couldn't compete with battle-hardened Takuda and his oaken staff, not if he was clever about . . .

Another blur, and a quick, biting pain in his shoulder. He looked down to see a slice in his coveralls, with blood coursing down his sleeve.

Yoshida hissed, "Get us out of here!"

At the sound of her voice, the sleepers awakened. They stopped their ghostly movement and turned toward her, all facing the center of the still rosette. The stone still passed among them, so quickly Takuda couldn't follow it in the half-light.

The girls' mouths popped open as one in their hideous grins.

If the stone gets to her before I do, they'll slice her to ribbons before I can stop them.

Takuda moved quickly, tossing the teeth-chattering girls aside with his hands and his staff. They made no sound except the sudden exhalations as he tossed them against each other.

As he reached Yoshida, the rosette broke and the girls crowded in on him.

"Tuck and roll," he said to Yoshida as he picked her up by the waist. "Land on your feet and run out the back door." Then he tossed her, shrieking, over the heads of the massed girls. Yoshida hit the swinging door with a bang, and he heard a clatter of pots that meant she had landed on the central table or the back shelves. Then the bang of the back door and a flash of bluish evening light from the outside stairwell. Yoshida was out the back door. Even if she had a broken hip, she was out. She would live.

Takuda, on the other hand, was surrounded by the grinning girls.

He felt the blade bite into the back of his leg, just below the knee.

Takuda went down, and the grinning horde piled on top of him.

CHAPTER 26

Monday Evening

Takuda stood in the half-light, blood running down his calf. The blade had bitten deeply into the back of his thigh, just above the knee. The pain had been shocking, but he had felt the blade bounce off his hamstring. Takuda was still flesh and blood —with bones and sinew slowly toughening into something entirely harder to destroy.

Meanwhile, the girls didn't know he wasn't crippled. *The Kurodama doesn't know.*

He pushed the girls back with his staff, tossing some of them almost out of the dining room, until he had a good staff's length between himself and the closest one. They stared at him with their awful grins until suddenly, as if in response to a silent signal, they started shuffling again. They were moving quickly now, as fully awakened as they could be, Takuda guessed. He stood on one foot, watching them pass through the pool of green light beneath the exit sign— feral things with matted hair and bloodied mouths, eyes glowing like half-seen creatures in passing headlights. Some came close enough to reach with the staff, and he thumped each in turn. They were predictable; they were running the rosette out at the edges of the room, and a few of them looped back inward toward the center, toward him, when the stone knife drove them to do so.

Takuda just needed to keep them back until he could start tracing the route the blade itself took among the girls' hands. That's why he was watching them in the light. If he could spot the blade, he could start to track it.

The alternative was smacking them down one by one with his staff. This just occurred to him as he stood on his one good leg, his back to the bone altar. If he could do it without killing them it would probably be the best thing for everyone there. He just needed to do it without cracking skulls—or exposing himself to that blade. The first thing he had to do was get out of the center.

He hurtled himself across the open space, windmilling at the sides with his staff. When he reached the kitchen door, he wheeled back toward the center of the room, leading with the butt-end of his staff.

The stone knife missed his face by a handbreadth.

The girl who had held it was right on his tail; she went down with a solid exhalation as his staff took her breath, and the knife slid away into darkness in another girl's grasp.

He dropped his staff at his feet.

They drew toward him, crouching, grinning, and showing their teeth in readiness to strip his flesh from his bones. They were all so close now that he could see the knife moving among them by the ripples in their ruined clothing. It passed from hand to hand so smoothly and so quickly that he was sure now that it was not under their control. They didn't even look at it. They only had eyes for him. They closed in on him slowly, deliberately, with no fear at all.

Easy.

He caught the first one under the jaw. She dropped without a sound, and one of her sisters stepped in from the right to close ranks. Takuda watched the blade—it was still moving almost too quickly to follow, and the path was too complicated to predict: right hand to left, left to left, behind the back, they passed it in every direction except up and down. At least it stayed a predictable distance from the floor.

Except when it's time to cut. That's when it breaks the horizontal plane, and that's what I have to let it do, if I don't want to knock out all but one girl and then wrestle it away from the last one standing.

The blade veered forward, and he caught the bearer with a punch to the solar plexus. She dropped, sucking air through that horrible grimace, then stood again when her breathing steadied. He punched her again under her left ear just as the knife reached her again, and the girls passed the knife onward, stepping over her sprawled form to reach Takuda.

The businessman went down easily, almost gratefully, it seemed to Takuda. He missed one girl, and she stood back, grinning. His forearm stung. He glanced at his arm glistening brown in the pale green light. She had sliced him from elbow to wrist.

Takuda continued to cut them down until there were only six standing amid the twisted limbs of their fallen sisters. The curved jewel continued to pass among them, still cutting a flat pattern a meter off the ground as it passed from hand to hand, still seeking a route to Takuda's blood, Takuda's bones.

They closed in on him suddenly, with no cry or outward signal. Takuda struck out fiercely at each girl in turn as the blade passed through his flesh—first along the ribs, then along the jaw, then along his hip bone.

Sweet Lord Buddha, they're slicing me to ribbons.

But another voice in the back of his mind said, *It's slicing for the bones. It doesn't care about bleeding you out or piercing your organs. Let it try to free your poor skeleton. When poor skeleton steps out, you'll be free to join them.*

Takuda was suddenly terrified. The voice wanted him dead.

No. I want you free.

He struck out in earnest. The blade continued to bite into him. He struck with his bones, suddenly understanding what the voice had told him, ignoring the musculature he usually used to form a strike. He flailed at the girls with his arms and legs, and they flew away from him, landing in heaps on their fallen comrades.

He paused when nothing came at him for a second. There were only two left, standing, and they crouched just out of the range of vision. Blood was running in his eyes now, and it was impossible to be sure where the remaining girls were.

There, said the voice. *From your left.*

Takuda struck downward, across his body with his right hand, slapping the stone knife from the grip of a pale, luminous paw. It disappeared among the bodies, and Takuda and the girls fell on the spot, digging for it.

Around them, other girls began to disentangle themselves from the pile on the floor. Takuda had knocked them out cold, perhaps concussed a few, but the knife would not let them stay down.

Takuda and the girls struggled to find the blade in the mound of sodden, bloody girl flesh where it had fallen. He felt for the knife between thin arms and scrawny knees, all the limbs so grimy and cold, as if the knife kept the girls' bodies only as warm as they needed to be for the continued functions of life.

A grinning girl rose to her knees beside him, a triumphant hiss whistling through her clenched teeth.

Takuda elbowed her in the face as the knife came swishing past his nose. He leapt to his feet as the blade slipped from her fingers, and he stepped on it. The crawling girls pried at his boot, the blade, the tile flooring. One girl closed on him and fell to chewing on the leather of his boot.

He streamed blood from a dozen slices. The girls piled onto his leg. He couldn't keep his balance for long.

The butt of his staff poked out from beneath a pile of fallen girls. He crouched low, keeping his weight on the stone blade as he reached in the opposite direction for the staff. His fingers closed on the butt and he drew it toward himself, centimeter by centimeter. He leaned too far, and the wound in the back of his leg opened. He lost his balance, falling face-forward into a pile of girls, still pressing his boot down as hard as he could.

The girls continued to pile on, and he felt his boot heel lifting.

The blade and his staff came free at the same instant. The girl with the yellow sandal stood with her hideous grin of victory and brought the knife in a slicing arc toward his throat.

He stopped the arc in midair with his staff. As the girl's ulna and radius snapped, her hand and the blade continued in a shorter, tighter arc around its new axis, Takuda's staff. The blade flew out of the girl's fingers.

Takuda caught the blade in midair. The naked girl reached for it with her broken arm dangling. They all reached for it. Takuda cut a wide swath with his staff, but they started to pile onto his back.

There were too many behind him, toward the kitchen. He had to go forward, through the front door, and hope he could open it. If not, he would have to fight his way back through, and he would probably kill at least a few of the girls.

It was difficult. The stone knife was cold, dull, and dead in his hand. The girls swarming him were cold as well, draining him of energy as he slogged toward the door. The stone was so heavy . . .

He slashed at the base of the bone altar, and it collapsed on them, knocking a few girls off their feet. It helped a little. He plowed onward, and they made a chain, trying to pull him backward.

One step at a time, he thought as the girls clawed at his face and tried to pull the stone knife from his hand. He dropped the staff and hugged the stone knife to his chest.

When he reached the door, he kicked it, and it banged open. He pulled the bloody girls with him up the stairs and out onto the sidewalk. He dropped to his knees and snapped the stone knife in two on the curb. The blade skittered off across the pavement. The girls watched it dully.

Takuda shook off the last of the clinging girls. A few dropped to their knees. The businessman made sudden retching, gagging sounds, as if clearing his throat to catch a breath.

Takuda, bleeding, sore, exhausted, slipped the lozenge of the handle into his left hip pocket. He hobbled across the sidewalk to retrieve the blade. His leg gave out as he bent to pick it up, but his hand landed on it, and he put it in his right pocket.

He pulled himself to his feet. On the sidewalk, on

the stairs, and inside the restaurant, the girls began to weep and moan. The knife's power was broken, and the horror of what they had been through was coming to them. By the time he got into the cafeteria to retrieve his staff, some of the girls had begun to scream.

In the dim light streaming in through the doorway, he saw the naked, bloodied girl with the shattered forearm shrieking in an avalanche of bones. He picked up his staff, turned, and left.

As he limped away on his staff, men in Zenkoku Security blues streamed out of the shadows. Takuda walked away, not even glancing at the security guards as they moved in to clean up the mess. It didn't matter. The girls who had survived the blade would make it home alive, and the dead were already dead.

And he had the broken knife. No matter what else had happened, the nightmare was over, and the jellyfish murders were finished.

The proof of that was in his pocket, banging against his wounded thighs with every step.

CHAPTER 27

Tuesday Morning

The stone knife lay in two pieces on the low table while Yumi examined Takuda's wounds.

"I don't know why we bother anymore," she said. "Most of your little cuts here seem to heal from the inside before I can get ointment on them."

Takuda frowned. Yumi and the rest had been horrified when he had come home in tatters the night before, but their horror had given way to intrigue when he had produced the stone knife.

Mori and Suzuki sat on opposite sides of the table, staring at the two pieces.

The whole blade, before Takuda had broken it, was much like a stylized comma from a fancy Western font, that or the yang of a yin-yang symbol. The outer rim would have described a perfect half-circle, thick as Takuda's thumb at the disc and disappearing to a pinpoint at the tip. That tip was the horrible business end, the part of the sharpened inner curve that left such neat incisions on the victims' bones.

It was a frightening object not only because of its mysterious antiquity but because of its clear, prosaic, horrible purpose.

The palm-sized lozenge that served as the handle lay a few centimeters from the snapped-off blade. Both pieces were a dull, velvety, midnight black, so black that they seemed to absorb light, casting a hazy ambient shadow around themselves, but the broken edges revealed slight variations, iridescent striations that shifted slightly with Takuda's viewpoint as if hidden dimensions had formed within the stone itself. It was entirely possible, Takuda thought, that this relic of some prehuman time had built itself by accretion, layer on layer, as a way to make itself real and visible in our world.

The characters, if such they were, were intricate beyond the simple sketch in Suzuki's begging bowl or the one in Thomas's notebook. *Even mad foreigners can't do this thing justice*, Takuda thought as he and Yumi joined the others at the table.

The characters were no more than a finger's width at their most robust, near halfway down the blade. They were raised or incised or both in some cases, apparently in an effort to create depth. Some were rude and angular, some curved and delicate, but none seemed Asian in origin, nor were they linear in the manner of runes or Latin, nor were they curvilinear in the manner of the scripts adapted to languages native to Japan. Some were disorganized, random lines like jackstraws tossed by a dimwitted child. One was quite hideous, almost toothed in aspect as if poised to bite the hand of any who dared write it. Another was so smooth and rounded Takuda thought to caress it off the stone and into his palm.

The characters started at the center of the discus, fully formed but so tiny it was hard to imagine them being carved by human hands, then spiraling out onto the blade, each character by that time the width of the blade itself, each character's proper orientation as unknowable as its meaning or origin, each character incised in strokes shifting and shimmering as if with the hidden dimensions hinted at in the stone's broken edges. It was hypnotic, following the characters from their tiny origin, following the tight spiral of the discus to the freer arc of the blade, then tightening again as the characters neared the point of the blade, disappearing into the miniscule and reappearing, Takuda realized, in the center of the discus as if the blade had incised the letters itself in an unending litany of self-creation. Takuda thought that if he just edged the pieces together, the string of characters would be unbroken, a little easier to study . . .

Mori flipped the disc with his forefinger. It clunked on the table: dull, dead stone. Now the characters on the reverse of the disc didn't match up with the characters on the obverse of the blade. The order had been disturbed. Takuda fought the urge to flip the disc back over.

Yumi glared at Mori. Suzuki laughed out loud.

"Well," Mori said, "if I hadn't done something, you would have sat here staring at it all day. Until someone went to get the glue." He shook his head as he stood up. "You said it yourself. It's broken, the girls snapped out of it. We drop one half in Hakata Bay and the other in the Inland Sea, or we catch a ferry to Busan and dump both halves in the trench. Let the deep-sea fish worry about it."

"Well, we can't just throw it out," Takuda said. "Even those characters may be dangerous."

"And the stone itself may not be inert," Yumi said. "We don't know what happens if the pieces come back together."

Suzuki's stomach growled.

Yumi nodded. "We have to do something about that, too."

Mori looked exasperated. "Well, I have to work. I'll see if I can find out anything about the fallout from the cafeteria break-in. It might be completely quiet, just because Zenkoku was on the scene. Waiting, were they?"

"It seemed like they were waiting, yes," Takuda said, rubbing his healing jaw. He stood as well. "They let us find it, and when we did, they swooped in to clean up. That cafeteria is sanitized right now, even if they had to burn it to the ground to sanitize it." He pulled on his shirt. "It's unclear if they know the stone is broken, and that it's all over." He pulled on fresh Ota Southern Protection Services coveralls, even though it felt as if some of his cuts were opening up again. "We don't have anywhere else to take it right now," he said, "but that's okay. We know they can't do anything about it. They can't touch it."

Mori shifted his weight from foot to foot. "They could send someone. They could find a way."

Takuda zipped up his coveralls. "If they could take care of it that way, they would have done it already." He stepped to the entrance pit and pulled on his shoes. "I'm beat, completely wiped out, but I have to find out about Yoshida. She was cut up, but she was okay. She'll know what happened with the girls, if any of them entered the system. I don't know what we could do about it, but I need to know."

He and Mori walked together as far as the convenience store. "We shouldn't leave them alone with the blade," Mori said. "Even if it's broken, the priest could . . . I don't know. Come under the spell."

"What spell? It's broken." Takuda stopped walking. Everything hurt. "Suzuki is stronger than you think. He's stronger than you are, maybe stronger than I am."

Mori bowed deeply, a frown carved around his mouth. He was angry, bitterly angry, and he was not going to hide it.

Takuda thought about it all the way to Yoshida's office. He didn't know what to do about Mori. Maybe this was the end of the line. Maybe they had been at the end of the line the whole time. Maybe none of it had meant anything at all.

Yoshida was sitting at her desk with a bowl of noodle soup. "It was a deep cut, but not life-threatening in any sense. Stitches, all shallow, no staples." She sat back, breathing a little heavily. "You tossed me well enough that I landed right on my feet, and I ran like a scalded cat out that back door. I thank you for saving my life."

He bowed in return, but he grinned at her when he straightened up. "You're a fool for going in there alone. You know that, don't you?"

"I've always been a fool. How else do you end up doing a job like this one at my age?"

"You're talking to a soon-to-be unemployed security guard. I don't know where the rent is coming from next month."

She nodded. "The choices we've made, eh? I'm supposed to go to a hot spring with some old crows from school. I'll have this scar, if it's even healed up. They'll be talking about their husbands' retirements and their children's jobs, and I'll be making up lies about being slashed by a patient." She smiled. "They'll say I'm brave." The smile dimmed a notch. "Your wife is the brave one."

"Stop talking about her. I can't stand it."

"What are you going to do? How will you get out of all this?"

"I don't know. I don't even know how I got here."

She pushed her soup away. "There were a lot of questions, of course. I told them everything."

"Everything?"

"Everything and everyone. It was illuminating. For one thing, they were not interested in you or your friends at all."

"Who were you talking to?"

"A patrolman. No one I've ever seen before. He didn't even write down your names. He wrote the address of the restaurant incorrectly. Not even close. His report reads like he was drunk. It says I ran into a girl gang that used an abandoned cafeteria as a hideout."

"Girl gang? Yamaguchi Gumi Pink Faction?"

"Sailor Moon Subfaction." She almost smiled. "They released me to rest, but I couldn't rest, not with these girls out there. Some of them are already home, you know."

Takuda just blinked.

"They were cleaned up and dumped at their houses. That's in the news.

The runaways are back. The jellyfish killings were regrettable exceptions to the peace in Fukuoka City. They may have been committed by an unnamed foreigner who died in an accidental overdose in a mental facility, but the runaways coming back, that's the headline." She looked as if she would spit. "I've been calling around. A couple of them were picked up, not dropped off, one of them with a broken arm. But everyone was scrubbed, not a drop of blood in sight."

Takuda didn't know what to say.

She shook her head. "I still don't believe any of this is real. The doctor kept me awake while he was stitching me up—horrible process, just horrible—and I just lay there, thinking it was all a nightmare and that I would wake up and come to work and hang out with Nabeshima. No worries, it was all going to be okay. But now . . ." she ended with a small, helpless gesture. "You and your crew came and destroyed everything. And you'll move on, just as you always do, leaving chaos in your wake."

"That's just it," Takuda said. "You'll forget. We won't."

She snorted in derision.

"I'm serious," he said. "You'll forget we ever existed. As aware and awake as you are, you'll forget. Your mind will reconstruct this as a terrible aberration, a strange thing that happened with some local girls, and you'll forget about us, and you'll forget about the cause of it all."

"I'll never forget the inside of that cafeteria."

"You'll have nightmares, but those will be the memories working themselves out, like a bamboo sliver working out from under the skin. It will bother you for a while, and then, one day, it will be gone."

"You know this from experience?"

"Yes. People forget me and my friends much more quickly than you would imagine. So will you, and so will Nabeshima. So will all those girls."

"And do you think this selective amnesia is magic?"

"No, I don't. I think it's the human mind protecting itself from the outer darkness."

As if on cue, the lights cut off. The fan stopped,

and the refrigerator in the kitchen stopped its reassuring hum.

"That's strange," Yoshida said. "It's not even so hot yet that everyone's running their air conditioners. There shouldn't be brownouts, much less a complete failure."

The hair on Takuda's neck stood up. He locked the front door and started checking the windows. "Get up," he said. "Gather your things. I'll get you out the back way."

She started to protest, and he spoke from the darkness in the back of his mind: *"Get out."*

His right temple exploded with pain.

She said, "I suppose I really should be resting at home anyway. I was going to enter some notes on Nabeshima's workstation, but without the power, I can't even do that. You'll lock up?"

"I'll lock up," he said, almost shoving her out the kitchen door and locking it behind them.

"Very well," she said. "I'll put in a good word for you with your boss. I'm sure he will appreciate your taking care of the office . . . Good day."

He walked her to the end of the alleyway, and then he watched her go down the main road toward the train station. She didn't look back. It was as if she had already forgotten who he was.

He paused at the front door, holding his right temple. He could feel the bone rising under his fingertips, raising the ridge that would push the right canine tooth out as a new fang. *I'll be a pop-eyed, grinning demon by nightfall. All I'll need is a spiked club.*

When he let himself back in the office, Counselor Endo was waiting for him in the shadows of the main room.

"Well, I see you've survived your schoolgirl crush without great injury," Endo said. He stepped into the light from Yoshida's window. "Congratulations. Now, you and your friends have something I want. You should deliver it to its home immediately, before it kills you all."

CHAPTER 28

Tuesday Morning

"I beg your pardon for the interruption of the electrical current," Counselor Endo said as he clicked on Yoshida's desk lamp. "I have a medical condition that makes fluorescent lighting very disagreeable. It's usually fine in larger, newer buildings, but this . . ." He reached up and flicked the hanging fixture with a thick, blunt forefinger. "Two concentric fluorescent rings with three illumination settings and an incandescent button for mood lighting, a twenty-year-old model for home use. It's a Zenkoku product, of course, made to last." He smiled. "The buzzing of such little units really grates on my nerves."

"You don't have nerves."

"This one would send me all to pieces."

"A flickering fluorescent fixture wouldn't show you in your best light, would it?"

Endo regarded Takuda. "My vanity is a failing, but it is not at issue here."

"Vanity isn't part of your makeup. It's part of your disguise, the eyes on the cobra's hood. I'm talking about persistence of vision. Illusion. Deception."

Endo was frozen still as a photograph. For five full heartbeats, he didn't move at all. Then he said, "You, Detective, lack vision. You are laboring under illusion and deception, and you have no one to blame but yourself. You have deluded yourself."

"In what way?"

"You have deluded yourself that your friends and your family are safe."

Takuda wanted to leap across the room and strangle Endo, to squeeze the poison out of him, but the man was so poisonous that Takuda simply didn't know where to start. In his gut, he knew it would be like strangling a water balloon; a tight grip on the counselor here would just make him bulge more over there. Endo was more than elusive. He was somehow formless.

But the form he's chosen could not be more deadly.

"Are you threatening my friends and family?"

"No," Endo said, pretending to look around the squalid little office. "You are."

"Just how am I doing that?"

"Well, you're a payday away from homelessness. I could take care of that, permanently. You know I could."

"Rubbish. You wouldn't do it."

Endo spread his hands. "I've never offered directly because I knew you wouldn't accept."

"You would have moved us around to clean up your messes anyway."

Endo smiled as if to say he had already done exactly that. Takuda felt the heat rising to his face.

"So what kind of danger are we talking about?"

"Ah. Back to your friends and your wife. I didn't say they were in danger. I said you had deluded yourself that they were safe. It's an important if subtle distinction. Danger and safety. These conditions are not polar opposites or mutually exclusive. Continued existence is contingent, and a single mind's survival in the dark void of eternity, as brief and bright as each hideous spark may seem, is never a zero-sum proposition. Our friend Ogawa at this point would make a sophomoric reference to Schrödinger's cat, neither alive nor dead, in an indeterminate state. He still sees this existence, or human life anyway, as binary, and any deviation from that scheme as an aberration demanding referents in particle physics. Otherwise, it's all yes or no, black or white, danger or safety, life or death." He flicked the light fixture again, a little harder; Takuda heard the plastic crack. "There are, as it turns out, indeterminate states that are neither life nor death."

"Possession must be one of those. What possessed you? Were you ever human?"

Endo grimaced. "As much as you seem to enjoy verbal sparring, you're really not equipped. Not only do you lack the wit, you lack self-knowledge. And at this moment, you're running out of time. I'm trying to tell you something."

"So spit it out."

The counselor fixed him with a stare. "No matter how often I tell you, you don't believe that there are rules I must observe here. The fact that you are ignorant of these rules will not protect you, but that doesn't change the fact that I must protect myself and my interests. There are situations that would deteriorate in unexpected and potentially disastrous ways if I tried to control them directly. I know this from experience."

"So I have to ask the right questions. Perhaps I do lack the wits. I can't guess at what you're trying to tell me."

Endo nodded sadly. "If young Mori were here, it would go more smoothly, I'm sure. I wonder what Mori would do?"

Takuda folded his arms. "He would probably ask you to tell him about the Kurodama."

"Ah. The artifact—I'm sorry, but I really can't refer to it by terms already in use for fruit or candy or lumps of anthracite—is a sort of hideous spark all its own, an entity with its own karmic weight and destiny. You might even call it a soul, if you believed in that sort of nonsense."

"It's not a mind anymore, and if it has its own karmic weight, that weight carried it straight to the hottest hells. I killed it."

"*Bully! Bully for you!*"

"I don't know what this *buri* means."

"I apologize. Old jokes, old habits. Congratulations, Detective. And how did you destroy this mind?"

"I broke it with my staff."

Endo flicked the lamp's pull-string. "How resourceful and . . . um, virile of you, breaking it into . . . two pieces? Yes, two? All with your long, hard staff, right on the sidewalk outside the cafeteria. Yes, you were observed." He flicked the string again, now visibly annoyed. "This artifact, a literal comma that somehow slipped into the daylight world from the litany of everlasting midnight, brings with it some of that outer darkness. I can tell you that with no ill consequences. You know already that it spurred what some might call unnatural appetites, causing famous but unproven acts of cannibalism. You've read the supposedly fictional story of the priest of the Koyama family temple who cleaned a beloved boy's bones with his own tongue, thereby becoming a demon. I know that young Mori has opinions on the alleged consumption of the American airman's liver, and that he finds it significant that the charges of cannibalism were dismissed."

"You've been spying on us."

Endo didn't bother to reply. "There have been more recent dinners in that general locale, dinners that some would call unusual, special events held even right in the squalid cafeteria where you retrieved the artifact. For sensitive people, and I use the term *sensitive* in the best possible way here, the artifact has an attractive force. Mr. Thomas Fletcher is one of those people, even though his mental state seems to have precluded active participation in any acts of veneration. Your Reverend Suzuki may also be among those who are unduly influenced by this visitor from the outer darkness. Mind to mind, do you see? One mind affected by another in an attraction that breeds an insatiable hunger. Such an attractive force!" He smiled. "Like the electron's lust for the proton, it's really all about love, isn't it?"

Takuda hunched forward over the desk. "How can it be such an attractive force if it's broken?"

"Broken? There you are, thinking in binary states again. On, off. Black, white. Alive, dead. Broken . . . whole."

"You're saying it's not dead."

"Not by a long shot. Let's recap, shall we? The artifact is a mind with attractive powers, a hideous spark in and of itself, and it seeks self-actualization and self-expression, which our postmodern world seems to prize above all else. Ignore these needs of the artifact at your peril."

"And you're saying it might be calling out to the priest."

"He has been terribly hungry lately, hasn't he? Your grocery bill is getting worse and worse."

Takuda didn't bother to smile. "I'm supposed to run to the Kurodama and lead you right to it."

"Sunshine Heights, apartment 201. You left it there because no matter how obtuse you pretend to be about rules regarding matters such as this, you know neither I nor those in my employ can cross that threshold."

"So why are you here? You don't care about the danger."

"I do. You see, not only do I want the artifact back where it belongs, I want you back where you belong, conducting monster hunts until I need you for something big. I also need your friends. You would be useless to me pining for your wife in prison because you murdered the priest."

"You think the priest would hurt my wife. It's pretty ridiculous. Don't you need seven to kill the eighth? Critical mass, wouldn't you call it?"

Endo clicked off the desk lamp. "Even that incandescent unit makes a slight noise. Now it's very quiet, isn't it? You can hear a little traffic from the highway, even a little bustling commerce from the market across the main street. Do you hear the voices?" He cupped a hand to his ear. "I believe I hear a greengrocer calling out the prices of his eggplant. And something else, very high-pitched . . . do you hear it? A sort of wailing?"

Takuda strained his senses despite himself. He did hear the highway, closer traffic on the main street, voices filtering in from the market, and high above it all, sirens. Lots of sirens, far off.

"Sounds like they're up in the city," Endo said. "Maybe right in your neighborhood."

Takuda cursed. "You didn't come to warn me." He vaulted toward the door. "You came to distract me and slow me down."

As fast as he was, Endo was faster. Endo stood with his hand on the knob. "Remember," he said to Takuda.

"It isn't dead, not dead at all." He opened the door for Takuda. "There's a taxi at the corner, waiting to take you to your house. Don't worry. I've already paid for it. Take care, and I hope you find everyone well at your apartment. I hate to be the one to tell you this, but breaking it probably just made it angry. It will be wanting revenge."

CHAPTER 29

Tuesday Morning

Takuda took the stairs at Sunshine Heights three at a time. He had burst through a gantlet of officers in the parking lot, and now two uniformed officers barred his way at the door. They flew before him like leaves in a gust.

The apartment was a shambles. Every drawer had been opened, every cabinet ransacked. Dusty white footprints trailed across the straw mats in every room.

He shouted for Yumi. In the second bedroom, Suzuki and Mori's room, the wall had seemingly exploded inward. Shards of cheap, cardboard-backed sheetrock littered the floor. *Maybe she escaped.* Takuda dropped to his hands and knees to peer through the hole between two vertical beams.

The apartment next door was an abattoir. Blood had spattered every surface he could see. The feet of the emergency workers were covered with white, pull-on booties, but these were already smeared crimson and brown.

"Yumi!"

A face appeared in the hole—Kimura.

"Hey, look here. Special consultant or not, you can't just wander around in there. This is police business!"

"This is my apartment. I live here. I'm looking for a woman."

Kimura's face fell. "You live here? I mean, there? That apartment, 201? And you're looking for a woman. Ah. Wait right there," he said, fumbling for his telephone.

Takuda stood. The trip to the apartment next door was dreamlike, slow motion, like running underwater. His mind was racing even as he stood up. *She got away from Suzuki into the gambler's apartment—could Suzuki have squeezed in after her?* The two officers he had brushed off were on him again by the time he got to the doorway of the bedroom; he brushed them off again, destroying more wall and one of the sliding doors in the process. *She can't be dead. She's smarter and quicker than Suzuki.* Takuda ran to the door, but his body didn't seem to respond quickly enough. He could even feel the pulling of his wounded hamstring and the multiple new cuts from the girls in the cafeteria, all the cuts seeming to pull him backward as if scar tissue were somehow heavier than unmarked flesh.

More officers crowded the entrance pit. They had come up the stairs from the parking lot, and they all wanted to talk sense to him. He simply vaulted over them this time. Their hands followed him as if supporting him, and he shook off their grasping fingers as he lit on the concrete landing. He ran into the open door of apartment 203, and the stench of blood and emptied bowels hit him in the face. *So much blood. This thing is so hungry. It's even hungrier than Suzuki.*

He strode through a crowd of protesting officers toward the back bedroom, where Kimura stood with his back to the door. Next to Kimura lay a pile of butchered meat. It had been a woman.

Yumi.

Cut edges of flesh had begun to darken. It was an incomplete job; the corpse was flayed, but the exposed bones were not removed, not set up in a shrine to cradle the Kurodama. *He must have been interrupted*, Takuda thought. *It must take longer doing it on your own, passing it back and forth to yourself to make up for the other six...*

His knees touched the straw matting. Then his hands. He had floated down like a feather. There was no place to fall that was not covered in clots and shreds of Yumi, so he closed his eyes and stayed on his hands and knees, breathing slowly and evenly so he didn't pass out in the spattered remains.

The large, still voice said, *Take your time. It will all still be here when you compose yourself.*

"He says he lives here, right next door," Kimura

hissed into his phone. "I need you to call your friend Ota. Get him down here so we can keep this contained . . ."

Takuda raised his eyes. In the corner was a blue plastic sheet covering a body. *They cover Suzuki, but they don't bother to cover Yumi. I'll kill them all for that.* He thought to rise and whip the plastic off Suzuki to cover Yumi, but he saw small, almost dainty feet in men's black socks sticking out from under the sheet.

Suzuki has feet like paddleboats.

"That's not the priest," he said. "The priest is still loose. You have to catch him. You have to stop him."

Kimura jumped. He turned just as a rough dozen strong hands grabbed Takuda by his arms, his legs, his collar, and his midriff. They were going to carry him out.

"Wait, wait," Kimura said. "You thought this was your priest?"

"I thought the priest . . . yes, I thought it was him. Tell them to release me. I can identify these people."

The officers argued with Kimura, telling him what Takuda had done to them, until Kimura finally waved them off in an imperious and very insulting manner. They bowed stiffly and correctly as Takuda rose from the soiled matting, wiping blood from his palms with a discarded booty.

Kimura pulled the plastic aside. The gambler stared at the ceiling. Blood leaked from the corner of his mouth.

"That's the resident of this apartment," Takuda said. "I don't know his name, but I know he's been here several years."

Kimura grimaced. "You don't know your next-door neighbor's name?"

"My wife and the priest talked to him. The priest gave him money. I had to work. I didn't have the time to socialize."

"You missed your chance." Kimura let the sheet fall. "His name was Inaba. He killed himself as the first officers crashed the door. And this one . . . are you ready? There's no face. You'll have to find some identifying mark. If we have to roll her over, you'll have to wait, or we can do it from dental records."

Through the horror, over his heart hammering in his chest, Takuda had one clear, precise thought: *If that's not Suzuki, this might not be Yumi.*

He walked cautiously toward the head of the flayed corpse. All but concealed in half-gelled gore and chips of bloodied bone, the matted hair was gray, much grayer than Yumi's. The mottled flesh was not her flesh; the hands were not her hands.

"It's not her," Takuda said. "It's not my wife."

Kimura said, "Well, that's a relief. That would have made things much more complicated. We assumed it was Inaba's wife, although it will take some forensics work to determine without doubt. I'm sure that was a horrible shock for you—won't you take a seat for a second?"

Takuda sat on the only blood-free spot he could see, a squarish area that must have been shielded from blood by a low table or part of a sleeping mat.

"It's really a ridiculous coincidence, isn't it? Are you serious? You live in a place like this?"

"I'm a security guard."

Kimura frowned deeply. "We were told you were some sort of consultant. You didn't even suspect that you lived next door to the starfish killer?"

"You think he was a serial killer?"

"The victim is female. There's a lot of exposed bone. It fits the profile. Are you really just a security guard?"

Takuda sighed. "I never said I was anything else. What about the knife?"

"We think that's why he broke into 201 . . . your apartment. There's no knife in your kitchen."

"We only had one."

"I think it's in an evidence bag now, even if you ever wanted to use it again. I certainly wouldn't." He motioned for Takuda to stand. "Come on. Let's get you some fresh air. You've had a shock. This is quite gruesome even for me, and I'm a detective!"

Once Takuda was on his feet, Kimura hustled him out of the apartment. "Forensics, you know. Everyone has a job to do. We'll see if the landlord will handle the repairs to your apartment and the replacement of the flooring. Once that plaster dust gets into the straw mats, it never comes out."

Takuda stepped past the disapproving patrolmen

out onto the landing, and a wave of nausea overtook him. As he leaned over the railing, trying to keep from vomiting, the huge, still presence in his head gently mocked him: *Relief is too much for you. You know how to be alone and afraid, but simple happiness is beyond you. Actual joy would probably kill you.* And it boomed silent laughter that echoed back through his life to a time before his birth.

Takuda spoke back to it with his eyes squeezed tightly shut and his jaw clamped to keep his breakfast down: *How would you know anything of joy?*

It retreated with a rushing like water, but there was mirth in its passage.

When he opened his eyes, Mori was at the bottom of the stairs.

"Come on," Takuda said, holding the railing as he descended toward the parking lot. "They aren't in the apartment. They got away somehow."

"Who?" Mori stood back to make way for him. "Yumi and the priest?"

"Maybe they weren't even there when the attack came."

"Attack?"

Takuda pulled Mori into the parking lot, away from the steady stream of uniformed officers going in and out of the apartment. He hissed to Mori, "Endo delayed me at the satellite office. Someone went right through the wall from the gambler's apartment, into the priest's bedroom. Next door, the gambler's wife is hacked up to look like the jellyfish killings. As if the gambler did it with our kitchen knife and then he killed himself when they entered his apartment."

"Why did they enter his apartment?"

"I didn't ask why they broke in. It doesn't matter why. Endo knew it was coming. He stalled me at Yoshida's office, but he was listening for the sirens. That's what brought me back."

"The police radio brought me. They were so hot to get here that they even broadcast the address. Half the prefectural police is here, and all the city police. Chief of Detectives Ishikawa is down at the corner trying to bring some order to it, but it's chaos. I just walked right through." Mori shook his head as if he had bees. "Where are Yumi and the priest?"

"I don't know where they are. Maybe Endo's people needed them to leave with the Kurodama because they can't touch it themselves. The rules."

Mori threw his hands above his head in frustration.

"I need your brain now, Mori. I need you to think. Where would they take it? If Endo needed Yumi and the priest to carry it somewhere, where would that be?"

Mori sank to his haunches with his head in his hands. "Aaahhh, let me think, let me think." He ran his hands through his hair. "First, I don't even know what's happened. Is it still active? The Kurodama?"

"Endo says it is. He says it's a mind, and that it's exacting revenge."

"I told you so. I told you it was a bad idea to leave the priest alone with it. He's so weak-minded that it probably possessed him. Or maybe it lured the gambler through the wall."

Takuda grabbed him by the collar. "Think! Where would they take it?"

"I don't know how to figure out where they're taking it." Mori shook himself free, still squatting. "Endo dropped hints about where it was, but not where it was supposed to be . . ." He looked up suddenly. "He dropped hints about the cafeteria, but also . . ." He stood so quickly his knees popped. "We need the priest's papers. That map. The old map and the tourist map. It's . . . Endo gave us everything we need. He gave us too much probably. I know he did. We just need to sort it out to figure out where they took it . . ."

A familiar voice came from behind them: "Where who took what?"

CHAPTER 30

Tuesday Morning

Takuda spun. Yumi and Suzuki stood two meters away with their arms full of shopping bags.

Takuda held Yumi tightly as uniformed officers swarmed around them. The groceries lay scattered at their feet.

She struggled in his arms. "What has happened? What's going on here?"

Mori was badgering Suzuki. "Where is the Kurodama? Did you take it with you? Speak up, Priest!"

"It's on the table in the apartment," Suzuki said. "Release me now. Control yourself, please!"

Yumi pushed Takuda away. "Tell me what's happened! There are police everywhere. They wouldn't let us in the parking lot until one of them recognized the priest."

"The gambler in 203 was taken by the Kurodama. That's going to be the official story anyway," Takuda said.

Yumi pulled free of him but still held his hand tightly. "He . . . what? Old Inaba? He was taken? Possessed?"

Takuda told her everything he knew.

Her eyes set hard when she heard about the hole in the wall. "And the Kurodama is gone."

Mori had released Suzuki. "So I assume the two of you left the apartment to get the priest some food."

"It was a great deal," Suzuki said, "too good to pass up. The assistant manager of the Marukyo by the station came by to tell us we had won the grocery lottery. Everything we could gather and carry out ourselves for one thousand yen, but we had to be at the store in ten minutes."

Takuda and Mori exchanged a glance. "You decided to leave the shards behind," Takuda said.

"I was starving," Suzuki said. "I couldn't stand it. But we didn't want to take that thing out in public, whether it was dead or not. And you said the counselor couldn't do anything about it, not directly. So we thought it would be safe in the apartment by itself until we decided what to do with it."

"I just wanted to get out," Yumi said. "Between that thing on the table and the priest complaining of his hunger pangs, I just couldn't take any more."

Takuda turned to Mori. He was gone, nowhere to be seen.

"Yumi, Priest, where did Mori go? He was here just a second ago."

They looked in all directions, but all they saw was Chief of Detectives Ishikawa striding toward them, his face set as grim as a kabuki mask. "Did you call this in? Did you? We got an anonymous tip that your neighbor was killing his wife, but no one else is home. Every other apartment in the building is empty."

"Maybe they won the grocery lottery, too," Suzuki said helpfully.

Ishikawa ignored him. "You've engineered this whole thing, haven't you?"

Takuda squared his shoulders. "Baseless accusations aren't your style. Someone told you all about us, just this morning, right?"

Ishikawa sneered. "You deduce all this based on your distinguished career as a detective. A detective who quit in disgrace. All you do is go around making messes for others to clean up."

Takuda smiled. "You received a dossier of some sort."

"I did," Ishikawa said. "You need to stay as far away from police business as possible from now on. Unfortunately, this morning, you're in the middle of it." He held up an evidence bag. It contained a bamboo-handled kitchen knife.

Bright red blood had pooled in the bottom of the bag. Endo's thugs had actually used his kitchen knife to butcher his neighbor.

"Do you recognize this knife?" Ishikawa was waving the bag. His face was an angry purple, making Takuda think of venous blood once again . . .

"It looks like our kitchen knife," Yumi said. "It's a very common kind of knife, though, the kind you buy at Daiei or Topos."

"We're not responsible for this," Takuda said.

"You show up everywhere, even on the security tapes of the mental hospital where Thomas Fletcher died, but I can't prove it because the tapes were mysteriously wiped clean right in our evidence room." He drew a breath. "So now your near-indigent neighbor proves he was the jellyfish killer or the starfish killer or what-the-hell-ever. Meanwhile, his neighbors, who were there every step of the way, had nothing to do with it." He brandished the evidence bag. "Except you had everything to do with it, didn't you?"

Takuda tried to show no expression at all. Suzuki rattled plastic behind him.

Ishikawa looked them over. "Stay close. Tell your Mori I said so. Don't skip out, or I'll hunt you down like rats."

"We won't," Suzuki said. His mouth was full. "We love Fukuoka."

Ishikawa stared at Suzuki for a second over Takuda's shoulder, and then he spun on his heel and strode back to the apartment.

They stood in the parking lot as the forensics team finished in their apartment and the coroner's team carried the body bags out of apartment 203. Uniformed officers continued to keep the reporters out of the parking lot. Takuda ignored their shouted questions.

Suzuki continued to devour the groceries.

Finally, a small knot of uniformed patrolmen wearing white surgical masks descended the stairs. They surrounded Kimura, who turned from one to the other of them, confused. He asked them where they were taking him, and they refused to respond.

"There it is," Takuda said. "They've got it, and they've got Kimura."

The patrolmen hustled Kimura into the back of a van. As he clung to the doorframe before they pushed him in, Takuda saw a bright blue sparking. Kimura's hand clenched on empty air, and the patrolmen bundled him in.

Two patrolmen carried cloth bags tied to the ends of sticks.

"The Kurodama," he hissed. "They've got it, and they're taking Kimura as well."

Takuda sprinted toward the van. The last man at the door of the van spotted him: the head of the Zenkoku Security force, now dressed as a city policeman. He slammed the van door and drew the old Russian pistol. Takuda set his heels to dodge right, but pain shot down his leg. He dropped to one knee in the parking lot, meters from the goal.

Ogawa grinned down at him as the van pulled away. He held a long, forked device, an enhanced cattle prod. He leaped into the driver's seat of a black sedan. As Takuda struggled to his feet, the sedan sped through the cordon after the van, scattering reporters and patrolmen in its wake.

They sat in the Lotus Café waiting for Mori to show up. "It's getting worse," Suzuki said. "I'm hungry all the time now. There's obviously something wrong with me."

Takuda was relieved that Mori wasn't there to agree. "You both did the right thing, leaving the Kurodama in the apartment. It might have gone badly if you had been carrying it."

Yumi looked at him severely. "You don't call that going badly? We've been doing this too long, then. You've forgotten what it looks like when things go well."

He flushed. "Well, at least the priest didn't leave you alone there. No telling what would have happened then. And he hid his sword. That's a good thing. You wouldn't want to get caught with it."

"It's up in the rafters in the second bedroom," Suzuki said. "There's a loose panel in the top of the bedding closet, and my arms are long enough that I can get the sword up over the second ceiling rafter, where no one could see it even if they were looking for it." He sighed heavily. "Mice are chewing off the sharkskin wrapping."

Mori slid silently into the seat beside Suzuki.

"Thank you for helping us with the detective," Yumi said acidly.

"None of you seemed to see him coming," Mori said. "I hoped we could keep at least one of us out of custody to help the others."

"Or you were just tired of us," Takuda said.

Mori frowned. "It was time to leave. I couldn't believe you were all still standing there."

"It wouldn't have mattered," Takuda said. "The Kurodama was on the property the whole time." Takuda told Mori of Kimura's disappearance in the van.

"So Endo got his artifact back," Suzuki said.

"And we have nothing. Nothing," Mori said. "After three years on the road, fighting the forces of darkness, we'll have no work, no prospects, moving along at the whim of Counselor Endo. If he wants us out of Fukuoka today, we'll have to leave. We'll wander the islands, following the little jobs we're allowed like sparrows after fallen grains of rice. We'll be only as prosperous and happy as he allows us to be, until he needs us to clean up another mess, and then we'll move there to do his bidding."

Suzuki looked up, his eyes blazing. "We must capture him."

Takuda glanced over at Yumi, who stared at Suzuki. "You mean," she said, "we must capture Counselor Endo?"

Suzuki nodded eagerly. He bared his teeth in an unpleasant grimace. "We should bind him with sutras and throw him in a well. Or a pit. Something to separate him from his base of power. That's the way to start."

"That won't stop him," Takuda said.

"No," said Suzuki. "No, it won't. If we want to stop him, we have to kill him. We have to eat him."

Takuda and Yumi sat back. Suzuki had crossed an invisible line. As narcoleptics slept and kleptomaniacs stole, so Suzuki ate, and his hunger devoured his rational thought. He believed that he could eat his problems. Suzuki had finally gone mad.

"It's not such a bad idea," Mori said. "That would take care of the evidence right away." He took the lid off a jar of seaweed flakes and peered inside. "We'd still have the bones to contend with, if there were bones." He frowned at Takuda. "You seem to think he isn't human. Do you think he has bones? Would we make soup?"

Takuda heard his own knuckles popping under the table. Yumi laid a cool hand on his forearm.

"I'm committed to not finding out about anyone's bones today," Takuda said quietly.

Mori feigned disappointment.

"You're mocking me," Suzuki said, "but it's the only way to stop him. I'm serious."

Mori leaned halfway out of the booth, away from Suzuki. "You're not going to eat me for disagreeing, are you?"

Suzuki grinned at him, a strange rictus of the mouth that Takuda had seen before. *Maybe it's more than madness,* Takuda thought. *Maybe the Kurodama set him off.*

"Well," Takuda said. "At least there are groceries to

hold us through tomorrow, and tomorrow's going to be a busy day. I have to attend the cremation . . ."

"Whose cremation? Inaba the gambler's?"

Takuda bowed. "They have no friends or family. It's going to be rushed, of course, to beat the press, and I feel obligated to serve."

"I could go," Suzuki said.

Takuda hesitated. "You're not invited," he said finally, "and you need to look for work. After the ceremony, I'm going to talk to Ota again." He pretended interest in the tabletop. "Maybe he can find us something." *Even if I have to beg,* he thought. *I can't ask Yumi to keep living like this.*

"And I have work tomorrow," Yumi said, "until the phone call comes that I don't. That will be any day now."

"Well," said Mori, "I can pay for one more dinner here, if your Koji ever comes to serve us."

Suzuki flushed. "He's not *my* Koji."

Takuda was satisfied. If the worst Mori did was tease Suzuki about his crush on the waiter, that was more than acceptable. But as Mori and Suzuki bickered, he leaned over and whispered to Yumi, "Make sure the priest has enough groceries tonight. Let's not let him get *hungry.*"

CHAPTER 31

Wednesday Morning

"It's really a nuisance," said the apartment manager. "Their social services caseworker should be here, but he said he had to make the rounds, roust the unemployed, and get them out looking for work. I don't envy him that job. A never-ending struggle."

The crematorium waiting room was silent except for the apartment manager, and Takuda ate his boxed lunch while the man talked. The lunch was a stale, soggy mass of rice and fried vegetables that was supposed to be tempura but tasted of curry. He thought several times just to set it aside, but as he was unsure where his next meal was coming from, he kept eating.

"This is a depressing place, isn't it? Cardboard coffins, old ambulance gurneys to transport bodies, stale box lunches." The apartment manager tossed his aside. "This is the only kind of place that accepts the charity cases the city sends them, I suppose. What a sad place to be disposed of."

Takuda didn't look around. He had seen it all, from the dusty, ailing plants to the discolored imitation granite flooring. Takuda himself had never even been to a crematorium with a waiting area, but he was a country boy, and from a backward area, at that. Even when he had been a detective in the capital of his home prefecture, the mourners had dispersed when the body was removed for cremation, returning after the bones had cooled enough to be placed in the funerary urns.

This crematorium was so cheap there was no attendant to stay with the bodies. Takuda had waited alone, with the bodies in cardboard coffins perched on their battered gurneys. Of course he had peeked.

Inaba the gambler's wife was in a black plastic body bag, for which Takuda was immensely grateful. Inaba himself was under a white sheet. He had a cheap nylon shirtfront and suit, a one-piece thing that opened at the back. It was tucked in underneath him very poorly, but it was all going to burn in a few moments anyway. Fake plastic shoes had been jammed on his feet. His face was puffy and greenish, as if he had died of liver disease rather than blood loss. His nostrils were stuffed with cotton to prevent leakage, and his jaw had been fixed shut. Maybe his teeth had been glued together. Takuda didn't want to know badly enough to touch the corpse. Inaba's slashed throat was covered with a beige bandage through which the rough, black sutures bulged visibly.

Like my new scars coming up, Takuda thought.

Takuda had let the sheet drop and closed the cardboard coffin again just as the apartment manager had arrived. The attendants had wheeled the bodies off to the cremation chamber on his signal.

"The whole thing is inconvenient, that's all," the apartment manager said as Takuda finished the dismal boxed lunch. "They had no family, no friends, no one but a neighbor and a landlord's proxy to mourn them." He looked at Takuda, sizing him up. "They were always late with the rent, even though I knew exactly when they got it. These subsidized cases are a real handful sometimes, especially when they get in on a regular lease and then things go sour. You can never get them out. Never." He sighed. "They said your brother-in-law helped them out sometimes. The tall one." He sipped coffee. "He stays over a lot, doesn't he?"

"He's a priest in a small sect. He's got calls all over the northern part of the island, sometimes farther south," Takuda said. "He sometimes sleeps over for convenience and safety. It's always nice to have a priest on the premises, isn't it?"

"Didn't help much this time, did it? Where did you say his temple is, or did you say?"

A sleepy-eyed youth in a tight, shiny suit cut for nightclubbing stepped in to tell them that the cremation was completed.

They followed him out across the grimy lobby.

Ahead were brass-bound double doors. The attendant in the nightclub suit opened the doors with a smooth, practiced air. He escorted them into a spare, dim room. A young monk with mild acne stood at the foot of the gurneys, which now held stainless steel trays covered with bones.

Takuda drew closer. The bones were laid out more or less in the shape of human bodies, with the tumbled toe bones facing the young monk, the ribs and vertebrae laid out neatly in the middle, and the skulls sitting at the heads of the trays. Each gurney was overarched by a rolling tray, a repurposed over-the-bed hospital tray table. On each of these tray tables was a plain ceramic urn that Takuda and the apartment manager would fill with the bones of the dead. Takuda assumed they would push the tray tables along as they went.

"Are you family of the deceased?" the monk asked.

"No, we're not," the apartment manager said. "I really have to go soon. Would you please start chanting?"

The monk blinked, then reached into his robe for his beads. He started to chant the "Expedient Means" chapter of the *Lotus Sutra*. Takuda realized he was a monk of the Tendai sect, the sect Suzuki referred to as "the heretics of Mt. Hie."

Another reason it's good I didn't bring the priest. It would have turned into a brawl.

"Look," the apartment manager whispered, "I know this is unusual, but why don't you take one, and I'll take the other? I have to dash, so I'll leave you the hyoid bones and the skulls, okay?"

Takuda bowed in assent. *The less this man touches the bones, the better.*

Using oversized chopsticks designed for the purpose, they put bones in the urns, starting with the toe bones. The apartment manager all but pitched them in, moving quickly from phalanges to metatarsals to shattered long bones. The bones the apartment manager worked on were grayish, shadowed almost blue, but the bones on Takuda's table were pearly white, almost as white as the urns themselves. The long bones had been broken up for ease of loading into the urns, but as Takuda picked up one length of femur, he noticed an indentation along the length of the bone. He held it up to the light; it was an incision. It was the woman's femur, and the knife had cut into the bone.

My kitchen knife, or the black stone knife? He stood holding the bone in the oversized chopsticks for a long moment while the apartment manager tossed bones into his urn.

. . . *clunk* . . . *clunk* . . . *clunk* . . .

How many died because of that stone knife?

. . . *clunk* . . .

The boy Haruma, almost surely.

. . . *clunk* . . .

Thomas Fletcher.

. . . *clunk* . . .

The girl at Able English Institute.

. . . *clunk* . . .

How many at the cafeteria? I never even counted.

. . . *clunk* . . .

The gambler and his wife.

. . . clunk. . .

Kimura. Poor, conceited Kimura.

. . . clunk. . .

He dropped the fragment into the urn and worked his way up to the shattered hip bones.

The apartment manager sidled over to him. "Okay," he whispered, "you have the hyoid and skull over here . . . still on the ribs? I must have gone too fast, but I do have to be elsewhere. I'm honored that I could take part at all." He bowed to the monk, bowed to Takuda, and then bowed toward the gurneys while holding his palms together and muttering prayers from a different sect altogether.

After he left, Takuda transferred bones. They echoed over the droning of the young monk.

Finally, Takuda reached the hyoid bone, the delicate arch of bone from the throat that allows speaking, swallowing, and breathing. He placed it gently on top of the other bones.

It was time to break up the skull. He looked around for the attendant. There was no one to help. The young monk droned on, pretending not to notice Takuda's dilemma.

Makes sense, Takuda thought. *Just a drunken reprobate and his wife. No one cares about a hanger-on at the boat races.*

There was no one else to do it. He plunged the oversized chopsticks into the brittle skull of the gambler's wife. It split with a muffled crack.

Just another drunken gambler. He stabbed again.

. . . crack. . .

Just another silly schoolgirl.

. . . crack. . .

Just another mad foreigner.

. . . crack. . .

Just another gay boy.

. . . crack. . .

The skull lay in plates, ready to line the top of the urn. He placed them carefully.

He moved to Inaba's tray. The hyoid bone was often placed by two mourners using two pairs of funerary chopsticks. Takuda did it by himself, just as he had for the wife. As he prepared to break up Inaba's skull, he noticed a tiny bit of bone at the base of the urn. The apartment manager had been in such a hurry that one of the smaller bones had missed the urn altogether.

Takuda picked it up. A toe bone, it seemed, too small for a finger, one bone from Inaba's tiny, delicate little feet. Takuda sighed as he placed the bone in the urn. It was all backward, a toe bone going in the top of the urn instead of the bottom, where it should have gone in.

Something about the toe bone nagged at him as he began to break up the skull.

. . . crack. . .

Something about those little feet sticking out from under the blue plastic sheet.

. . . crack. . .

Black socks. Tiny feet in black socks. Takuda paused

with the chopsticks hovering above Inaba's skull like the bill of some hideous, bone-puncturing bird. Inaba had been wearing black socks when he died in his apartment, Sunshine Heights 203. The Kurodama had been in Takuda's apartment, Sunshine Heights 201. Whoever had burst through that apartment wall had spread plaster dust all over Takuda's apartment. The apartment manager had personally vacuumed up as much as he could, with a promise to have the mats professionally cleaned or replaced. The footprints Takuda had seen were prints of stockinged feet, but much too big to be Inaba's feet.

Inaba's socks hadn't shown a trace of plaster dust. Inaba had been framed in his death.

Proof positive that someone had gone through Inaba's apartment to get to the Kurodama. Someone had butchered Inaba's wife and then stabbed him in the throat to frame him for the jellyfish killings.

Pointless.

. . . *crack*. . .

It would have been easier to just steal the Kurodama.

. . . *crack*. . .

Perhaps it wasn't so simple. Perhaps there was some truth to Endo's claims that he couldn't affect these things directly. There was a blood debt to pay. Endo had been willing to pay the price with other people's blood.

Takuda was angry, but his hands were steady as he placed Inaba's skull in the urn. When he was finished, he put down the funerary chopsticks, recited a verse of the *Lotus Sutra*, and walked out. The stylish attendant rushed after to hand him a certificate of cremation, which he refused.

He had made a decision. He had more pressing responsibilities to the dead.

CHAPTER 32

Wednesday Afternoon

The old castle grounds were deserted. Takuda, Mori,
and Suzuki walked in silence, first up the hill past the
old moat and then into the winding gardens planted
among the remaining fortifications.

"So it's all pretty clear from the newspapers," Mori
said. "They pinned the jellyfish killings on Inaba the
gambler. It all wraps up pretty neatly."

"Not neatly enough," Takuda said. "There was
really no need for anyone to die. Thomas Fletcher
wasn't going to talk to Japanese officials about the Kurodama, and if he did, who would believe him? The
gambler and his wife were just a ruse."

Suzuki said, "Maybe it was a cover so that Endo's

masters couldn't see that he was bending the rules he always talks about."

Takuda looked around as they climbed winding roadways to the highest point of the castle ruins. The massive granite blocks were a perfect backdrop for summer foliage. With the droning of early cicadas a reminder of the hotter summer to come, the shaded walk up to the top of the stonework was a pleasant break from the sweltering concrete downtown.

They wound upward through the fortifications, now a garden of azaleas, camellias, and begonias in the shade of plum, cherry, and dogwood trees. The walkway narrowed to a gravel path. The stone ramp of the castle's upper keep rose to the north. The ramp doubled back on itself and led them to a narrow stairway of dressed stone. At the top of that stairway lay a cramped courtyard and the stairs of a steel superstructure rooted into the highest level of the castle ruins. At the top of those stairs, a ten-meter square of boilerplate steel let them look out on the city from the castle summit.

Low, rounded mountains rose green in the south. Takuda looked north for a glimpse of the bay, but the buildings were just too dense. He breathed it in, enjoying the break from the city, surprised that a little oasis like this wasn't crowded, even on a weekday.

"What are we looking for?" Takuda asked Mori.

Mori stood still in the center of the boilerplate, his feet spread wide and his fists deep in his pockets. "First, we have to talk about history and geography."

Suzuki struck an attentive pose.

Mori pretended to ignore him. "Right over there, where the old baseball stadium is, stood the Korokan, a seventh-century waystation for travelers going to and from China. Much of our culture came through this gateway from Japan to the rest of the world. Our written language, our drama, our weaponry, our basic social structure, all flowed through the Korokan. The light of Buddhism entered here. The light, and also darkness."

Takuda looked at the needlelike tower at the beach, kilometers to the northwest. Suzuki gazed at the billowing summer clouds.

"When the Korokan was built, it was at the beach. You see? The beach was here. Now the water is a twenty-minute drive away. It's landfill. Reclaimed land."

Suzuki nodded. "All that beach to the northeast, Momochi, where that needle-sharp tower stands next to the shiny new baseball stadium? That was all ocean a few years ago. We fill in the bays to make more land."

"And what happens when we hit an island?" Mori asked.

Takuda decided to play, partly because he thought he knew where Mori was going. "We usually end up with a hill." Takuda searched through the trees. "See there? See that hill way over there? It's a shrine way up at the top of a long set of concrete steps just north of Nishijin. That shrine used to be on an island, I'll bet."

"It's not exactly at Nishijin, but that's the idea," Mori said. "Sometimes we end up with hills, but sometimes the islands aren't that high." He sank to his knees on the boilerplate. He drew a sheaf of papers from his hip sack. "Here's a copy of a map of the bay from the twelfth century, the one Yumi found in her bicycle basket. Come look."

Takuda stood so that his shadow cut the glare on the paper. It was strangely thin copy paper, so dark that the black boilerplate beneath made it harder to read, glare or no. Suzuki stood off to the side, looking at the mountains to the south.

Mori concentrated on Takuda. "Here's where we are now," he said, pointing at the map. "The old Korokan was right here, where the old baseball stadium is now, and this little inlet of water became the castle moat a few hundred years later." He pointed out in the bay to the west. "Here's that shrine you're talking about, the one on the hill that isn't in Nishijin. That hill used to be an island."

Takuda grunted. On the map, the island was rendered rising conically from the bay with a tiny shrine and two windswept pines perched atop.

Mori's finger drifted back east. "This is the island of the Devouring God."

It was an irregular patch on the map, an errant blotch outlined in red ink. The only marking was a clearly modern notation in English: *twelfth-century location, conjectural.*

"Priest, is this your father's writing? Would you recognize his writing in English?"

Suzuki said, "I'm not sure it's his." He hadn't even

glanced at the map. *Perhaps he's pored over all this in private*, Takuda thought.

Mori continued: "Here's a prewar map. The street names are different, but it's recognizable. It's not one-to-one, of course, but the scale is close enough to do an overlay. Notice how much farther the land extends out into the bay."

This was a map from the days when the castle had come and gone. The land was a puzzle of trapezoidal properties cut with major roads. The conical shrine-island had been absorbed, with neatly plotted land extending outward to meet it, but the smaller island was still a blotch in the bay, much smaller in proportion to the rest of the map than in the twelfth-century version. The map itself carried no notation for this island. The modern, handwritten notation, in English, said: *Site of Baron Asano's 1925 footage, confirmed by M. and P.*

Mori laid it over the twelfth-century map, centered on the red-circled island. The beach was much closer to the island in comparison.

"You see what's happened here," Mori said. "We've been doing it for centuries. That's how Japan gets new coastline. That's how we get new airports and bridge footings."

"Eventually, Japan will be one big island," Suzuki said.

Mori snorted.

"Let's forgive the exaggeration," Takuda said. "What does this mean to us, Mori? Where's this Devouring God island now? How close is it to shore today?"

Suzuki unfolded a cheap tourist map. "The proportions aren't perfect, but the scale is close enough, and it has the landmarks we need. Castle ruins here, your shrine up on the hill here . . ." He slipped the tourist map beneath the tracing paper and lined up his landmarks. Then he sat back so Takuda and Mori could examine his work.

They saw the progression: the beach continued to move northward from the twelfth century to the early twentieth century to the present, and the red-inked island, the Island of the Devouring God, was now landlocked.

"Okay," Takuda said. "That's where we are right now, that's where the island used to be, so it should be right over . . ." He raised his eyes to the northern horizon. "Let's see . . . wait a minute . . . no! No, no, no!"

He turned away and walked to the southern end of the platform, staring out at the purple mountains.

Suzuki looked down at Mori. "What? What's happening?" He scanned the northern horizon. "What did he see?"

Mori pointed north. "Look straight north. See, right past the little junior college?"

"I don't see a junior college."

"Right in front there, there on Meiji Avenue. Peaked green roof, broken clock."

"Oh! Able English Institute. Yes, I see it."

"Look behind it, a little to the east."

"There are just a lot of . . . oh. Oh, no."

A few blocks behind the college with the broken clock stood a squat, gray building. Just barely visible at this distance was a red Z in a red circle, the corporate symbol of Zenkoku General.

"That's right next to the cafeteria where you retrieved the Kurodama from the girls," Mori said.

Takuda turned. "What do you mean, right next to it?"

"I mean, right next to it. If you look on the map, they seem to be adjoining. They might have adjoining walls."

Takuda sat on the rubberized surface. "So that's where it came from originally. It's been trying to go home."

Mori said, "Counselor Endo had us right in the building. Foundation of everything we do indeed!"

"Cornerstone of the organization." Takuda could have spit. "If I had even looked up when I was coming or going from that cafeteria, I probably would have seen the Zenkoku logo."

"No, not from the street. It's too tight. You have to be up high, like this. But it wouldn't have mattered. There was no way to know where that island was, or how it had been absorbed, until we put all this together."

"I was right," Suzuki said. "Right around the corner from the Officers' Hospital, where they ate the American airman's liver with soy sauce."

Mori sighed.

"Allegedly," Suzuki said. "Maybe this isn't the first time it escaped the basement. Maybe it wasn't involved at all."

Takuda turned to Suzuki. "The basement, you say. Why the basement?"

Suzuki frowned. "Well, it's obvious, isn't it? The cafeteria where the foreigner taught the girls is in the basement. The Zenkoku classroom where he taught employees is in the basement. The foreigner is the link. I'll bet the cafeteria used to be a lunchroom for Zenkoku staff, and I'll bet it shares a wall with the basement of the Zenkoku building."

Takuda looked at Mori. "Does this make sense?"

Mori looked solemn as he folded maps. "I suppose it does." He handed the bundle to Suzuki. "From what we know, the Kurodama usually doesn't attract people who don't touch it, but Thomas was sensitive. Whether that's related to his mental illness is unknown. But at least one of his private students was sensitive as well. She stole it back from him and took it to the cafeteria."

Suzuki cocked his head at the high summer clouds. "You know what Counselor Endo was lying about?"

Takuda and Mori glanced at each other.

Suzuki shaded his eyes as he gazed toward the Zenkoku building. "He said he needed the Kurodama back to keep his sales team sharp, but he went on too long about how he hated the copy editors, a truth to cover the lie."

Mori opened his mouth to speak and then thought better of it. He stared at the Zenkoku building as well.

"He's experimenting with corporate assets again," Suzuki said. "Just as he was with the Kappa."

Mori shook his head. "What are we going to do about it?"

"We're going to do the same thing Counselor Endo did," Takuda said. "We're going through the wall."

CHAPTER 33

Thursday Morning

Takuda, Mori, and Suzuki drifted along the sidewalk, ghostly shapes in the predawn stillness across from the Able English Institute. Mori and Takuda wore their Ota Southern Protection Services coveralls, and Suzuki was in his robes. Mori and Suzuki carried their swords in fishing tackle tubes, and Takuda carried his staff slung over his shoulder.

"A cruiser already came around twice," Mori said. "It's two hours before the first bus. I think we should move along."

Takuda led them across the deserted avenue past the side entrance to Able English Institute and into the dense warren of side streets beyond.

"So we're just going to walk along, fishing tackle

slung over our shoulders like boys on holiday," Mori said.

"Exactly," Takuda said, swinging his staff over his shoulder and swaggering in the pale fluorescence of the streetlights. "Just a few guys out for a stroll. We could whistle to make the apartment dwellers think we're burglars passing signals."

Mori snorted.

Takuda led them past the Zenkoku building on its east side. "That's where we're going," he said. Then he led them around to the cafeteria. There was a narrow, trash-strewn alley between the buildings.

"They don't adjoin," Mori said. "We're back to square one. Are we going to dig underneath the alley as well?"

"They don't adjoin above ground," Takuda said. "We'll see in a moment what we'll need to do."

The front door was barred and padlocked, with a sign that told them the cafeteria was closed for renovation. The kitchen door was sealed as well. They walked around the building twice before Suzuki spotted an unbarred window on the second floor.

"Let's go," Takuda said, crouching down to boost Mori up to the windowsill.

Mori pried the ancient casement open with a dagger Takuda had never seen. *Still full of surprises, this Mori.*

Takuda pushed the gawky priest up the wall and waited. He only had time to glance at the alley around him before the female end of a stout electrical cord fell at his feet. He tested his weight against it. Mori had obviously anchored it well, so he began to scale.

He pulled himself through the window and brushed off his coveralls, as if he wouldn't get dirty retrieving the Kurodama.

I'll be lucky if it's just grime from a windowsill when we're done. . .

He had tidied and straightened and untied the electrical cord from his staff when he noticed the stillness of his companions.

They were staring into the shadows of this upstairs room. The skeletons shone in the darkness.

"What the hell has happened here?" Mori said.

Suzuki pointed at the door. The characters were visible in the light from the corridor, reversed on the frosted glass:

Southern Medical Supply
A Zenkoku Company

"They're plastic," Mori said, running a finger down a shining femur. Takuda's eyes were accustomed to the darkness now; he saw the racks and shelves of synthetic skeletons and anatomical models lining the walls. He had a fleeting memory of Thomas's inside-out sculpture of Kaori Nabeshima. He pushed the thought aside.

Mori slid to the glass door. Takuda saw the dagger flash, and the door swung open at his touch.

The stench of chlorine filled the stairwell. At the

bottom of the stairs, the cafeteria door was propped open with a *Wet Floor* sign.

"You should have seen the bodies down there," Takuda whispered as they crept down the stairs. "No amount of bleach could clear that up."

"Sounds like a sushi place I used to visit in the Naga Valley," Suzuki whispered back. Mori chuckled, to Takuda's surprise.

The lights stuttered on at Mori's touch. The concrete floor was completely bare. There was a strong smell of disinfectant, not chlorine. Something industrial and pleasant, perfumed cleaning solvents. Takuda let out his breath. He hadn't realized he'd been holding it against the stench of blood and entrails that had filled the air the last time he had been in the cafeteria.

Takuda pointed. "Kitchen to the south." He turned. "Front door to the north." He turned again. "We just came from the stairwell to the west, so . . ."

He turned again. In the east wall, a section of paneling was outlined in darkness, with a yawning gap at the bottom. The panel hung on hidden tracks, a "pocket door" of the type popular in the 1950s. Takuda slid it aside, and the darkness gaped before him.

It took longer to find the light switch in this room. No linoleum or carpet had ever covered the bare cement. A single rough-hewn table stretched the length of the room. Benches of time-darkened cedar hunched beneath it.

Suzuki wheezed a husky laugh. Takuda and Mori looked at him, then their gaze followed his: High on the wall before them, the fare was painted in broad strokes on cedar shingles. Most of the shingles were hung facing the wall because the dishes were sold out, but a few items remained.

Hocks.

Shoulder.

Tongue.

Liver.

"Not chicken liver," Takuda said.

"And not beef tongue," Mori answered.

"And that's just the leftovers from the last special dinner," Suzuki said. "I'm glad we don't know what's on the shingles they've turned to the wall." He turned to Takuda, smiling. "It will be a pleasure to end this dinner for good. We're like spiritual health inspectors, shutting down the worst restaurant in the world."

"You're like a child playing some damned game," Mori said. "Let's see if we can get through this wall."

Suzuki pointed toward the northeast corner. "There we go. Another door."

Takuda slid the door aside to reveal another yawning darkness. It took all three of them to find the light switch this time.

When the fluorescents stuttered into life this time, they found themselves standing in a long, narrow kitchen.

"Another kitchen," Mori said, "for those special dinners."

The twin sinks were ancient, chipped porcelain. The drain boards were tin. The oven, range, and rotisserie were massive affairs built from the same steel used to occupy Manchuria.

The south end of the room was the solid steel door of a massive walk-in freezer. Suzuki moved toward it, and Mori made to stop him, but Takuda put a hand on Mori's arm. "Let him look," Takuda said.

The freezer door swung open when Suzuki pulled, and the plastic scrub brush that propped it open fell onto the floor. The freezer was empty, with nothing on the shelves, nothing on the meat hooks. Clean and dry, not recently cleansed like the main dining room.

"This is the place . . . I just know it," Suzuki said. He ground his teeth; Takuda winced at the sound.

Mori tapped his foot on the drain in the floor. "Who the hell has a floor drain below sea level?"

"Someone who plans ahead . . . and pours a deep, deep foundation. Around two separate lots," Takuda said. He pointed to the east wall ahead of them. "That's plain brick right there." He moved his finger southward, where the bricks became rougher, less regular. "Back there, it's dressed stone."

"It's behind the stone," Suzuki said. "I can almost smell it."

Takuda said, "I think there's nothing but brick between us and the basement of the Zenkoku Sales building, and we're underneath the alley between the buildings."

Mori just shrugged and nodded at the bricks.

Takuda turned to the wall with the butt of his staff at the ready. At the first blow, a brick cracked, leaving a crater of shattered clay and chipped paint. Half of it came down into the sink. At the second blow, it broke free of its mortar and buckled inward. At the third blow, the brickbats shattered, leaving a dark rectangle. Takuda ran his staff into the hole until it hit the inner wall. "It's only about twenty-five centimeters inside here. Maybe they were going to fill it with concrete."

He ran the staff back in the rectangular hole and broke a brick out of the inner wall. After they killed the lights in the kitchen and dining room, Takuda peered in with his flashlight.

"I can't see anything," he said. "A little reflection a long way off, like a glint off a high window."

"That's it," Suzuki said. "Make a hole big enough, and we'll be in."

Takuda knocked out bricks one at a time, widening the hole downward, hoping that would keep the wall stable. "It's just occurring to me that this isn't a supporting wall for the building, but it might be holding up the alley."

Mori stood on the drain board and tapped the ceiling. "It's solid, very solid, like plaster on lathe." He took out his dagger, but Takuda told him to stow it.

"Let's just hope it's strong enough to hold up a few feet of earth."

When Takuda had made the hole large enough, he helped Mori through, then Suzuki. The lights went on in the basement of the Zenkoku Sales building.

It was a large, rectangular basement. Folding tables and chairs stood stacked against the far wall. The bare concrete floor sloped downward to a steel-grated drain running the length of room. A track in the ceiling ran parallel to the drain in the floor.

"Looks like they had some special dinners here as well," Mori said, gesturing toward the track. "A real assembly line."

"No, this was for kitchen prep," Suzuki said. "A long time ago, these basements connected." He pointed toward a section of brick just below the section Takuda had knocked out. Those bricks protruded slightly from the rest. "They filled it in from the cafeteria side."

They both turned toward something Takuda couldn't see: the older stonework section. "It's an old iron door," Mori said, "older than the kitchen stove even. This is Meiji-era shipyard work. You have to see this thing."

Takuda started knocking out bricks again. He was too big to get through the hole he had made for Mori and Suzuki.

They moved out of his line of sight while he worked on the bricks. He heard them arguing about whether to open it or not, whether to wait for him, Suzuki becoming insistent that he wanted the Kurodama, had to have it . . .

Takuda started kicking in the bricks. They shattered under his boots. He was almost ready to step in when he heard a low shifting, almost too low for his range of hearing, and Mori crying out in surprise.

Oh, you stupid priest, you're going in without thinking.

He used his knees to smash away a section of half a dozen bricks.

Suddenly, Mori stood in front of him on the other side, gesturing for him to come through the hole. Just as he was about to yell for Mori to get Suzuki away from the iron door, Mori grabbed the front of his jumpsuit.

It was too late. Mori's hands were swept away as a wall of falling bricks and shattering plaster drove Takuda to his knees. The alley had collapsed upon him. He was covered, smothered, and darkness closed in on him.

CHAPTER 34

Thursday Morning

The bricks and shattered plaster covering Takuda were surprisingly comforting. The warm, reassuring weight of it made him sleepy, so sleepy he barely noticed there was no air, no light, and no real warmth. He barely noticed the brickbat corners digging into his skull. He barely noticed that he was dying.

Something pulled him. It forced his fingers to dig, forced his back to bow under the weight of masonry and earth, and forced his knees to draw up beneath him. He wanted only to lie there and sleep, if only for a few moments, but the massive presence of which he was only a tiny part forced him to stand in a flood of rubble.

When he finally opened his eyes, Mori and Suzuki

stood gaping at him. Suzuki still held a brick. Mori finally released the length of rotted rafter he'd been digging with.

"How long was I under there?"

"Minutes," Mori said. "Just a few minutes."

Suzuki dropped the brick. "You're getting stronger," he said. "I didn't think it possible."

"That should have crushed you," Mori said. "It should have broken your skull and flattened your rib cage."

Takuda rubbed dust and brick chips out of his hair. He wondered idly if the horns and the extra bone in his face had protected him. "At least it wasn't a supporting wall for the Zenkoku Sales building."

Suzuki laughed in appreciation and relief. Mori sat suddenly, losing his balance at the end and falling sideways. They grabbed him by the collar so he didn't hit his head on the concrete floor.

Takuda waded out of the bricks and rubble as Mori made the feeble gesture of fighting off Suzuki's help. Takuda brushed himself off while watching them. His uniform was dusty but unmarred. *Ota isn't stingy about the uniforms, at least,* Takuda thought. *Good old Ota. Maybe we should take him up on his offer.*

Takuda looked around. The room was the size of a tennis court. The walls were white, all I-beams, concrete pillars, and exposed plumbing. Folding tables and chairs stood stacked against the far wall. Block-and-tackle rigs on pulleys long since painted immobile hung on rails running the length of the ceiling above a long drain set into the painted floor. At the end of the drain, to Takuda's right, a low, ornate iron door was set into the irregular stones of the wall. The other walls were modern cinder block, but the wall to his right was of much older construction. The ornamentation of the door itself suggested prewar fabrication, perhaps even from the nineteenth century. The iron door was black, as if it had been oiled or varnished. It had been taken care of.

Takuda walked to it. The latch was simple. He lifted the latch, opened the door on silent hinges, and stooped inside.

There was sand. There were scattered bones, human bones. There was a low, rectangular stone altar. Mori and Suzuki suddenly crowded the entrance, shutting off what little light came in the door, so Takuda took out his flashlight. Beside the altar lay an elaborately decorated human skull, gaping at Takuda as if surprised to meet him in this dark, sandy place.

Takuda flipped the lid off the altar. A corner of it smashed the skull. One wood-and-ivory eye popped out into the sand.

The Kurodama lay in the altar. Takuda grasped it by the blade and rapped it against the edge of the altar. It took three tries to break the lozenge-shaped handle off the blade. Takuda realized it would have been easier had he simply taken it out of the enclosure. It was strongest here, in its home.

He was surprised he was immune to its powers, he thought as he turned to the door. His immunity really made it unnecessary to carry it in two pieces. He really should rejoin it just for the sake of convenience . . .

Oh, you cunning little rock, I know all your tricks. You have no idea how many demons have spoken into my head.

"What are you grinning about?" Mori asked as he stepped out of the shrine enclosure.

Takuda just shook his head. "I got it." He handed both halves to Suzuki. "Let's figure out how to get out of here."

"It's almost dawn," Suzuki said as he slipped the Kurodama shards into the sleeves of his robes. "We're going to run into employees. This could get nasty."

"It could," Takuda said. "Hang on while I dig out my staff."

Mori was at his elbow the whole time he dug down into the bricks looking for his staff. "You're leaving the Kurodama to the priest? It's a bad idea. A bad, bad idea."

Takuda thought to answer, but he had just found his staff. He wormed it out carefully. He was strong enough to pull it out in one go, but there was no way to be sure it wouldn't crack under the strain rather than simply passing among the bricks and rubble on the way up. *Slowly but surely. . .*

"You're not listening to me at all," Mori hissed.

"That's true," Takuda said. He ran his hands down the staff. A few nicks and deep scars. He was unreasonably pleased with himself. He and the staff were both buried, and he came out better than the staff.

"Just think about it," Mori said. "Do we know if it

was Inaba or Zenkoku Security that put the two pieces of that stone knife back together? Are we sure it wasn't the priest?"

"I'm not sure of anything. But if the priest put it back together, that means he walked out of the apartment and left it there. That makes him safer than most, doesn't it?" He smiled and hefted the staff over his shoulder. "Let's get out of here."

The double doors were locked tight. Takuda strained against the knobs, which came off in his hands. He could not budge the steel doors themselves, and the hinges were buried in poured concrete within the hollows of I-beams.

"The ceiling is even worse with those slabs between the steel beams," Mori said. "What did they build this room for anyway?"

"We might have to scramble back up," Takuda said. He pointed up the heap of rubble. A ragged hole at the top showed a tiny glimmer of predawn light.

Suzuki and Mori exchanged glances. "You can try it," Suzuki said, "but you'll need to bring us a rope and haul us up. We're not like you."

"Right. Right." Takuda turned and turned, looking for a way out. "We don't have any wall to go through."

Suzuki pointed at the cinder blocks beside the door. "What's that?"

A sheet of paper was taped to the wall at chest height. The painted concrete floor was smeared with hastily swept concrete dust.

Takuda poked his finger through the paper. "There's

a whole cinder block missing here," he said. He stood back as Suzuki ripped the rest of the paper free and tried to stick his head through the wall. "Allow me," Takuda said, aiming the butt of his staff at the cinder block below the hole.

The noise was tremendous, and they were sure security would come running. When they were done, Mori pushed between them to be first into the hole. "I'm smallest," he whispered as he wriggled in feet first. "Putting the priest in here would be like shoving a noodle through a straw."

Takuda resisted the urge to push Mori through by the top of his big, brainy head.

"It's a broom closet," Mori hissed through the hole. "Come on through."

As Mori wrangled Suzuki through the hole, Takuda looked again at the chest-high hole they had started with. He stood before it and then turned slowly until he faced the cracked and yellowed projection screen hanging from the pulleys above the drainage trough. Someone had been watching murder movies in this awful place. That person had written a precise description of a murder movie and dropped it into Suzuki's begging bowl.

"Come on through," Mori hissed.

Takuda squeezed in. There was no sign of a projector, just a broom closet. They cracked the door and crept out.

It wasn't a hallway as much as a tunnel. The stone walls were painted an ancient tapioca green and lit with incandescent bulbs in tiny cages, the lighting itself powered via rusting conduit pipe strapped haphazardly onto the stone. The tunnels wound around pilings and boiler rooms, past padlocked storerooms, piles of worn furniture, and a security office with security camera monitors turned off. An aged security guard with his shoes off and his feet up slept at the desk. They dropped to their knees and crawled past carefully.

After the security office, the tunnel went up three steps, continued for two meters, went down three steps, and then took a hard right into darkness. There the tunnel narrowed to shoulder-width. Takuda went first, trying to keep away from the left wall, covered as it was with water pipes and electrical conduit. The tunnel took a ninety-degree right turn and opened into a tiny elevator lobby. There were no stairs.

Mori swore so eloquently that even Suzuki looked impressed.

"We must have missed something," Takuda said. "There has to be another way out of the basement."

"There was nothing else," Mori retorted. There was no other way to go.

They both turned to see Suzuki moving a dusty plastic plant and a folding screen to reveal a steel door. He turned the knob quietly and grinned at them over his shoulder. He opened the door before they could whisper for him to stop.

He looked in, then turned to them and whispered, "Stairs."

The fire door at the next landing up had a narrow, reinforced glass pane looking out into the darkened lobby. Mori reached for the knob, but Suzuki touched his sleeve.

Out in the lobby, a burly security guard strolled past the circular reception desk toward the elevator bank. They waited till he had gone in and the door had closed behind him before they tiptoed out into the lobby.

All but Mori. He ran to the reception desk and vaulted over. "In the Tenjin office, they keep the keys . . . right here." He tossed the jingling ring of keys to Takuda, who was halfway to the massive, curving glass doors. Takuda caught them with his right hand and tucked his staff in his left armpit. The third key fit . . . and nothing happened.

Suzuki stood back and waved his arms at the sensor, and the doors slid open with a hiss of muffled servomotors.

"As easy as that," Takuda said, tossing the keys into the shrubbery.

"As easy as that," panted Mori, catching up to them. They walked quickly and quietly back toward the college, past fallen earth between the Zenkoku Sales building and the abandoned cafeteria.

"We forgot to turn the lights out," Mori said, pointing toward the glow coming from the disturbed earth. Suzuki laughed and clapped Mori on the shoulder, and Mori didn't shake the hand off this time.

As they neared the park, Takuda thought he was

glad, very glad, that Suzuki was keeping the two pieces of the Kurodama separate. Suzuki really was the best man for the job, having shown a virtual immunity toward it. It only made him hungry, really, and why not? He had a very fast metabolism. He was always hungry. Perhaps they should stop and get him some breakfast so he could carry his burden without undue strain . . .

Takuda stopped in the darkened street. "Priest, where is the stone?"

"It's in my sleeve, of course. I mean, they are. In my sleeves. The two pieces."

Takuda brought his staff around. Cicadas awakened by dawn's first rays in the treetops shrieked their greeting to the sun.

"Priest," Takuda whispered, "bring out the stone."

Mori held out a restraining hand. "Now, now, it's safest in the priest's robes. He really is the perfect man for the job."

Takuda felt a thin wedge of panic in his chest. "Priest, let me see it, or we're going to have problems. Right now."

Suzuki, grinning shyly, drew the stone knife from his sleeve. It was whole again. "I couldn't help myself," he said. "I'm just so hungry."

CHAPTER 35

Thursday Morning

Takuda struck the Kurodama from Suzuki's hands, and Mori stripped Suzuki of his sword. Suzuki dove for the stone knife with a cry of anguish, but Takuda drove him backward with his staff.

Suzuki was drooling. "Just give it to me. This is what I was born to do. Don't you see? This explains my hunger, my constant, raging hunger."

He squared his shoulders and stared into Takuda's eyes. He was breathing hard, almost panting with the effort of keeping away from the curved jewel. "This explains everything."

Mori stood back with the swords. He had tried to keep Takuda between Suzuki and the curved jewel the whole time. He held his own sword at the hilt guard, ready to whip off the scabbard if Suzuki came at him.

Takuda spread his arms as if to protect Mori. "Priest, why do you think it's safe with you?"

Suzuki all but wailed in frustration. "Because nothing can survive my hunger!"

Takuda shook his head.

Suzuki said, "Just let me have the Kurodama, and I'll eat it, bit by bit. I can see evil now, you know. The curved jewel is all aglow with it, but there are little spots of it in everyone, hideous sparks of evil hiding in their hearts." He leaned around Takuda to leer at Mori. "Some people have more than others."

Mori whipped the scabbard off his blade. "That's it. You want to eat my heart? Come on."

Takuda turned and took Mori's sword out of his hands. "It's not time for drawn swords," he said.

Mori growled and made to draw the laundry-pole sword. Takuda took it away as well. Mori stood unarmed, glaring at Takuda.

Suzuki leaned over Takuda's shoulder. "Just give me the curved jewel. I'll scrape it down bit at a time. I won't be bothering anyone."

Takuda stepped away to look at Suzuki without turning his back on Mori. "You're sure, Priest? You're sure it won't just possess you from the inside out?"

Suzuki laughed out loud. "I'll grind it into sand and then into paste and then into jelly to fill my stomach. Believe me, it will not possess me." He beamed. "I was born to possess it . . . in my belly!" Suzuki pointed to his laundry-pole sword. "That blade will last long enough to shave it down."

"You'll ruin it for good," Mori said. "That'll be worse than the time you tried to pry open a window with it."

Suzuki shook his head. "No one cares about that. I was born to consume evil, and this is the biggest evil I've ever seen. I'm ready. And I have the perfect place."

Mori retrieved his scabbard from the bushes. "We have to move. It's almost dawn. Traffic is already steady out on Meiji Avenue."

Takuda said, "Priest, where is this place?"

"Some of my friends, the beggars on the street, told me about it. It's an abandoned warehouse on the waterfront, on the other side of West Park."

Mori wrinkled his nose. "That's all refineries and yacht slips and so forth. It's all fenced and gated."

"Not this place," Suzuki said. "It's right on the water. We just go through the park and under the expressway and walk along a little road, and then we walk right to it. It's a group of abandoned warehouses, and the gate has come right off the hinges. Maybe my friends helped with that, but I don't ask." Suzuki leaned forward. "Here's the best part," he whispered.

Takuda leaned forward, ready to smack him down if he seemed possessed by evil.

"To get there," Suzuki breathed, "we pass through the grounds of a little Zen temple, and we go past an elementary school, which will of course be consecrated, and then we go right up the road to West Park, which is a shrine road! The whole path is actually holy, though not for the reasons the pagans think." He sang a snippet of the *Toryanse*:

> Going in is easy, but returning is scary.
> It's scary, but you may pass, you may pass.

Suzuki laughed aloud, but Mori scowled. "Enough children's songs, Priest. We need to get this thing to deep water."

Takuda looked at Mori, and quick as a wink, Suzuki snatched the Kurodama from the pavement and secreted it in his sleeve. Mori moved on him, but Takuda held him back.

"Priest, can you do this thing? Are you sure about this?"

Suzuki nodded deeply, silent as a naughty child. He had his arms crossed tightly over his chest to protect the Kurodama, and he cut his eyes at Mori as if he expected the attempt at any second.

The huge, dark presence in Takuda's mind was wholly mute, as if it were asleep or absent. Nothing his parents had ever said helped him in this situation, nor any of his police training. *But Yumi still likes Suzuki even when she's frustrated*, Takuda thought. *She's never steered us wrong.*

Takuda nodded and slammed the butt of his staff on the tarmac. The sound rang out in the narrow street. "Right, Priest. You have a lousy sense of direction, but if you have a route, let's go."

The rusted pulleys shrieked as Suzuki slid the ware-house door closed behind him, cutting himself off from Takuda's view. When it slammed against the concrete stanchion at the end of its track, it hung on its pulleys, its steel sheets shuddering and booming as if they contained a tiny thunderstorm.

The whole situation was faintly ridiculous. It reminded Takuda of period dramas in which robed nobles secluded themselves behind paper-paned doors to prepare for battle, but Suzuki was no warrior, and he wasn't preparing for battle. He was the battle. In the abandoned warehouse with the Kurodama, now whole again, he was grappling the oldest, strangest, most seductive evil they had ever faced.

And his plan was to eat it.

Or it will eat him, Takuda thought, *and then everything will be lost.*

"This is insane," Mori said. "We should catch a ferry to Busan and just dump it on the way."

Takuda shrugged. Despite everything, he felt serene and hopeful. He had been drugged, Tasered, maced, and slashed. A concrete wall had fallen on him. Yet he was alive and whole, and the three of them had gotten this far. It was all up to Suzuki, the daydreaming priest closed up with the Kurodama. It was out of Takuda's hands.

"We could break it into a hundred little pieces," Mori said. "We could encase each one in concrete, in little film canisters. I can get boxes and boxes of those.

Then we could dump them into the bottoms of lakes and bays and canals and crevasses where they could never come together again."

Takuda closed his eyes, imagining a huge and subtle web of evil, the pieces calling to each other across the kilometers and across the years, affecting not just a handful of schoolgirls or a few salesmen but every man, woman, and child in the archipelago, turning Japan into a land of cannibals, savages, murderers. *Not again*, came the unbidden thought.

He shook his head. "It just won't do."

"How about a kiln? I know a potter over by Children's Hospital who would fire his kiln up for us, if we paid for the propane. I'm sure he . . ."

"A kiln?" Takuda was incredulous. "It's bad enough at room temperature. Let's not go heating it up."

Mori folded his arms. "Deep water. We hire a fishing boat and get it out to a trench. A drop-off. It would at least buy some years. Decades, maybe centuries."

Takuda turned on him. "Centuries to spawn monsters in the deepest oceans to bring it back to bloodletting. No, it has a mind of its own, even if it isn't fully awake, and it won't lay down for temporary solutions. Neither will I. I don't want it out of the way. I want it dead."

"Then you've gone the wrong way with the priest," Mori said. "He doesn't have it under control. He'll come out of there grinning and chattering, ready to strip the flesh from our bones, and I'll have to strike him down because you won't do it, or maybe he'll stay in there and start working on himself, flaying to the bones until he bleeds to death. We don't know. We don't know what happens when we leave someone alone with that thing."

Takuda nodded. He was sure Mori had not seen the fire blazing behind Suzuki's eyes. He could not see Takuda's new . . . fangs? Tusks? No, Mori had no idea what might be happening to the three of them. Takuda decided it wasn't the time to tell him. Instead, he said, "It's nice to finally get confirmation that you don't want the priest dead, either by his own hand or by some other agency. There is some comfort in this situation after all."

Mori scowled. "You've already given me the lecture, and you pushed me around and disarmed me this morning to soften me up. I hear you. I should be nice to the priest. But I tell you, leaving him alone with that thing is not being nice to him. It's going to kill him. The ferry is right over there." He pointed east. "Ten minutes by taxi. We don't have our passports, so we could just grab a ferry for Nagasaki or the Goto Islands."

Takuda was tired of the conversation. "I'm going to grab us some food. You just keep out of sight and cover the door." He turned, hopped off the loading dock, and strode off across the parking lot. He felt Mori's eyes on his back. As he turned the corner and headed toward the shops, he felt other eyes on his back. He saw nothing, but he knew they were there, in the forests of pallet stacks and among the rusted forklifts and empty cable spools, up on the rooftops, in the gaping windows. Suzuki was wrong. They had been followed, and they were being watched, but the watchers wouldn't move on Mori. That would be against the rules.

Or so he hoped.

Takuda was two blocks away before he realized he had left his staff leaning against the loading dock. He didn't even feel the need for a weapon anymore. He was in a different kind of fight.

While he walked, he ran his tongue over his fangs, smoother than his other teeth, and felt with his fingertips the new bone and emerging horns. He only noticed the differences when he felt for them.

A man can get used to anything. He passed his own pop-eyed, demonic reflection in a shop window. *Almost anything.*

It was the first chance he had to think about the presence in the back of his head. It was part of him and yet it contained him, like a puzzle picture where foreground and background shifted places. It was new, and yet it was old, like a place just discovered that he had always known. It was the source of all déjà vu.

The darkness in his head stirred at that thought, but it remained silent.

Takuda directed the thought to the stirring: *What are you?*

It remained still, and the stillness enraged Takuda. His body coursed with the silent fury he had felt when his only brother, Shunsuke, had been pulled cold and dead from the waters of the Naga River valley. He clenched his fists with memories the pain and suffering he and Yumi had gone through when their only son, Kenji, was pulled from the same waters many years later. A deep growl rose from his throat.

Takuda had worked too hard and sacrificed too much to be possessed by some phantom. Who did this this thing think it was, that it would occupy his mind and speak from his mouth without explaining itself? It could not be. He would not allow it. He would cut out his own heart before surrendering. He remembered the triumphs, the times when he had pushed through the pain to do a man's job, like the time when he had been poisoned by the Kappa in the Naga River valley, his blood full of a psychoactive poison that had bent his mind in a spiral of grief, and he remembered how Reverend Suzuki's voice in his head had brought him back from the brink of suicide, pushing him onward to face the beast . . .

Sweet merciful Buddha, Takuda thought. *That wasn't Suzuki in my head. That was you.*

The darkness within remained silent.

The mind that watched as if in slow motion the split second of the car crash, the mind that noted with dispassionate satisfaction that Takuda's body had survived a fifteen-meter fall into a cave full of human bones, the mind that assessed the heat and noted the damage as Takuda wrestled a fire demon into the surf . . .

The dark mind had always been there, always part

of him, always protecting him. It was not awakening. It had always been awake. He was now just awakening enough that he could hear it and feel it.

His frightening strength, his luminescent scars, his nascent horns and budding fangs—the changes in his body were just reflections of his true nature.

Takuda slowed to a stop in the middle of the busy sidewalk on Meiji Avenue. The realization hit him like a hammer. He wasn't becoming a monster. He had always been a monster.

CHAPTER 36

Thursday Morning

When Takuda got back to the warehouse, Mori had his ear pressed to the warehouse door, and he didn't hear Takuda as he climbed the loading dock stairs. Mori jumped when Takuda spoke.

Mori cursed with an Osaka gangster's flourish, straight from the movies. Takuda had to laugh. He needed a laugh, and the thought of what he must look like with his bulging eyes and wicked fangs made him laugh even harder.

Mori was beside himself. "You think this is funny? What the hell is wrong with you? Suzuki is in there screaming and crying and carrying on. It's driving him insane. We need to get in there."

Takuda put the bags of food down on the concrete.

"You should have pulled up some crates to sit on at least. Have you done anything while I was gone but stand there with your ear to the door?"

Mori was beyond listening. "I can't get the door open. He's locked it from the inside."

Takuda sighed and took out one of the boxed lunches. He doubted Suzuki would eat, but there was a can of hot tea to help him wash down the Kurodama. As he reached for the door handle, a length of pipe fitted vertically to the steel plating, Takuda wondered himself why he was so casual about this situation. Trapped with their backs to the water, obviously watched by the enemy, dependent on the victory of their weakest link, why did he feel such a deep-seated and resounding . . . joy? Yes, joy. There was no other word for it.

Takuda rejoiced silently for a second and then he wrenched the door open. It resisted briefly from the inside, then gave with a snap and a splintering of wood and squealing protest from the pulleys above. Takuda crossed the threshold into darkness, kicking aside the shattered broomstick Suzuki had used to jam the door shut.

The warehouse was a filthy tin shed attached roughly to concrete stanchions, the kind of metal box that's a few degrees warmer than the outside, winter or summer. Soiled sleeping mats, sake bottles, and plastic food containers were piled in the corners. Suzuki had cleared the floor, and he sat on a stack of pallets in the center, an emaciated Buddha on a makeshift dais, weeping like a child.

Takuda approached Suzuki. "Priest," he whispered, "can you do this, old boy? Can you end this thing?"

The sobbing priest raised trembling hands bandaged with strips torn from his brocaded sash, the silken symbol of his vocation and ordination. The silken strips were soaked with blood.

"It resists," Suzuki wailed. "It is stubborn and uncommunicative. It is very old, and it cannot fathom that its own end has come!"

Suzuki's laundry-pole sword lay unsheathed and bloodied at his side. A full third of the blade had broken off. The remaining length was so deeply scratched and marred that it could never be fully restored, even if the squared end were ground off to form a new tip. Takuda was pleased to see the beautiful antique ruined. *Good riddance to it.* Suzuki had always cut himself more than he had cut anything else. He was hopeless as a swordsman.

"Priest, I brought you food. Do you want something?"

Suzuki laughed till his face was purple and tears streamed down his cheeks. "I'm so hungry I can't stand it. Every bite I take just makes it worse. I'm a hole! I'm the eye of a cyclone! I'm a blazing furnace!" He shrieked and rocked back and forth on the creaking pallets, his bandaged hand on the hilt of his ruined sword. "Oh, oh, I'm so hungry, but if I stop for a snack now, all this evil will turn into needles of volcanic glass in my belly! I can't stop for . . . what is that, chicken cutlet?" He peered at the box lunch in Takuda's hand. "It smells like chicken cutlet."

"We'll save you some," Takuda lied. He placed a can of hot tea on the corner of the pallet, within easy reach. "Just in case you get thirsty."

Takuda bowed and backed out, still bowing. He really should have kowtowed and crawled away backward, he thought, because Suzuki was doing such a hard job. For a split second, he wondered if that was the Kurodama talking, worming itself into his mind. The dark presence stirred in the back of his mind, spinning off a single word: *veneration*. Takuda smiled. Yes, veneration is finally due this addled priest.

At the door, he glanced up, and he was arrested for a second by Suzuki's blazing stare.

"You're a good man, Detective," said the skeletal Suzuki. He sat ramrod straight in his ruined robes, gazing at Takuda. "You've always done your best for me."

Takuda bowed again as he slid the door closed. He was suddenly very glad that Suzuki and he were on the same side.

"Man, he looks weird," Mori whispered. "Did you see it? Is he eating it? How much is gone?"

Only then did Takuda realize that he had not seen the Kurodama at all. He told Mori, just to see the younger man's horror and disbelief.

They ate their lunches with their legs dangling from the edge of the loading dock like a pair of children, accompanied by shrieks, howls, and cackling laughter from the warehouse. Takuda ate his own lunch, Suzuki's, and a chicken cutlet and pickled radishes from Mori's. He thought he might have to be careful about eating with his new fangs, but his whole face seemed to have accommodated nicely. While he ate, he watched the rooflines of adjacent warehouses. He saw shimmering movement, and he saw shadows against the pale blue summer sky, shadows that had no referents in the daylight world. He pointed out the distortions and the host of gathering shadows to Mori, who did not see them.

"Maybe you're just seeing the heat rising from those clay tiles. It gets pretty hot up there."

Takuda nodded as he watched a wayward shadow sneak toward them, darting from one darkened space to another. He borrowed Mori's sword. "Maybe they're just curious about the feast in the warehouse," he said as he jumped down to the tarmac and unsheathed the sword, sending reflected sunlight toward the fleeting shadow. It darted away toward a jumble of loose cable. "Maybe they're just harmless scavengers."

"Maybe your imagination is a little overactive," Mori said.

Takuda sheathed the blade and handed it to Mori. "We've been out here all morning, and we haven't seen as much as a security guard. You know we're being watched."

"Not by shadows."

Maybe not only by shadows. Takuda bowed in agreement. It wasn't worth arguing with a blind man.

"You're treating this like a game," Mori said as Takuda climbed back on the dock.

"I am," Takuda said, "because Counselor Endo has taught me to do so. You're a brainy fellow, so you might enjoy imagining we're in a giant game. Each of the players has different strengths and weaknesses . . ."

"Attributes."

"Attributes, yes, like good to evil, or neutral to chaotic . . ."

"That's alignment. You're talking about alignment, not attributes."

"Okay, yes. Alignment. But attributes are also important." Takuda stifled a sigh of frustration. "They are all continua, though, right? Like perfect good to absolute evil, omnipotence to impotence, like that."

"There could also be special attributes. Special powers."

Takuda considered. "Let's leave that alone right now. Let's say these powers are all reflections of the same thing. Power is power, no matter how it manifests itself."

"Like the ability to push people around or . . . like appetite." Mori's smirk was only in his voice.

Suzuki's sustained, juddering screams interrupted Takuda's deliberations on slapping Mori unconscious. He folded his hands in his lap. "If the priest walks out of there alive, will you grant that appetite can be power?"

Mori stripped off his glasses, rubbed his eyes with his knuckles, and then pinched the bridge of his nose. "Okay, sorry. I'm sorry. Please continue."

"Our biggest weakness is awareness. Our lack of

awareness. That's where we're almost off the charts. Or barely on the charts. You know what I mean."

Mori frowned. "Self-awareness, or other-awareness?"

"Both. I get glimpses." He told Mori again what he saw in mirrors and about his vision at the old moat, the dark fires of sacrifice sending pillars of suffering to the empty heavens. He didn't mention the animal spirit in the bar girl's body. He didn't know where to start.

"But glimpses don't tell us what we are or what our enemies are. We are ignorant, so ignorant, of ourselves and the invisible realms around us. That's how Endo plays us according to rules we don't understand."

Mori stared off at the roofline, where he probably saw nothing unusual. "We don't even know what there is to see. There are five worlds that we know of: the world we were born into, plus the one only you can see, the one you almost see, the unseen . . .

"And on the other side, the gloriously bright, upon which we cannot yet bear to look."

Mori blinked. "The priest says there are somewhere between ten and thirty-one worlds, but that's storybook Buddhism . . ."

"Don't bet on it."

Mori turned to him. "So if we're playing the priest's game, what's the point?"

Takuda didn't miss a beat. He couldn't afford to. "The point is to send enemy players back to 'Start,' straight to hell so they can burn off their evil karma. Then they'll come back to the neutral middle so we can help them past us, all the way to the other side of the board. We're here to help them leave the game altogether."

Mori looked him full in the face. "You think we're saints sent to help others achieve enlightenment. You know how crazy that sounds, right?"

"That's the problem with such low self-awareness," Takuda said. "We don't know yet whether we're saints on the way down or demons on the way up."

Mori gaped at him.

Takuda shrugged. "I think it's an important distinction. Something to think about anyway." He elbowed Mori and pointed to the long, black car speeding toward them through the deserted warehouses. "I'll bet you a bottle of sweet potato liquor that's Counselor Endo. Time to stow away this talk of games, because the black king has arrived. Let's see if Suzuki can demote him to pawn."

CHAPTER 37

Thursday Afternoon

Mori came to Takuda's side. "We'll split up and hit them from the blind spots. You take the back, and when Endo gets out, slam the door on him. Take him out. I'll get Ogawa."

Takuda at first didn't intend to answer, but it wasn't Mori's fault that he was in the dark. Takuda himself couldn't have explained how he knew what he knew. "Counselor Endo is unarmed. He doesn't need weapons." He felt Mori's incredulous, challenging stare, but he didn't take his eyes off the black windows of the sedan in front of them.

Mori hissed: "The priest can't do anything now. He's helpless in there. We have to hold Endo and Ogawa back. We have to give him more time."

Takuda said, "He'll have exactly the time he has, no more, no less. Let's hear what Counselor Endo has to say for himself."

The left rear passenger door opened, the far side from the loading dock. Endo's head rose above the car's roof as he stepped out onto the pavement. "Mere steel cannot shield me from your disappointment at my arrival, I know, but I hope putting a little distance between us may help you temper your reactions." He raised his empty hands as he strolled around the car toward Takuda and Mori. "A little time to think, a little time for dispassionate discourse."

"We've had lots of time to think," Mori said. "Be careful. Another step means war."

Endo grinned. He was dressed for the warehouse district, but not for a Fukuoka summer: a black turtle-neck sweater with a short, squarish black leather coat and cheap, boxy shoes. It was insane to wear such an outfit in southern Japan at any time of year, but in August, it was suicidal.

"Are you masquerading as KGB or Stasi, with those Eastern Bloc shoes?" Mori's tone was harsh and challenging. "You'll pass out from heatstroke in ten minutes."

"I won't pass out," Endo said, "and I doubt I'll even be here ten minutes."

"He won't pass out," Takuda said. "You need a pulse to get heatstroke."

Endo laughed aloud. Mori stared at each of them in turn.

"Please," Takuda said, "empty the car. Let's see who you've brought today."

Endo bowed. "I regret that I cannot comply. I don't want to spoil the surprise."

Mori started forward, but Takuda checked him with a raised hand. "If you want surprises, keep approaching without telling us what you want," Takuda told Endo.

"What I want is simple." Endo beamed. "I want harmony and wholeness. I want a shining accord between us and a new understanding of how we may cooperate to deliver our entire nation from ignorance, oppression, and mortal danger."

"You want the stone knife."

Endo bowed. "At your earliest opportunity, please."

Takuda said, "Now that you're getting it back, will you tell us where it came from?"

Endo spread his hands and widened his eyes as if mystified and amazed. "Who could say where such a thing came from? Across frozen seas of endless time or something like that, I would imagine. From the markings, I assume it's older than human language and perhaps the progenitor of bone script, but since you are said to bear the same markings on your ample and well-muscled frame, could the same be said of you? Really, since you and the artifact share a common language, I should be asking you these questions." He leaned forward, eager for new knowledge. "What is it? Where is it from? Are your shared markings the equivalent of an origin label? *Not Made in Japan?*" He laughed, pleased with himself.

"*Not Made in Japan*," Takuda said. "That's very clever. So how did it come here?"

Endo tried on a serious frown. "Shall I tell you an illustrative story?"

"Will this illustrative story tell me how the Kurodama came here?" Takuda asked.

Endo raised an eyebrow, which was no kind of answer. "Pacific islanders used to expand habitable territory by releasing piglets on snake-infested islands. When the rains came, the snakes were forced out of their hiding places, and the piglets gobbled them up. When the settlers returned, the pigs were fat, and new islands were ready for habitation." Endo smiled as if pleased with the explanation.

"So the Kurodama was sent to help clear land for conquest, but it got out of control. Somehow your predecessors managed to contain it to an island in the bay," Takuda said, "until we were in place. You could test-drive it a little once we were here to retrieve it."

Endo looked at his watch, perhaps only admiring it. "Think of the artifact's recent excursions as a sort of performance review." He looked up brightly. "I'm not allowed to say which of the functional components involved were being assessed."

"But this isn't the first time it got loose," Mori chimed in. "The cannibalism of the airman's liver. The butchery of the Mongol invaders when their fleet was destroyed by the Divine Wind."

Endo made a dismissive gesture. "You underestimate the creative exploration of the Japanese people at play." He rocked back on his heels. "Perhaps it's just as well that you have remained ignorant. If you knew a fraction of what I know about the artifact, you would have dumped it into the South China Sea as soon as you got your hands on it—which would have caused an entirely different set of problems." He nodded as if to himself. "Best just hand it over."

Takuda said, "Is your sales force still losing its edge?"

"I'm losing my patience. Let's have it." Endo started toward the landing dock.

Mori buttonhooked behind Takuda as if to intercept Endo, but Takuda stopped him with an open palm. Mori tried to brush it way or move past it, but Takuda didn't let him do it. With a fraction of his strength, it was like controlling a kitten.

As Endo neared the concrete slab, Takuda said, "You shouldn't just walk in there. I really don't advise it."

"What, will the priest say sutras at me?" Endo leapt up onto the loading dock, more than a meter straight up. No normal man could manage that jump flat-footed. Takuda and Mori stepped back.

Endo grinned at them. "I hope your hungry priest is burning the right kind of incense."

"Your mockery and impiety don't serve you here," Takuda said.

"They don't serve me anywhere," Endo retorted. "I serve them." He indicated the warehouse door with a nod. "Step aside, and I'll have a word with your priest."

On impulse, Takuda stepped aside. Mori's mouth dropped open.

Endo bowed graciously and reached for the vertical bar that served as the handle on the giant warehouse door. He hesitated with his fingers centimeters away from it and then drew back his hand in a knuckle-popping fist. "Is your Reverend Suzuki alone in there?"

Takuda grinned, trying to mimic the counselor's frequent display of large, yellow teeth. He doubted the imitation was convincing. "Slide open the door and find out," he said. He pulled the struggling Mori farther from the counselor and the door. He had never seen Endo hesitate, never seen him afraid. He didn't know what Endo would do if he were truly frightened.

Endo backed away from the door. He reached toward Takuda and Mori quickly, without turning his head, and laid a finger on Takuda's wrist. "Please tell me what he's doing in there," he whispered.

Takuda and Mori looked down at Endo's finger on Takuda's wrist, then they looked at each other. Mori raised his eyebrows to show that he didn't understand the significance either. Takuda shrugged. "He's eating it," he told Endo.

Endo turned his head by degrees. "You can't mean that he is physically eating the artifact," he said. "Not with his mouth."

"Exactly what I mean," Takuda said. "He's using an antique laundry-pole sword to shave bits off it, and he's swallowing those bits one by one. He was having a hard time of it, but he's gone quiet." Takuda reached for the door handle, careful to keep Mori at arm's length from the counselor. "Allow me."

Endo shrank from the door as Takuda grasped the handle, ready to throw it open.

The door flew open on its own, ripping the handle from Takuda's grasp. It slammed into the stanchion at the end of its track and hung shuddering and booming on its pulleys.

Suzuki stepped pale and skeletal from the gloom. Both hands were still bandaged with strips of his priestly sash. The blood in the silk had gone brown. In his right hand hung the remains of the sword, less than half its original length, broken off clean, the remaining steel marred and hazed with deep scratches from shaving down the stone.

"Reverend Suzuki, how nice to see you again," Endo said. "I hope that blunt little blade isn't meant for me."

Suzuki turned his sunken eyes toward his own hand as if just noticing the remains of the sword. It hit the concrete with a dull clunk as if contact with the curved jewel had somehow ruined its temper. It rolled to Mori's feet, losing chips and flakes of lacquer from its hilt guard as it spun on the concrete. Mori picked it up, frowning deeply as he examined it.

"Thank you, Reverend Suzuki. I hope you'll release the artifact in your possession just as easily. I've brought someone to collect it from you." Endo motioned toward the car, and the driver's door popped open.

It was Hiroyasu Ogawa. Takuda felt a sharp phantom twinge in his neck and a dull throbbing in his thigh, and he looked away. He had to.

Ogawa scampered up the concrete steps past Endo. He held out a broomstick with a cloth satchel hanging from its end. Takuda opened his mouth to tell Ogawa that simply not touching the Kurodama wouldn't protect him from its effects, but Endo motioned him to silence with a conspiratorial wink and a finger raised to his lips: *shhh.*

It was so brazen and horrible that it actually worked. Takuda found himself on standby, waiting to see what would happen.

Sweet Lord Buddha, am I experimenting with the Kurodama, too? But when he looked at Suzuki, he knew he didn't have to worry about the Kurodama. *He's taken care of it. Somehow, he's done it.*

It showed in Suzuki's face. He was grim and gaunt, with no softness in his sunken, blazing eyes. Ogawa held the sack up to him like a child begging for treats. Suzuki towered over Ogawa. Then he smiled. Takuda thought at first Suzuki had something in his mouth, but those were his teeth, gray and metallic, like pencil lead. He looked quickly at Mori, Ogawa, and Endo in turn, but they looked at Suzuki expectantly, with no hint on their faces that he looked strange at all. He joined them, waiting to hear what Suzuki would say.

"You're awake now," Suzuki said. "I was a bit worried about you the other night. How are you feeling?"

Ogawa glanced at Endo for guidance.

"The artifact if you please, Reverend Suzuki," Endo said with a tolerant smile.

"Ah," Suzuki said. He reached into his robes and

withdrew a grayish, ovoid lozenge of stone. He dropped it into the waiting bag. Ogawa peered into the satchel and made a dismissive farting sound with his lips. He dumped the stone lozenge onto the loading dock. The soft stone cracked in half when it hit the concrete. Takuda recognized it as the same stone he had carried in two pieces, the stone that had tried to steal his soul and his sanity, but it was dead now, dried out, lifeless.

"Reverend Suzuki," Endo said, his voice so smooth and pleasant that Takuda couldn't mistake the effort, "this just won't do. This isn't the artifact that you and your friends stole from the Zenkoku Sales branch office. I really must insist that you give it back, or I'll be forced to involve local law enforcement."

Suzuki smiled even more widely. It made Takuda's skin crawl. "Counselor," he said, "I've complied with your request." He gestured at the shards at Ogawa's feet. "That's all that's left. I ate the rest."

Endo's smile did not waver. "You're lying."

Suzuki shrugged, an oddly normal behavior from a man with steel teeth, Takuda thought.

The counselor sighed an exaggerated sigh. "Very well. If you won't cooperate with me, perhaps you will have to answer to the head of your heretical sect." He motioned Ogawa toward the car.

Suzuki stood stiff and unsmiling as Ogawa scampered off. Takuda watched Suzuki for some clue as to what the Kurodama had done to him. Mori hefted the shortened sword, looking between Takuda and Suzuki as if awaiting instructions. The counselor studied his fingernails and did not seem entirely displeased with what he saw.

Ogawa pulled a heavy man in robes from the backseat. The man's hands were manacled to a heavy belt around his waist, and he wore a silken hood. Ogawa led the hooded figure to the loading dock, cajoling and cursing the whole way, all but dragging him up the concrete steps.

Ogawa left the hooded man standing unsteadily in the center of the loading dock. Endo smirked and motioned for Ogawa to turn the hooded figure toward Suzuki. As Ogawa did so, Takuda noticed the figure's priestly sash. It looked identical to Suzuki's.

"Priest," Takuda said to Suzuki, "go back inside. We'll deal with this."

Endo laughed aloud. "Please don't send him away. I've been waiting for this."

The silken hood moved with the bound priest's labored breath, in and out, in and out.

"Here's someone who can explain why you must return the artifact," Endo said, and he motioned for Ogawa to remove the hood.

The hood came off, revealing the livid face of an old man, elaborately gagged and blinking in the shade of the loading dock awning. His eyes adjusted after a few blinks, and then they locked on Suzuki. They narrowed to slits of rage and pain.

As Ogawa began to remove the manacles, the counselor made a grandiose gesture that included Mori, Suzuki, and Takuda. "I believe you have met all these heretics at different stages of their careers. Heretics, I present to you Abbot Suzuki."

The younger Suzuki's lips were pale, almost blue. They twitched upward in a tight little grimace that was almost a smile. He whispered, "Hello, Father."

CHAPTER 38

Thursday Afternoon

"**H**eretics. Blasphemers. Liars." The abbot spat out the words like angry little nuggets as he looked at Mori, Takuda, and Ogawa in turn. His eyes lit on Suzuki. "Traitor," he hissed.

Suzuki stood very still, but Takuda saw something pulsing beneath the surface of the man himself. It was not vision as such. Takuda now saw as if with some primordial organ that predated the evolution of the eye, that or some sense wholly unrelated to his physical body. The pulsing he saw was a consuming fire raging inside Suzuki. It was the hunger. Suzuki's hunger was a force in itself, like molten lava straining against the crust that held it in place.

The force straining for release from the abbot was

of a different sort altogether. It was a hideous spark of fear and resentment and misery that burned deep in the man's heart. The abbot growled as Ogawa loosened his bonds. Takuda wanted to reach out and squeeze the spark out of the old man, just as he had wanted to shake the anger and the bitterness out of Mori over the last few days. There had been no hideous spark in Mori, though, no palpable substance to squeeze out of him. With the abbot, Takuda could feel it waiting to be squeezed, waiting to be snuffed out. Just looking at the old man made Takuda's palms itch.

Ogawa finally finished removing the old man's manacles and belt. Without warning, the old man slapped his son across the face. It was a stinging, resounding slap, and even the counselor seemed abashed in the silence that followed.

Ogawa giggled.

Suzuki hadn't flinched. He stood just as before.

"I hate you," the abbot said. "You are a disgrace, the greatest disappointment of my life."

"That's surprising," Suzuki said. His sunken cheek hadn't even gone pink from the slap. If anything, it seemed more pallid than before. "You've had so many disappointments that I can't imagine myself being the greatest. The failure of the temple, for example, and the extinction of our sect in its home valley. Surely those were harder blows."

"Those were your doing."

"Perhaps, but in the end, I believe your master drove us to ruin," Suzuki said, indicating the counselor with a courteous gesture. "And if all that was not enough, I would imagine that the disappearance of my mother was a greater disappointment than my existence could have been."

"Your mother! The horrible devil of a woman!" The abbot turned away from his son. "If she's alive, imagine what a shark-skinned old hag she must be! She looked so young for so long, never changing a hair, but I'll bet all her sly, mischievous ways finally caught up to her. No, she was a liar and a thief, but you were a complete waste of my time. Fooling around just to make us all late, slacking off for the sake of slacking off, betraying for the sake of betrayal. You were a disgrace, an embarrassment."

Suzuki bowed without irony. "And yet you are the greatest traitor of all."

The abbot turned. "What did you say?"

"You heard me. My mother didn't run off just to see the big city. She loved the order, and she loved her boys. But she sensed the evil in you, and she knew you would feed her to the river." Suzuki's eyes flashed with the dull fire very near the surface now. "You call me a traitor, but you are the greatest traitor I've ever even heard of. You only failed to deliver your wife to the Kappa of the Naga River because she was too quick for you, but you delivered your sect and your sons directly to enemies of the *Lotus Sutra*. The only way in which you failed to betray your family was in abandoning your youngest son. I kept the order alive long enough to kill the Kappa."

The abbot looked up at his son. His rage had cooled to something sweet and venomous. Takuda wanted to squeeze it out like toothpaste.

"You know," the abbot said, "our order is still going, safe and sound and secret. We still fight the fight you abandoned in your misspent youth." He smiled. "Your brothers are all with me. Your brothers are worthy. You, I left behind. You aren't good enough." The abbot turned away again, leaving the silent priest looking down at him.

Counselor Endo cleared his throat delicately.

"Well, this family reunion isn't as heartwarming as one could have hoped, but I think it might still serve its purpose. You see, the artifact must be returned to its proper place. The workings of a great mechanism depend on this single cog. It provides the livelihoods of many citizens in this great nation. Of course, no single man may stand in the way of that process."

He stepped to the center of the loading dock. Takuda, Mori, and Suzuki stepped back toward the edges of the concrete, leaving Endo beside the abbot with Ogawa skulking at his shoulder.

"So here is our situation," the counselor said, folding his hands in preparation for a formal summation. "The three of you are apparently immune to the effects of the artifact, as expected. We already knew that madmen had some protection—who knew madness such as yours would grant complete immunity?" His laughter then was more for punctuation than pleasure, which made it all the more insulting to Takuda.

"Anyway," Endo continued, "this really is a ludicrous situation. You seem to want the artifact for yourselves. The abbot knows that it cannot remain with you, no matter how he and I disagree on its final disposition. Therefore, I propose a solution. If the artifact is returned to its place in the Zenkoku General Sales office, Abbot Suzuki will take his son and whomsoever his son shall choose as permanent residents at the head temple."

The abbot snorted and turned on Endo. Endo silenced the abbot with a forefinger on his liver-spotted wrist.

"If, however, the artifact is not returned immediately, the abbot's life is forfeit."

The abbot stared at Endo.

"Yes," Endo continued, smiling at Suzuki. "The artifact returned to the place from which you stole it, or your father dead at your feet."

Mori stepped forward with the ruined swallow-cutter in his left hand and his sword in his right. He had drawn so silently that Takuda hadn't even heard. Endo stepped away from the abbot, his hands raised. "Swords or guns or bombs can't stop this. It will simply happen."

The abbot glared at Suzuki, a look of pure hatred on his face. "You have done this to me. You've killed me."

"How can you say such a thing?" Suzuki said, his face a perfect picture of curiosity and wonder. "How can you believe me responsible for this other man's actions?" He peeled the bloody rags of his priestly sash from his hands—fully healed but hideous, even longer than before, with tapering fingernails of bluish-purple, like burnished claws. He grasped the abbot's robes at the throat. *He's going to squeeze it out of him now*, Takuda thought with satisfaction.

The abbot struggled, but Suzuki drew him close and grasped his head between those pale, hideous claws as if to crush it between the palms. The abbot flailed and kicked, but Suzuki was suddenly strong, horribly strong, and the light Takuda had seen earlier shone from his eyes like a searchlight into the old man's soul.

"I see the evil in you," Suzuki said. "I cannot explain how, but I see it, and I see that it is not yours. It was somehow planted in you, and it can be removed as the sin was removed from the heart of Muhammad."

"Blasphemer," the abbot snarled.

The priest grinned steely gray. The gaunt, pallid creature with its glowing eyes and shining teeth was no longer Suzuki. In Takuda's eyes, it was no longer human.

Suzuki has crossed over, Takuda thought, a wave of sadness passing over him. *He has become something inhuman, as I have.*

Of those on the loading dock, only Takuda saw the change. Mori was watching Ogawa, Ogawa was looking to the counselor for instruction, and the counselor regarded Suzuki and his father with bemused tolerance. No one had noticed the sudden shift in the world.

"Priest," Takuda said, not sure if the being before

him was really Suzuki at all. "What has happened? What are you?"

Suzuki's grin widened as he stared at his father's head pinned between his palms.

He hissed: "I . . . am . . . hungry!"

He opened his mouth wider and wider, as if his jaw would unhinge. It was a shocking display of cutlery. He drew the struggling old man toward him in a yawning, sucking kiss.

CHAPTER 39

Thursday Afternoon

They watched Suzuki seemingly suck the life out of his struggling father in an obscene and deadly kiss. Mori shuffled forward and back, a sword in each hand, as if unsure whether to advance or retreat. Takuda watched with a mixture of wonder and simple satisfaction as Suzuki drew the evil from his father's heart in a great, squirming lump. He saw it pass smoothly from the old abbot's heart to his windpipe and into his mouth, whence it passed directly between Suzuki's cold, blue lips.

Suzuki released the old man. As the abbot collapsed to a quivering heap on the concrete, Suzuki folded his hands in an attitude of prayer. He wore an expression of ecstasy, his eyes nearly rolling back in his head. The lump in his mouth, meanwhile, moved frantically against the insides of his cheeks as if in a bid for escape. Takuda saw the impressions of tiny body parts on Suzuki's sallow cheeks, as one sometimes sees the shape of an unborn child's foot move across its mother's belly. These impressions were in no way so wholesome as an unborn child: here, a splayed claw; there, a half-furled wing; there, a tiny, snakelike head.

"Reverend Suzuki," Endo said, stepping forward with more haste and concern than Takuda had ever seen him display, "that belongs to me. It is, in fact, very precious to me, and it could be very dangerous to you. You must listen to me. In the next few seconds, you must spit or swallow, one or the other. Do not allow my tiny friend to choose its own path. That would be ruinous for all involved. If you swallow, simply opening your throat, new worlds will become yours. You will become a prince in an invisible empire, as was your father before you. If you spit, no harm has been done. We would all start over, though there may be similar opportunities in the future. But please, please, choose quickly. Spit or swallow, it's all up to you."

Suzuki opened his eyes. They blazed with the fires of dark worship Takuda had seen so often of late. Suzuki looked at each of them in turn, even sparing a glance for the collapsed abbot at his feet. He smiled then with great mirth and warmth, despite his terrible mirror-bright teeth, prison bars for the tiny thing still struggling in his mouth. Then Suzuki closed his bluish lips tightly and, as Takuda had half expected, he chewed.

The thing in Suzuki's mouth shrieked, a high-pitched, mewling wail above the bone-deep crunching and popping. Red-and-black froth appeared at the corners of Suzuki's mouth as his jaw crushed and minced the living evil until it fell silent and Suzuki swallowed it down in three great gulps.

Counselor Endo stood still as stone. Takuda watched him for a few seconds before he realized why this stillness was so unnerving: *Counselor Endo is so surprised that he has forgotten to pretend to breathe.*

"Reverend Suzuki," Endo finally said, "I beg your pardon. I thought I knew who you were, but I do not. I do not know who you are at all. Please be so kind as to tell me your name. Your true name."

There was an echo of command in the counselor's voice that made Takuda think to tell him Suzuki's given name, just in case Suzuki himself didn't volunteer it quickly enough. Whatever Suzuki had become, however, he was unmoved by words alone.

"I have no name," he whispered. He drew a cotton handkerchief from his robe. *Hello Kitty.* He dabbed the bloody froth from the corners of his mouth. "I come from times before all names, even before the figures scratched on your old stone knife. However, I shall continue to be called Suzuki." He grinned dark blood and steel. "That's Reverend Suzuki, to you."

Endo lowered his head like a bull about to charge.

"Yes, about the artifact you mention," he said. "I would like you to return that now."

Suzuki shook his head. "It's done a great deal of damage, but that's all over now. You may recall, or you may have heard, that our strong friend here used it to carve protection for himself in his own flesh." Suzuki indicated the silvery scars on Takuda's forearms. "That was a very, very long time ago, another partial foiling of the stone knife's original purpose. I was curious to see if the scars would disappear with the destruction of the knife. What would you say, Counselor?"

Endo did not glance at Takuda's forearms, but Takuda knew the counselor didn't need to turn his head to see. "Some scars never heal. You're not making sense, Reverend Suzuki. You mention the destruction of the artifact, an impossible event."

Suzuki smiled a thin and knowing smile. "My guess is that you don't see some of the amazing changes in the former detective."

Takuda's hand raised involuntarily to the horn growing down into a fang.

Suzuki looked at Endo with dull, burning eyes. "Counselor Endo, I think you've got one foot in hell, and you can't see half of what you pretend to see of this world or any world beyond it."

The counselor stepped forward and laid a forefinger on Suzuki's wrist. "Tell me now: What is your name, your true name, and what have you done with the artifact?"

"My name, if I ever had one, is lost across oceans of

frozen time, to use your phrase. As for the Kurodama, I ate it bit by bit, from the tip of the blade to the handle, and then I sucked the evil from that shrunken lozenge like syrup from shaved ice. It was delicious. As you will be."

Suzuki flipped his hand so quickly that even the counselor couldn't escape his grasp. Now Suzuki gripped the counselor firmly by the wrist. The counselor's whole body seemed to shiver apart and come back together more quickly than Takuda's eyes could make sense of the change. Endo tried to pull away from Suzuki, but Suzuki was far too strong. The counselor strained and shuddered until he finally pulled away from Suzuki with a snap. He stared at Suzuki's hand. Everyone on the dock stared at Suzuki's hand.

A small creature struggled between Suzuki's thumb and forefinger. It was pale and moist, eyeless, unformed. It sprouted flapping wings, then reabsorbed them when it failed to escape. It grew a mouth to bite Suzuki, and then the tiny maw collapsed upon itself. The miniature demon struggled for freedom, but Suzuki would not release it.

Mori's sword flashed. The pieces fell from Suzuki's fingers.

Suzuki looked down at it mournfully. Endo turned on Mori.

"You will pay," he said. He widened his attention to the whole group. His eyes were black, like a shark's. "You all will pay."

Mori stood stock-still, his blade still at the ready. Suzuki looked at him with cool disdain. "That's not the first time you've come between me and a square meal." Reddish fumes boiled slowly from the outer corners of Suzuki's eyes. They rose in delicate, tapering columns past his forehead. Takuda realized for the first time that he might be unable to protect Mori from the hungry priest.

There was sudden motion at their feet. Small distortions in the air, mirages like those Takuda had seen on the eaves of the buildings surrounding them, burrowed across the reality of the concrete deck. The bleeding halves of the creature Mori had cut disappeared without a trace.

"Nothing is wasted in this secret economy," Suzuki said without a smile.

"You will wander," the counselor said, backing toward the edge of the loading dock. Ogawa moved to Endo's side, eyeing the edge of the loading dock. "You can just say goodbye to this gorgeous Fukuoka City right now, because you will be leaving very, very soon. You will find no work here. Even your begging bowl will be empty, Reverend Suzuki. The three of you will find no sustenance. You will find no solace, no succor. Every door will be closed to you, and you will be visited by pestilence, famine, suffering, and death."

He stepped backward off the dock, and the limousine door opened for him. He flowed backward into it, his eyes still on Suzuki. The door slammed, echoing off the opposite buildings, the echo finally losing itself in the sounds of distant traffic and nearer seagulls.

Suzuki grinned his terrifying grin. "Show-off."

CHAPTER 40

Thursday Afternoon

They gathered once again in the Lotus Café to wait for Yumi. Suzuki sat still and gaunt while his father, the abbot, jabbered apologies meant to atone for decades of abuse and neglect.

"My son, my son, I don't know how you can ever forgive me, or how I can ever forgive myself. We abandoned you. We left you alone to continue the fight in that nasty little valley. It's unforgivable."

Suzuki laughed, an abrasive echo of his formerly breezy self. "There's nothing more to be said about it, Father. You were possessed. Possession is an understandable phenomenon. You acted more or less against your own will."

The abbot blinked. "More or less?"

Suzuki cocked his head in return. His smile seemed fixed, a calculated expression unrelated to human pleasure. "Yes, more or less against your own will. Being possessed by a demon is certainly an extenuating circumstance, but you have to admit that it just barely counts in this case. After all," he said, "it was a very small demon."

Suzuki winked at Takuda.

Takuda felt a surge of relief, and he felt the grin spread across his own face, despite any embarrassment it might cause the abbot. *Thank the Lord Buddha, Suzuki is still Suzuki, no matter what else he may have become.*

After the third heartbeat of silence, the abbot burst out laughing. He laughed until his face turned purple. Takuda hoped this stress-driven hilarity wouldn't devolve into tears. Finally, the old man settled into a steady chortling. He sat back wiping tears of mirth from the corners of his eyes.

Mori pretended to study the Lotus Café's one-page menu as if he had never seen it before. His hand shook slightly.

The abbot leaned forward when he had recovered his breath. "But the three of you, you and young Takuda, and this Mori who severed the water-imp's finger . . ."

"He cut off its arm later, and I lopped off its head."

The abbot beamed. "That must have been something. But what happens now? We need you in the order. We've been thriving up in the hills. We have converts and satellite temples and . . ."

"And your luck has run out," Suzuki said. "You were living in a fool's paradise, and now it will come crashing down around your heads. Counselor Endo had you all under his thumb, all in the same place where he could see you. Now that your eyes are open to his evil and his villainy, he must either possess you all over again, if that is even possible, or he must destroy you and everyone else involved in the order. I doubt that he will leave you in peace or leave a single brick of your temple standing. He doesn't do things by halves, this counselor."

"But he gave us the temple outright," the abbot said. "He can't just . . ."

"Don't think for a second that you know what he can and cannot do," Suzuki countered.

The abbot spread his hands. "What can we do? Will the three of you come and assess the situation? Perhaps we can keep the temple, with your help?"

Suzuki looked at Takuda and Mori. "We don't seem to have much else going on right now. Shall the four of us take a trip with my father, if Yumi agrees?"

Mori nodded distractedly. Takuda bowed to the abbot and said, "We would be honored to be of service, if there's anything to be done. You understand, of course, that having us there might be the single most dangerous thing you could do."

The abbot jumped out of the booth. "Let me make a call. Where's the nearest pay phone?"

They pointed him toward the Heiwadai Hotel, next to the college. He took off at a trot.

Mori said, "Is it wise to let him run off by himself?"

Suzuki said, "I don't know, but we can't hold his hand forever. He has to go to the bathroom. Fairly often, I'd guess, judging from his age." Suzuki looked pensive.

Mori turned an exasperated look to Takuda.

"He'll be fine," Takuda said. "Fukuoka is a good city, and the shadow of evil is gone. Don't you feel it? Can't you feel that it's lifted?"

Mori shook his head.

The three of them sat for a few moments. "So," Mori said, "where does this leave us?"

Suzuki looked back and forth between them. "What do you mean?"

"I mean, what have you become, and where will it lead us?"

Suzuki looked steadily at Mori. Reddish fumes slowly wafted from Suzuki's head, radiating more than they drifted. It wasn't smoke, and Takuda had no idea what to call it.

Suzuki continued to look at Mori. Suzuki smiled, and Mori finally looked away.

He sees, Takuda thought. *Maybe not as much or as clearly as I do, but he sees.*

"You recall that our Takuda had the water sword, the massive blade with the hilt guard with a pattern of overlapping concentric ripples."

"Yes, yes, of course."

"And the hilt guard of the one I used? The laundry-pole sword?"

Mori pulled a shard of the broken hilt guard from his pocket. The lacquer had chipped off completely. "As you see, great triangles like gnashing teeth. It made me think of your hunger. You eating us out of house and home."

"It looks more like massed mountains meeting the sky," Takuda said.

"I think so as well," Suzuki said. "I believe this was the Earth sword. Ironic for a swallow-cutting sword . . . yes, I know, Lieutenant, I should call it a sword designed to make the swallow-cutting stroke. But I don't think the swords have much to do with the abilities of their bearers. It's the nature of their opponents."

"As the water sword was made for the water-imp, so the Earth sword was made for the Kurodama."

"Exactly."

Suzuki gazed at Mori. "And what is on the hilt guard of our one remaining sword?"

"I don't know," Mori said. "I haven't looked."

Suzuki's smile didn't waver. "I see."

Mori flushed.

Suzuki's smile broadened, revealing the leaden glints on his teeth. "I would guess it is the fire sword, even if the element has more to do with the opponent than the bearer. You are much like fire, like the wind. So quick and consuming, so mercurial as well."

"Stop it. You don't know that I am even the correct bearer of this sword."

"Oh, but I do. I see it in you."

"You see now more than I do."

"I do indeed. I see much more."

Mori shifted in his seat. "Then what do you see in me, Priest? Some evil to be sucked out, like the evil from your father?"

"You are a normal mix of fears, weaknesses, virtues, and strengths. A little heavy on impatience and pride, but that's to be expected."

"You see all that?"

"I wouldn't need second sight for all that." Suzuki smiled at Takuda, who pretended to be signaling Koji.

Suzuki said to Mori, "Your anger is understandable. You know the existence of infinite love and infinite mercy, but all you can see around you is an imperfect reflection of those beautiful truths. Now you are engaged in a great struggle on behalf of those truths, and you must act as a votary of the *Lotus Sutra*, but your vision is clouded by the vagaries of this illusory world. You are a perfect being in an imperfect shell, an angel trapped in a gorilla suit." Suzuki laughed at his own joke. "If I could show you, just for an instant, the world beyond this illusory realm of death and pain . . ." His bony, blue-veined hand rose as if of its own accord toward Mori's forehead.

Mori recoiled. "I would rather wait, if you don't mind. Maybe I've already seen as much as I need to see in this life."

Suzuki's hand floated to the tabletop. "As you wish," he said. He grinned, the thin lips peeling back to reveal a mouth full of chisels. Takuda had to look away.

"You will see worlds beyond imagining to you now," Suzuki said to Mori, before turning his attention to Takuda. "And so will you. All will be revealed." His teeth gleamed. "And then you and I will have a long-overdue reckoning."

Takuda wasn't sure what Suzuki meant, but the dark presence in his head shoved him aside to use his voice: "I'm looking forward to it, old friend."

The pain was immense, just as it was every time the presence spoke through him, but Takuda was getting used to it. *A man can get used to anything*, he thought. He pushed his temples together with his palms to make sure his head didn't actually split down the center.

While Takuda recovered, a group of surly youths strolled in, bush-league punks reverse-slumming on the nice side of town. They wore their hair slicked back, and they were all dressed in baggy double-breasted suits in improbable colors.

Takuda saw nothing out of the ordinary, but the priest's eyes glittered. "Sometimes, now, I see things differently. I wonder, when I see someone out of balance, if I couldn't just . . . tinker a little bit."

One of the lads bowed to Suzuki. Another, with his back to Takuda, twisted in his seat to look at Suzuki. He had too many nostrils, and cloudy membranes blinked sideways over the slitted pupils of his yellow eyes. A forked tongue slipped out to test the air around Takuda, Mori, and Suzuki.

"That's more than an issue of balance," Takuda said.

"Oh, that one? No, he's none of our business. Probably just passing through this life on his way to one of the frozen hells, I'd say. But the boy across from him, he could be saved."

"But he's none of our business either, is he?"

"That's a good question. Other than seeing to my brothers, what is our duty? And what is that growing out of your face?"

"What do you mean?"

Suzuki picked up a coffee spoon and smacked Takuda in the center of the forehead. Takuda cursed to wild laughter from the table of punks. As Takuda rubbed his forehead, he felt it: the beginning of a thick, horny growth. It was as though the skin had thinned and melded with the bone, thickening to shingles of rough, nail-like substance.

Takuda was growing a third horn, a broad one, right in the middle of his forehead.

"I'm a man, not a devil!"

One of the punks said, "Did you hear that? He said he was a man, not a devil!"

"He's neither," said the reptilian creature. He turned his head completely backward to stare at Takuda with his deadly yellow eyes. "He should come to this table if he wants to meet one or the other."

The table erupted in laughter as an indifferent Koji brought the punks their beer. One of the punks asked if Koji had come to their table to meet a man or a devil. They made kissing noises at him.

Suzuki made an odd whistling noise between his

teeth. "I shall now introduce them to the mysterious love of the *Lotus Sutra*," he said, rising from the table.

Mori caught him by the sleeve. "Not now. Not here."

Suzuki stared down at Mori. Takuda saw something new flaring behind Suzuki's eyes, a deadly mix of anger and hunger. He didn't know if he could handle the hungry priest in his new state.

"I don't appreciate the way you speak to me sometimes," Suzuki said.

Mori lowered his eyes. "I don't understand any of this, but I think we must be very careful with any . . . new powers we . . . remember."

Suzuki wavered.

"We don't know much," Mori said, "but we know the surge when it comes. This isn't it."

Suzuki sat, and Mori released his sleeve. Mori was sweating.

Good, Takuda thought.

Mori stood and bowed formally. "For my rudeness, for my impatience, for my lack of faith, I most humbly apologize. For the way I have spoken to you before our strange little family and before outsiders, there are no words to express my shame. Please forgive me, though I do not deserve your forgiveness."

"About time, too," Koji muttered, bringing another round of beverages. "You work him to the bone—look at how thin he is—and you keep him away from me for days and days, and then you bring him back just as I have to endure this ridiculous junior gangster convention. Yes, I am talking about you in your avocado-green suit, and you'll just accept that if you want clean food." Koji turned from scolding the hooting punks to lavish his attention on Suzuki. "So you, my priest, you just take his apology as good as gold so we can build up your strength. Then you can tell me again about the sutras and this universe of yours, this place of infinite love and infinite justice and infinite mercy."

"He's forgiven, of course." Suzuki looked at Mori with genuine warmth.

"Well, then," Koji said, scooting in beside Suzuki. "Let's talk about appetizers. You first, Reverend Suzuki, as you are looking so thin."

"Dear Koji," said Suzuki. He smiled with a mouth full of beveled steel and placed one blue-veined claw over Koji's pink, pudgy little hand. "Dear, dear Koji. Right now, I couldn't eat a bite."

ACKNOWLEDGMENTS

Thanks to Thao Le of the Sandra Dijkstra Literary Agency for her energy and enthusiasm, and thanks to Rebecca Lucash of Harper Voyager for bringing out the best in this story.

Special thanks to the kind and generous people of Fukuoka City for putting up with me for the duration of the 1990s. Thanks also to David Hughes, an unsung beta reader of *The Drowning God*, and to Honeycomb Jack, the APE Records forum troll who helped fuel my determination to keep writing.

ABOUT THE AUTHOR

JAMES KENDLEY, author of *The Drowning God* and *The Devouring God*, has written and edited professionally for more than thirty-five years, first as a newspaper reporter and editor, then as a copy editor and translator in Japan (where he taught for eight years at private colleges and universities), and currently as a content wrangler living in northern Virginia with his lovely wife and two fascinating and wonderful children.

kendley.com

Discover great authors, exclusive offers, and more at hc.com.